Miss Manners When Avoiding a Rake

Fenna Edgewood

Starwater Press

Fenna's Newsletter

Sign-up for my newsletter at www.fennaedgewood.com to receive the latest book updates, opportunities for ARCs (advance reader copies), giveaways, special promotions, sneak peeks, and other bookish treats, including a FREE special extended epilogue for the Gardner Girls series coming in late 2021, exclusively for subscribers.

To my real-life Gardner Girl sister.
If only there were four of us!

Contents

A Word of Caution...   I

Chapter 1   2

Chapter 2   15

Chapter 3   23

Chapter 4   33

Chapter 5   48

Chapter 6   56

Chapter 7   71

Chapter 8   78

Chapter 9   87

Chapter 10   105

Chapter 11   114

Chapter 12   120

Chapter 13   135

Chapter 14   151

Chapter 15   157

Chapter 16   165

Chapter 17	182
Chapter 18	200
Chapter 19	208
Chapter 20	223
Chapter 21	233
Chapter 22	240
Chapter 23	258
Chapter 24	283
Chapter 25	287
Epilogue	290
Thank You	293
A Sneak Peek at The Seafaring Lady's Guide to Love...	294
Other Books by Fenna Edgewood	306
About Fenna	308

A Word of Caution...

Although it cannot be denied, Dear Reader, that there is a veritable plague of young rakehells, rogues, and blades in the fair city of London, it has come to the attention of this publication that many youths, young women in particular, believe the country to be lacking in men of such vices.

With so many unwed ladies and impressionable young men in the vicinity, we feel it is our duty and in the interest of the public good to expunge this misconception and to assure our local youths and their Mamas and Papas that nothing could be further from the truth.

We therefore humbly present a list, Dear Reader, of hazards to avoid, of questionable company to be wary of, of the dangers which may lie not so very far from home. A list, in other words, of mistakes not to make...

The Beauford Chronicle, May 12, 1818

Chapter 1

*T*o begin, Dear Reader, we know that the kind of reading which young people are naturally most fond—those fictitious stories, novels, that so enchant the mind—may also inflame the youthful mind with unseemly passion, and rather than educate in moderation and restraint encourage the opposite. For in these stories, youths enter a world full of deceit and falsehood, where few persons or things appear according to their true nature and where vice hides its deformity beneath the garb of borrowed virtue. We therefore urge our youth to guard against such reading.

The Beauford Chronicle, June 1818

"Dash it all!" Claire swore under her breath, gritting her teeth and removing the sharp needle from her finger.

She was sewing while trying to read simultaneously. Something she had believed she had finally mastered.

However, having reached a particularly engrossing passage, she had lost concentration. She was on the third volume of *The Romance of the Forest* and Theodore had just been wrongfully imprisoned. Although the book was nearly in tatters for she had read it more times than she could count, she had nevertheless been wrapped up in the story once again.

Where did Mrs. Radcliffe come up with her wonderfully horrid ideas? Why was it so much more enjoyable to read about terrible events than to live them? Claire would not wish to live within a novel —she had already come closer than she had liked the previous year while helping to extricate her sister Gwendolen from her own series of misadventures.

While Gwendolen had recovered and moved on with her life, Claire felt irrevocably altered. It was one thing to read about evil villains in a book, and another thing altogether to encounter one in real life. Her impression of the male sex, not particularly favorable to begin with, had not been improved by the experience.

There was a firm rap at the door.

Claire jumped. Had she imagined the sound?

She waited in silence.

She had an imagination, but it was not generally overactive to such a degree.

The knock came again.

"For Heaven's sakes!" The exclamation came out before she could think properly. Whoever it was, she was not interested in a visit.

Had she really said it out loud? Possibly she had only thought it. If she stayed quiet, perhaps they would simply go away.

In annoyance Claire envisioned her quiet afternoon being eaten up with tea and small talk. It was just her luck to have unexpected visitors on the day her mother had gone into town, and she was alone at Orchard Hill with only Gracie for company.

There were a few seconds of silence.

"Pardon me, Madam?" A muffled male voice came from behind the door. It was not a familiar one. "We were wondering if we might impose upon you for some assistance."

She sighed. When one wished to live within polite society, one must play by the rules no matter how tedious they may at times be. Or so her family kept telling her.

She rose and entered the hall to yank the door open—rather more forcefully than she had intended.

"Good afternoon," she said smoothly, hoping she appeared more gracious and unruffled than she felt.

Two men stood on the step. She had never seen either before.

The man closest to the door had his arm up as if he had been about to rap again. Claire was tall for a woman, but he was taller. He had a friendly smiling face. The sunlight shone on his light brown hair. He appeared to be no more than ten years older than herself, perhaps around thirty.

His companion looked younger and was more striking. Taller, darker, with thick black hair curled in natural ringlets around his face, making him look quite Byronic. Claire would have found him handsome were it not for the scowl on his face.

Both men were dressed in fashionable riding habits, not quite suitable for muddy country roads. Londoners then.

"Good day, Madam." The fair-haired man inclined his head. "My name is William Campbell, and this is my brother, Thomas. I am sorry to impose upon you, but we have been out riding nearby and one of our horses has gone lame. We are new to Beauford. We recently purchased a house nearby, on the other side of the village. As we are to be neighbours, we wonder if we might impose on you already for some neighbourly assistance? I do apologize for the intrusion, but it is some miles back to the house..."

"Yes, of course." Claire answered automatically. Then she remembered. "I mean, no."

The men looked confused.

"My mother is out with our carriage," she explained. "And our servants have the afternoon off."

"Oh." William glanced at his brother as if wondering where to go from here.

Realizing they might be put off on her account, she exclaimed, "But I am not here alone. My younger sister is with me. Gracie."

Although she was not sure how reassuring that would be. Gracie was not much of a chaperone when it came down to it, being only eight-years old. Also, Claire had no idea where she might be.

"You are bleeding." The darker man spoke abruptly, staring at her hand.

Claire glanced down. There was quite a bit of blood dripping onto the stone step. She hoped none had gotten onto the baby bonnet she had been trying to finish for Gwendolen. It felt as if she had been working on it forever.

"I am sorry, Madam, but I do not think you have mentioned your name. Miss...?" The fair man smiled expectantly.

"Oh, yes, my apologies. I am Claire. Miss Gardner, Miss Claire Gardner." Could she not get out a complete sentence today?

"My mother should return with our groom quite soon. I am sure Arthur would be happy to help when he comes back. If you would like to come in and sit while you wait." She gestured to the room behind her.

"An excellent notion. We appreciate your hospitality," said William, stepping inside.

His younger brother made no comment but followed. He had not greeted her either.

Claire rolled her eyes as he passed. So that was how it was to be. She had no patience for rude men, no matter how handsome. She hoped Thomas Campbell would at least be civil to her mother when she returned or she might have to poke him with her needle.

She followed the two men into the room and looked about for a piece of linen with which to wrap her hand.

Before she could sort through her work basket to find a scrap, the younger Mr. Campbell turned to her with his handkerchief pulled out.

"Allow me," he said, stiffly, reaching for her hand.

"I am quite capable..." she started to snap, then closed her mouth. Likeable or not, these men were guests in her home. "What I mean is that... although I am capable, I would not wish to stain your handkerchief. Thank you for the kind off—"

But Thomas had already reached for her hand was pressing the cloth against her bleeding appendage. She resisted the urge to snatch it back. He had removed his own gloves and his skin was warm against hers. Standing so closely she could smell the masculine scents of leather and sweat. Not a completely repulsive combination. Rather an agreeable scent.

"Thank you very much, Mr. Campbell," she said briskly, finally pulling her hand away. "Please, make yourselves comfortable." She turned to her place on the sofa where her book and sewing still lay. There were spots of blood on the white muslin. "Hang it all..." she began. William began to cough loudly behind her. She tucked the bonnet into her work basket with a sigh and pushed the book aside.

"Keep the pressure on it until the bleeding has stopped," Thomas commanded shortly as he sat down.

"Yes, thank you. I would never have considered that." She fluttered her eyelashes, hoping she looked sufficiently stupid. Clearly that was what he expected. She wondered if it was Thomas's horse that had been lamed. If this was how he spoke to animals as well as women, she had the utmost sympathy for the horse.

Nevertheless, there was something about him which suddenly made her self-conscious of the fact that she had not glanced at a mirror since that morning. She looked down at her rumpled dress, quite wrinkled after being curled up on the sofa for hours. Hopeless, utterly hopeless. She put a hand to her hair, smoothing back the auburn strands as best she could in what she hoped was a subtle way.

"What a pretty little room." William seated himself in an armchair near the hearth and looked about. "You must receive excellent light here in the mornings. Look at the picturesque view this bay window provides, Thomas. Your apple orchard must be lovely in the springtime, Miss Gardner."

Thomas did not appear in the least bit interested in the view or the orchard. Instead, he was scrutinising his surroundings as if he expected the old house to collapse at any second.

"Yes, we think so." Claire turned a smile on William.

"Have you and your family lived here long, Miss Gardner?" William inquired politely. At least one of the brothers could make civil conversation. Claire appreciated the effort. It must be difficult to have to constantly compensate for the rudeness of one's sibling.

"Since my father passed away eight years ago. We moved houses a little after. Gracie was only a babe then." She remembered how peculiar it had felt to have to welcome a new life into the world while they were all still passionately grieving the loss of another.

"I am very sorry," said William quietly.

"Oh, please don't be. It was a long time ago. We have been very happy in this house. It is a beautiful part of the country."

"Indeed! I could not agree with you more. Charming neighbours and lovely country. I hope we shall see one another often." Claire smiled at his enthusiasm. What a contrast these brothers were.

"Is Gracie your only sibling, Miss Gardner?"

"There are four of us girls in all."

"Four girls?" Thomas appeared quite shocked.

"Yes, that is what I said, Mr. Campbell. Four. Girls. There are four of us." She emphasized the words slowly, raising her voice a little, choosing to pretend he was simply deaf instead of misogynistic.

Thomas glared at her from behind his dark brows.

"My younger sister, Rosalind, is in London right now visiting our eldest sister, Gwendolen and her family," she explained, turning her attention back to William.

"It must have been enjoyable growing up with so many sisters. Thomas and I have but one. Elizabeth is only fifteen. She has remained behind with our aunt in London for now."

"How nice," Claire said mechanically.

William was an acceptable albeit unexciting conversationalist, but she could still feel Thomas glowering at her from across the room, and if he did not stop soon, she was not sure what she would do. Nothing good.

She glanced at the clock on the mantle and wondered when her mother would be home. Or a servant. Or Gracie! Where on earth had she gone off to? Claire hoped she was not stuck up in a tree like last week. By the time they found her, it had been almost pitch black.

Gracie chose that precise moment to storm through the front door.

"Claire! I found some baby frogs. May I put them in a jar? Oh, and there are two strange horses outside!" Her apron was wadded up in her hands... and it was wriggling.

"Gracie! Did you bring frogs into the house?" Eying the apron with amusement, Claire tried to stifle a smile. "You are soggy. And muddy. Go upstairs and change and then come and greet our guests." Gracie curtsied quickly, glancing curiously at the two men, before dashing upstairs.

Thomas looked after her with a furrowed brow.

"Are you fond of frogs, Mr. Campbell? Perhaps Gracie can spare a small one for you," Claire asked him sweetly.

He turned his head towards her. She swallowed. He was fine looking; she would give him that. A powerful blend of dashing and dangerous. His gaze was so intense she felt herself begin to blush.

She quickly shifted her gaze to the older Mr. Campbell, who, of course, was smiling. Did he ever stop smiling? At least he would make some woman a very pleasant husband.

"May I offer you tea?" Claire asked, endeavouring to do her duties.

"You said your servants had gone out." Thomas's stare was accusatory.

"I did," Claire said slowly, turning unwillingly to look at him again. "I am quite capable of making us tea, however, Mr. Campbell. Do you mean to say that you think a lady to be incapable of boiling water? You will not find ones quite that high and mighty here in Beauford."

A cold stare was the only response she received.

"I shall go and see about the tea." She rose, feeling only slightly regretful about her rudeness.

Returning shortly with the tea tray, Claire paused in the hall as she heard the two brothers speaking.

"...a charming pair of sisters, do you not agree?"

"The girl is ill-bred and her older sister mulish, if that is what you mean by 'delightful,'" came the reply.

"Yes, well, you are not being exactly gentlemanly yourself. Kindly remember that these are our neighbours now, Thomas, and act accordingly."

Well, this was what she got for eavesdropping. Her mouth twitched a little. Mulish was not an altogether inaccurate description, although coming from Mr. Thomas Campbell's mouth, it was obviously meant as an insult. At least he had received the scolding he deserved.

"Tea?" She smiled brightly as she entered, placing the tray on the low table in the middle of the room and sitting down to serve.

"What has brought you to our area, Mr. Campbell? You mentioned you have recently moved to Beauford." Claire made sure to look only at William as she spoke. She sat back to sip her tea.

"Yes, we have family interests in the vicinity. Thomas and I agreed that being closer would be more convenient than London." Mr. Campbell glanced quickly at his brother at he spoke, before switching subjects. "I look forward to showing you the house, Miss Gardner. I think it is charming. Lovely grounds. Formerly owned by a Sir Arthur Darby. I am sure you will have heard of it, living so close— Northwood Abbey."

"Oh, yes, that is a grand old house. The Darby family was well-known in these parts. My sisters and I used to walk the grounds when we visited Sir Darby's two daughters. They are older now. One is married and one is in London for her second season. A good-natured family and well-liked in the area. We were sorry to see them give up the estate."

"Not," she added hastily, "to say that you will be any less agreeable as neighbours." At least not the elder.

"Why are you not in London for the season, Miss Gardner? Unless I am mistaken you are, what, nineteen? Twenty years? Do not all girls long for gowns, balls, and husbands at your age?" Thomas made no attempt to keep the disdain from his voice.

William looked embarrassed.

"It may surprise you, Mr. Campbell," Claire answered sweetly. "But not all women are, in fact, the same. Some enjoy reptiles and climbing trees, for instance, while others do not put finding a husband above all other interests." She was not about to tell him that she would be sent to London for a season the following year when her mother could better afford it. Or that marriage was one of the least appealing things to her right now.

"Oh, pardon me." He did not sound the slightest bit sorry. He gestured to the book beside her. "I merely assumed that as you enjoy reading such fanciful stories your head was as full of romantic nonsense concerning love and marriage as most girls your age. And—"

Thomas looked about the room before continuing. She followed his gaze. It was a cozy little sitting room but would probably be considered small by the Campbells' standards if their expensive riding habits were any indication of the size of their fortune. While there were no wide cracks on the ceiling, there were a few smaller ones. The carpets were faded with age and use, as was much of the furniture. Four young girls could be quite as rough on a house as four young boys. The walls alongside the fireplace were covered in shelves which were filled to the brim with books. Fresh flowers Gracie had picked the day before were in a vase on the mantle. The fireboard had been painted by Rosalind with a lovely *trompe l'oeil* scene of Paris—well, what Rosalind imagined Paris to look like. None of them had ever been further than London.

Overall, Orchard Hill was more cottage than manor. It was a pretty estate, if one could call such a small piece of land an estate. But it had plenty of space for their needs. With only a cook, one maid, and a groom it was not as if they required expansive accommodations. Nor did their situation allow for it. Her older sister, Gwendolen, had married well and wished to be generous to her family, but Claire's mother would not accept more than a modest contribution. She was a practical, modest woman who believed in living within her means. She had no grander ambitions of a larger or more ostentatious home. Particularly when they were all so settled, and the house held so many fond memories.

"—I would have thought the conditions in which your family live would make the finding of a husband a priority for..."

"Yes, Thomas," William interjected.

Claire's mouth had dropped open. She stared at Thomas, astounded by his rudeness and presumption. How could these two be brothers?

He looked back at her indifferently, as if he had not given cause for offence. In fact, she believed his lips were twitching.

William was rushing on. "I for one am glad to be away from London this season. So many people all gathered, gossiping and gawking. I prefer the quiet of the country. I think we shall be very happy here. Thomas enjoys the outdoors a great deal, Miss Gardner, as do I. Walking, riding, hunting, and the like. Not that we do not enjoy the company of good neighbours as well. In fact, I have been considering holding a dance quite soon at Northwood. You and your family will have to attend."

Claire still simmered with rage but managed to return her attention to Mr. Campbell. Unfortunately, she had missed most of what he had been saying.

"A dance, Miss Gardner? Would such a thing be to your liking? And to your mother's, of course." He looked at her a little anxiously.

Claire tried to smile. "I do enjoy dancing, yes, Mr. Campbell. That is a very kind thought, to hold such an event for your new neighbours."

"It is a plan then. You shall receive a card very soon, Miss Gardner."

He was so charmingly sincere that Claire could not help but return his warm smile.

"Does your mother permit you to waltz, Miss Gardner?"

Claire was a little surprised. "The waltz is not often danced here, Mr. Campbell, though I know it is quite the thing in London. I do enjoy the quadrille, however. It is very popular in these parts, especially with the young people." Although confused by the interest he was taking in her dancing preferences, she was glad to see her response pleased him.

"You are not in London anymore, William," Thomas spoke up. "But I'm sure you'll find your fair share of fortune hunters wherever you go in England."

It was an odd remark to make at that junction. Thomas certainly had his back up against the female sex. She was opening her mouth to issue a harsh rebuttal when, providentially, the front door opened once more.

"Claire!" Her mother's voice rang out. "Oh! Good afternoon." She stared at the two men with surprise as she stood in the entryway, beginning to unfasten her bonnet. Caroline Gardner was a warm, maternal-looking woman. Petite and plump, she shared the same dark auburn hair as her second eldest daughter.

Claire and the Campbells rose.

"Gentlemen, may I introduce my mother, Mrs. Caroline Gardner. Mother, this is Mr. William Campbell and his younger brother, Thomas. They have acquired Northwood from Sir Darby."

"What a lovely place!" Her mother beamed.

Claire knew she was simply glad to have the Darby house occupied again but looking over at Thomas she worried her mother's enthusiasm might be misinterpreted by such a cynical young man.

Gracie ran downstairs to join them. Soon it became apparent that she had merely transferred her frog offspring to a new apron. Claire was grateful to be spared any further arrogant comments from Thomas for the remainder of the visit. A little while later the Gardner's groom had made arrangements to transport the men and their horses back to Northwood and she and her mother saw the two brothers on their way.

Once they were gone, Claire determined not to spare them another thought.

Chapter 2

*T*rust not those with depraved reputations

Upon gaining knowledge of the individual who has unhappily sacrificed their character to depravity and vice, take the first opportunity to show your disapprobation by a silent gravity. Suffer not a contemptuous sneer or ill-bred superiority of manner from one who is known to deal in unrestraint and folly. While superficial attractiveness of person may be compelling to many young women, we urge, Dear Reader, that you exercise caution and be not deceived by spurious appearances which may lead to unwary intimacy.

The Beauford Chronicle, June 1818

Claire paused to catch her breath as she came over the top of the hill. It was only mid-morning but the June sun was brilliant overhead. Gracie had been walking with her but had dashed into a field chasing a rabbit or some other fascinating creature and not yet returned. They were only about a mile or two from home, halfway to the small town of Beauford, which was where Claire was heading. She had promised her mother she would check if the parcels of dresses for Gracie that her older sister Gwendolen had promised to send had arrived. Gracie was growing like a weed and wore through her clothing faster than any of her three older sisters ever did. Claire had no doubt Gracie would find her own way home again when she wished to or else catch up along the road.

After Gracie escaped from her tutor one too many times, Mrs. Gardner had decided they must take on the little girl's education themselves. Claire would teach literature, geography, and history; Mrs. Gardner would cover music and sewing, while Rosalind would give instruction in poetry, drawing, and French. With the weather so warm and beautiful the past few days, however, even threats and warnings could not keep their young pupil in her seat for more than a few minutes at a time.

When Gracie had continued to sneak away whenever she could, Mrs. Gardner had thrown up her hands and announced she might embark upon a "natural" education, at least temporarily, until Rosalind returned from visiting Gwendolen and her family in London.

The eldest of the sisters, Gwendolen had left for her season in London almost seven years ago. She had been married by the end of it, which many might call a success. Claire was one of the only people in the world who knew what a true catastrophe Gwendolen's season had actually been.

No, Claire was not impressed by the quality of men in London. Or England for that matter.

Claire was not averse to the idea of a loving union like her parents had shared. But she was determined not to settle for a scoundrel who would hold all power over her life and happiness.

Besides, Claire wanted for nothing and was exceedingly happy in her present state of singlehood. She enjoyed her family's company, which was more than many could say. While Rosalind was interested in travel and adventure, maybe more than was wise for a young woman, Claire was content. Completely.

Perhaps even boringly so.

Rosalind would tease and accuse Claire of merely being too frightened to leave. Perhaps there was truth in that. Certainly, she was not looking forward to a season in London and still held out hope that she could change her mother's mind. The money necessary for such an extravagance could be much better spent on a season for Rosalind or for Gracie.

As Claire walked alongside meadows and fields of grazing sheep, she neared a piece of land she had always admired. Set a way back from the road on a rising slope, framed by a grove of ancient oak and elm, stood a lovely stone-roofed house, a little larger than Orchard Hill. Behind it lay a wooded area that led down to a pebble-beached brook. Claire remembered trying to catch fish in that brook as a little girl, standing barefoot on rocks and crouching down to scoop with her hands. She and Gwendolen had come home soaked that day, without any fish, but thoroughly happy.

For years, the house stood uninhabited and local children used the grounds as another place to roam. Now Claire could see signs of occupancy. Lace curtains hung in the windows. Croquet mallets lay strewn on the lawn.

A little girl in a flowered muslin dress sat on a blanket on the grass with a doll and some books.

As she passed by, the little girl looked up, smiled, and waved. Claire returned the gestures.

Some impulse made her pause, then she marched up the lawn towards the girl. She had a lonely expression. Perhaps she could be a new friend for Gracie.

"Good day." Claire smiled down as she reached the girl on the blanket. She was a pretty child, slight and slender, with dark curling hair and dainty features. Delicate in comparison to Gracie's sturdy build. "I wonder if you have seen another little girl pass this way. She is about your height, with fair hair."

The little girl shook her head, smiling shyly. "You are the first lady Matilda and I have seen this morning."

Claire crouched down to the girl's level. "Is that Matilda?" she asked, pointing to the doll. "My little sister, Gracie, used to have a doll like that."

"What happened to her?" the child asked curiously.

Claire laughed. "Gracie is quite rough with her toys and I believe her Matilda is now lying at the bottom of a pond." She decided introductions were in order. "My name is Claire. Miss Claire Gardner. My sisters, my mother, and I live a few miles down the road from you, at a house called Orchard Hill."

"My name is Isabel Notley. We have just moved to this house. My governess is still unpacking inside. Her name is Mrs. Mowbray and she is lovely."

Claire could not help laughing again. "How wonderful to have a governess one actually likes! My sister, Gracie, has only ever run away from her governesses and tutors, and she always called them the most horrid names you could imagine."

Isabel looked quite shocked, and not a little fascinated.

"I would never call Mrs. Mowbray names. She is the sweetest lady I have ever had take care of me."

"Where are your mother and father? Will they live with you and Mrs. Mowbray as well?" Claire quickly wished she had not been so inquisitive for the little girl's face fell.

"Mama lives in London, but she does not visit me often," Isabel said quietly. "When Papa last came to see us, he told Mrs. Mowbray that we must move to the country for the city air was what was making me ill and he would not have a sickly child."

Claire's heart clenched as she tried to imagine how different her childhood would have been with a mother who only "visited."

"Well," she said encouragingly. "Your Papa must be a very wise man for he has chosen a beautiful place for you and Mrs. Mowbray to live. I think you will be very happy here. I hope I may bring Gracie to meet you one day. We can walk to the brook that lies behind your new house."

Isabel's eyes lit up at this prospect and she nodded excitedly.

"I must be on my way," Claire continued, rising. "Good day to you and to Matilda." She gave a little curtsy in the doll's direction and Isabel giggled.

Half an hour later, Claire reached the village and entered the post office. The parcels had not yet arrived, and as there was nothing more she needed in town, she prepared for a pleasant walk back home.

Beauford was a quintessential village of the perfect size. It furnished every necessity while retaining a picturesque tranquility. Rolling hills replete with pretty gritstone cottages and stone bridges surrounded the town. Along the high street, one could find such establishments as a milliner's, a chandler's shop, and a draper's. The village square hosted a market for farmers and craftsmen to sell their wares. In the center of it all was a fine old church built over the remains of a much older Norman construction.

All that it lacked was a bookstore. But the Gardners' were used to ordering in the literature they considered a necessity of life, and now that Gwendolen was permanently established in London, she kept them even better stocked.

As she stepped out into the street, a lady and a gentleman coming out of the milliner's shop across the way hailed her. Claire cringed. Harriet and Charles Morton were quite possibly her least favorite people in the village, and since it was a small place, they ran into one another far more often than she liked.

Harriet was a well-dressed young lady, who officiated over Bauford with the attitude of an aristocratic dowager. Average-height, with an oval face and thin, straight nose, she might have been charitably described as pretty. Certainly, she held herself in high-esteem and had never suffered from a lack of self-assurance.

"Why Miss Gardner!" Harriet gushed. She inclined her long swan-like neck. "How delightful to see you this morning. Have you been out walking long? You look positively scorched. Really, you must bring a parasol on such hot days." Harriet looked her up and down from head to toe and tsked in a manner Claire found irritating.

"By Jove, Miss Gardner! Red as a tomato, it's true." Charles chortled. Blond like his sister and moderately handsome, Mr. Morton was a fashionable dandy whom some of the young women in the neighbourhood found attractive. The sly expression he frequently wore had never endeared him to Claire.

The Mortons' mother was not as social as her children and preferred a retired life, while their father was rarely to be seen in the region, much preferring the gambling dens of London.

Claire forced a cheery smile. "Thank you, Miss Morton. I shall have to remember that for next time. So nice to see you both. Will you excuse me? My mother will be wondering what has kept me so long."

"But Miss Gardner, wait!" Harriet exclaimed, stopping her before she could hurry away. "We understand you have made the acquaintance of the newest additions to Beauford. You cannot leave without telling us more."

Claire looked at her blankly.

"The Misters William and Thomas Campbell!" Harriet shook her head in exasperation. "Oh, Claire, come now, do not try to tell me they did not make a deeper impression upon you than that for I shall not believe you. We have already seen the eldest Mr. Campbell, although from a distance," Harriet conceded.

Claire wondered where they had been snooping from. Behind a lamppost perhaps.

"Mr. William Campbell is such a fine-looking gentleman! So pleasant-natured and generous. Or so all the shopkeepers have been saying. With five thousand pounds a year, I would expect he would make an impression on any woman." Harriet's tone was light, but there was a calculated look in her eyes.

The Mortons' fortunes had suffered lately under Harriet and Charles' father's profligate spending. Claire was not sure of the extent of the family's troubles, but suspected Harriet wished to marry well and marry quickly, to ensure her own future was secure.

Harriet lowered her voice. "But the younger brother! Quite the rogue, we have heard. Gambling, drinking, a spendthrift. Sparing no extravagance." Her voice dropped to a whisper. "They say he even keeps a woman in London. An actress! He has already run through everything their father left him. He is utterly reliant upon his brother. No wonder they have left London, with such reckless behaviour."

One could always trust Harriet to have the latest gossip. Surprisingly, her news was often more reliable than not.

Claire found this new information hardly surprising. It lined up with every perception she had received of Thomas Campbell. She was only sorry to hear that William was having to bear the brunt of his younger brother's foolhardiness.

"Yes, well, he did look rather the rakish sort," Claire acknowledged. No point in refuting what Harriet had said. "The elder Mr. Campbell was very kind and civil. It is nice to think of Northwood being inhabited again. The Darbys' used to hold so many festivities there…"

"Do you think Mr. Campbell will do the same?" Harriet interrupted eagerly.

"Mr. Campbell did mention something about a dance," Claire admitted. "Perhaps there may be something of the sort. Well, I must be off. So pleasant to see you both."

Feeling she had fulfilled the social niceties, she walked hastily away from the pair.

A mistress in London? Gambling? Of course, such things were not unheard of but they were less common in a sleepy place like Beauford. The Mortons' own father being an exception which Claire had thought it wise not to mention.

No wonder Mr. Thomas Campbell was so concerned with fortune-hunting women who might be after his elder brother. If he was completely dependent on William's goodwill for his own subsistence, then it made perfect sense. What a hypocrite.

Some women seemed drawn to rakish men like moths to a flame. But Claire had never been the sort to be taken in merely by a handsome face. As she recalled the feeling of her hand in Thomas's, she admitted she could understand the attraction. But she was quite capable of resisting those kinds of feelings. When she married, and she was in no hurry to do so, she would make a practical choice.

Chapter 3

A void immodest dress

   Be always perfectly neat and clean, both in your person and clothes. Remember that the clothing of a woman is necessarily decent and concealing. Be not swayed by ill-suited finery, excessive ornamentation, or worst of all, styles which reflect an indelicate mind and may lead to loss of innocence. We speak, Dear Reader, of the fashion of wetting one's dress.

   The Beauford Chronicle, June 1818

When Thomas came down to breakfast the morning after the brothers' impromptu visit to the Gardner residence, he was inexplicably irritable and ready to show it. Though recently showing signs of maturation, his was a temperament prone to passion rather than moderation. Entering the drawing room, he filled a plate before seating himself across from his brother.

William was sipping coffee while reading his paper. Thomas glared across the table for a moment, waiting for his displeasure be marked, before losing patience.

"I hope you were not serious about that daft idea of a dance."

William looked up calmly. "Woke up on the wrong side of the bed again, I see, Thomas. Why would I not be? Are you opposed to dancing?"

"I am opposed to the notion of providing an opportunity for every family in the neighbourhood to throw their single daughters at you."

William raised his eyebrows. "I hardly think I am that much of a catch, Thomas, but thank you just the same. Do you have anyone in particular in mind or are you referring to all women in the vicinity of Beauford?"

When Thomas did not answer immediately, William changed topic.

"Miss Gardner is a pretty girl, is she not? Rather a willowy figure, and that burnished chestnut hair... She is not a beauty, but there is something about her which makes an impression. I admire a woman with the ability to speak her mind. She certainly seemed to get your back up. Perhaps a bit of a temper, but then I am already used to yours." His lips twitched.

"Are you assessing Miss Gardner's temperament for any particular reason? I assure you I am not amenable to matchmaking."

"It was not you I had in mind. I do wish to marry, you know, Thomas. While you may have written off the entire female sex, I have not."

"Well, write off Miss Gardner at the very least, I beg you," Thomas growled. "Not only did she seem a foolish and impudent minx, but with a house as run down as theirs seemed to be, I'm sure her mother would love to get their hands on you. She was practically drooling over the prospect of Northwood."

"You have a very bleak view of human nature, do you know that, Thomas?" William sighed. "That was not the impression I received at all. I thought Mrs. Gardner was a sincere and friendly woman. Her enthusiasm was due to fond memories and an appreciation for Northwood's beauty. Nothing more."

"An appreciation you used to share, I might add." William looked his brother in the eye. "In a roundabout way, we are here because of your appreciation of beauty, are we not?"

He alluded to the family interests which had brought them to Beauford and which he was determined to keep under wraps for the time being. William wished to establish a rapport with their neighbours first and foremost.

Thomas scowled.

William softened his tone. "While I appreciate your concern, brother, please bear in mind that your experiences with love, painful though I know it has been, does not constitute a fair representation of the whole of womanhood."

Thomas's scowl deepened.

"I'm going out. I must meet with the steward." He stood and grabbed a roll from the side table to shove in a pocket.

"Put you off your appetite with all this talk of women and dancing, Thomas? They used to be two of your favorite pursuits." William grinned into his coffee cup, as his brother stormed out.

Driving along a country road a little later, Thomas's mind remained stubbornly focused on the same subject no matter how he tried to clear it. He had met with their steward, determined to alleviate some of William's responsibilities, and had discussed the collection of rents, the clearing of a particular field, and the repair of a tenant cottage inhabited by an elderly couple too infirm to now do the needed work themselves. For a while, he had been adequately occupied and distracted.

Now the image of Miss Gardner's lips curved in a sardonic half-smile was once again intruding on his vision.

In truth, he was not sure why the thought of Miss Claire Gardner was so infuriating. Perhaps he had been a little harsh in his addresses to her yesterday, but she was so easy to provoke that it had been irresistible.

Some might find her pretty—he would give his brother that much. She had a tolerable figure, a good complexion, and a sweetly shaped mouth. She also gave the impression of being willful, stubborn, and sarcastic—and thus completely unsuitable for someone with William's good-natured disposition. And in spite of her claims otherwise, her head was probably full of fanciful notions of love and marriage like any girl her age.

She was a foolish country chit, nothing more.

A raindrop rolling off his nose drew his attention heavenwards. There was hardly a cloud in the sky when he left the house. Now ominous dark clouds were brewing. He stopped to put up the top of the gig and don his cloak.

The rain increased to a torrent, swiftly turning the road to muck. Thomas considered stopping, but decided to press on to his destination, albeit more slowly. As the horse trudged past the village, a figure in the mist ahead caught his eye. A woman walking alone. Perhaps a farmer's wife returning from market.

Thomas determined he would offer the woman a ride. He could be gentlemanly when he chose, no matter what William might think.

As the gig pulled up alongside the lady, he leaned out. A very bedraggled-looking Miss Claire Gardner stared up at him. She had evidently not chosen her attire with bad weather in mind for she was soaked to the skin. Her wet muslin frock adhered to every curve of her body, the ivory an unfortunate choice in the rain. Once again Thomas silently acknowledged that hers was a tolerable figure. Perhaps even more than tolerable. The way the fabric clung to her shapely thighs and breasts was quite alluring. Good lord! He could see her nipples. He quickly raised his eyes.

In spite of her appearance, Miss Gardner wore a haughty expression.

"May I offer you a ride home, Miss Gardner?" he asked politely, reaching out a hand.

"Thank you, but no. It is not far to Orchard Hill. I prefer to walk." She spoke decisively but her shivering somewhat belied the effect of the words.

Thomas gritted his teeth.

"Miss Gardner, your home is at least a mile away. It is pouring rain and you are clearly not dressed...appropriately." He could not help glancing downwards again, only for a second. Miss Gardner had no idea of how unintentionally enticing she appeared in her wet frock.

She started to respond angrily so he continued with haste. "I mean, for the weather. Although this is England, apparently you did not see fit to bring along a cape or umbrella." Tactless but true. He really could not help goading her. The looks he received were priceless.

"Please allow me to escort you home before you catch cold." He held out his hand a second time. She hesitated and then took hold of it. Her hand was firm but slight in his. And very cold.

She wrapped her arms around herself as she sat down next to him. He could feel her trembling.

With a longsuffering sigh, he pulled off his cloak and began to drape it around her. When she moved to protest, he gently pushed her arm down.

"I insist."

They drove on in silence.

When it felt as if minutes were turning to hours, Thomas ventured a curious glance. Miss Gardner was mostly hidden beneath the cloak. She had pulled the hood over her wet hair. A few stray tendrils lay damp on her neck from which trickling droplets slid lower and lower down her chest.

Thomas wished he had not been so courteous with his cloak. His view would be greatly improved without it.

"There was not a cloud in the sky when I left," Miss Gardner said abruptly.

Thomas agreed, but did not particularly feel like saying so.

"One should always be prepared. Especially a woman. What are you doing walking out alone in the first place? Does your mother know you are out?"

Miss Gardner drew in a breath and puffed up like a furious hen. Now he'd done it.

"Pardon me, Mr. Campbell?" She drew her words out slowly. "I am a grown woman of twenty. Perhaps ladies in London are so delicate and timid that they go nowhere unescorted, but if I wish to walk alone, I assure you I will do so."

"Moreover," she went on, "My mother is aware I went out. We are familiar with all our neighbours. I was quite safe."

"There could be highwaymen along the road, Miss Gardner, despite what you may feel. In your present attire you would make an ideal target..." He gestured to her near transparent garment.

She sputtered. "You are truly incredible, Mr. Campbell. Does your rudeness know no bounds? Is there anyone upon whom you do not bestow your pessimistic insights? It is ungentlemanly in the extreme to comment on a lady's attire." Thomas recalled William saying something similar that morning.

"Pull to the side. I wish to get out." She made as if to rise off the seat, dropping his cloak behind her.

"Stop! Sit down this instant!" Thomas commanded. William was not going to appreciate it if the Gardners decided to shun the Campbells before he could even hold his infernal dance.

Before he could think, he grabbed hold of her arm. Miss Gardner looked down at his hand, her face a mask of icy disdain.

"Kindly release me, Mr. Campbell. I believe it is not highwaymen with whom I should be concerned after all."

Thomas let go. "I... am sorry, Miss Gardner." To his chagrin, he realized it was true. When had he begun to behave so abominably to every creature he met? Of late it seemed bitterness seeped from his every pore.

Moreover, Miss Gardner provoked his devilish side like no one else he had ever met.

"Please, I beg you, be seated before you topple out into the road."

At the speed the horse was going it felt as if they were hardly moving at all. But she could sustain an injury all the same. He would not have that on his head, for William's sake if nothing else.

"I will remain silent the rest of the journey if that is what you wish." He swallowed. He would have to go all the way, he supposed.

"I am truly sorry for having given offense. It was... ungentlemanly of me."

An angry snort was Miss Gardner's only response, but she slowly sat back down.

He made no attempt to return the cloak to her shoulders. She could freeze if she chose, obstinate mule of a girl.

The rain was beginning to lighten. He could see an opening in the clouds in the distance.

They would soon reach Orchard Hill.

Stealing another glance, he found himself hoping Miss Gardner would speak again. When she did not, he tried to think of something else that would ease the tension before she disembarked.

"I believe my brother is quite set on holding a dance at Northwood," he offered. If only William was there to see him now, trying to be polite to the woman he had scorned at breakfast.

"Oh?" Miss Gardner raised her brows. "I am sure many in the neighbourhood will be eager to attend." The grim set of her lips said she would not be one of them.

"My brother is a fine dancer. He is very popular in London." Good God, was he going to be the one playing matchmaker now?

"I am sure he is. Your brother seemed a very refined gentleman." She allowed a small smile.

She had noticed William then. Perhaps returned his interest.

They were pulling into the yard of Orchard Hill before Thomas knew it.

He jumped out and came around to her side to help her down. But Miss Gardner was already standing and attempting to step out. In her determination to avoid taking his hand, she lost her footing and slipped.

She let out a gasp.

Before he knew it, his hands were around her slender waist, holding her firmly before she could tumble.

As Thomas prepared to lift her down, she stubbornly made to pull away. He lost his grip. Her body fell against him with a cry and he struggled to catch her before she hit the ground. His hands slid along her wet dress, missing her waist, before clutching her rather lower and pulling her against him for a moment. She let out a sharp cry of protest and he quickly set her down.

For a moment, her hands rested where they had landed on his shoulders. Her warm body pressed against his, separated only by the damp muslin.

Miss Gardner's face was a radiant mix of shock and anger, her lips parted fetchingly.

Thomas was struck by a bewildering impulse to kiss her, but before he could move, she let go and stepped back.

"Thank you, Mr. Campbell. Good day." She turned and was gone into the house.

And that was that.

Claire sank onto the sofa. She felt oddly weak in the knees. Her body had begun to tremble again, although she was no longer cold. Her face was flushed. There was a curious tingling sensation throughout her body. It had begun sometime around when Thomas's hands touched her waist.

Perhaps she was becoming ill.

A panicked thought entered her mind. Her mind raced back to all of the books she had read and the very same symptoms they described. Could it be that she was attracted to Thomas Campbell?

Frantically she wondered if this was how it started. Alone with a man and the next thing you knew you were pressed up against his body with his hands clutching your... well, a word she would not think let alone say. And then—poof! You were a fallen woman, living in a house of ill repute.

She had read enough novels to know what they were called.

Thomas was obviously an experienced seducer. Perhaps he had planned this all along. Perhaps he drove along country roads intentionally looking for ladies walking alone.

She knew such thoughts were absurd.

Or were they? Everything had become a confusing jumble.

Ridiculous because up until now romances in books had been quite enough for her. As she had told Thomas the first time they had met, she was not urgently seeking a husband. Even if she was, she would never choose a man like Thomas.

Gwendolen's plight had driven home just how precarious a woman's situation could be when she found herself helpless in the hands of the wrong man.

And Thomas was most definitely the wrong sort of man.

No matter that he was so very right in other ways. From his black curling hair to his intense dark eyes to the strong, steely arms that had so easily wrapped around her to catch her effortlessly when she nearly fell. Not to mention his incredible arrogance, oddly intoxicating as much as it was infuriating. His gaze spoke of danger and mystery. Mysteries that were best left unsolved, if a woman did not want to become a rake's latest conquest.

It was not as if a man like Thomas Campbell would be interested in marriage anyway. Especially not to a naïve little country miss—and a "mulish" one at that. It was probably the last thing on his mind.

Seducing naive young women likely ranked much higher.

Or at least enthralling them into sinful thoughts and unspoken desires.

She resolved to avoid Thomas Campbell in the future as much as possible. Not only was he the most infuriating man she had ever met, he was also completely entrancing.

Chapter 4

A *void improper diversions*
    Time is invaluable and its loss irretrievable. Look on every day as a blank sheet to be filled with worthwhile pursuits. Diversions, properly regulated, are not only allowable for young men and women but necessary to youth. But when taken to excess, when they lead to indiscretion, a sort of infatuation, an excess of passions, they grow distasteful. In other words, Dear Readers, guard most carefully against that pastime some would consider innocent but which is unsuitable to your age and inclination, and which may be a danger to your modesty and even womanly chastity itself. We refer, of course, to that insidious fashion—the waltz.

The Beauford Chronicle, July 1818

If Claire had any doubts that Thomas Campbell was not as bad as she had first judged him to be, they were put to rest conclusively after the events of the Northwood dance.

Mr. Campbell's invitation had not come as soon as the next day, nor the day after. But it had arrived within a fortnight, and as the Campbells had only just moved into Northwood, it reflected the eagerness of the new owner to gain the acquaintance and favor of his neighbours with haste.

While Mr. Campbell had expressed a desire to meet Claire's sisters, she realized she had forgotten to mention that Rosalind was away in London. As Gracie was too young to attend, that left Mrs. Gardner and Claire. Her mother's company was always agreeable to Claire, and the women spent the carriage ride enjoyably, conversing and admiring the fine scenery.

Northwood was a stately country manor surrounded by cultivated gardens and a lovely, wooded park. Claire had fond memories of romping through the dense woodlands with her sisters and the Darby girls. The house was one of the largest in the area, with three-stories laid out in an H-plan, designed in the Jacobean style. Claire could not help but think it was a great deal of space for two single men. The servants must outnumber them by at least ten to one. A far cry from cozy Orchard Hill.

Entering the Northwood ballroom, Claire was accosted by a shy dark-haired young woman who touched her arm affectionately. Fanny Rutledge had been a good friend of Claire's since the Gardners had moved to the area. Hillcrest Hall, the Rutledge estate, bordered Northwood to the west and the daughters of both houses along with Claire and Rosalind had fond memories of days spent out in the overlapping parklands.

"There are so many people here, Claire," Fanny whispered, looking about with wide brown eyes.

Mrs. Gardner smiled at Fanny's nervousness, which she was accustomed to, and greeted her warmly before moving off into the crowd. Claire's mother was a welcome addition to any event for she was kind and considerate and happy to spend her time wending her way amongst the spinsters, wallflowers, and older folk. She had a way of speaking with each one and putting them at ease which Claire admired but had yet to master.

Claire was amused by Fanny's assessment. By London standards, the Northwood ballroom was not a large one. Nor would this evening's entertainment be considered a "ball" by *ton* standards. But it was a charming room, with large windows letting in plenty of the fading evening light, a perfectly sized dance floor, and ample comfortable seating for those who did not care to dance.

She squeezed Fanny's hand. "Are you looking forward to dance, Fanny? Mr. Campbell mentioned the possibility of a waltz when Mother and I met him."

There was no reason to mention her meeting with the second Mr. Campbell.

"Mr. Campbell? A waltz?" Fanny sounded breathless. "I am not sure Papa would allow... That is, I am not sure I will be dancing this evening." Fanny looked at her feet.

Claire immediately regretted her comment. How could she have been so careless? Fanny enjoyed dancing, but it was Claire's humble opinion that men did not ask her nearly often enough.

She thought Fanny a pretty girl, but men did not seem to appreciate her particular brand of beauty. Her curvy, fuller figure may not have been the style, but her wide brown eyes, rosebud lips, and glowing skin made for a pleasing combination.

What was more, Fanny had an amiable disposition and a kind word for everyone.

Which was more than some deserved, Claire thought uncharitably, eyeing the door as Harriet and Charles Morton entered the room.

Fanny blanched at the sight of the siblings. Miss Morton's tendency towards tactlessness was even more pronounced around Miss Rutledge. Claire stifled a groan as Harriet spotted them.

"Miss Gardner! Miss Rutledge! How lovely to see you both."

Claire forced a smile. "And you as well, Mr. and Miss Morton."

"Miss Rutledge, that frock is just the right shade of pink for you. It perfectly matches your unique complexion." Harriet tittered behind her brother's shoulder.

Fanny looked down at her dress uncertainly.

Harriet seemed to be alluding to Fanny's freckles, which Claire thought were rather sweet. But then, it was not her opinion that mattered. If she were a man, Fanny would be on the dance floor already.

"It is a lovely shade on you, Fanny," Claire agreed. "The rose color compliments your chestnut hair beautifully."

The remark won her a grateful smile from Fanny. Harriet tried to look pleased at having someone agree with her backhanded compliment.

Fanny's dress was, in fact, truly flattering to her darker coloring. A soft rose floral printed silk gauze over a deep pink muslin with small decorative rosebuds sewn over the bodice.

Harriet herself was dressed in a much gaudier style—a bright yellow striped silk gown covered with yards of white lace. A tall orange ostrich feather capped her hair. Claire thought the colors made her look sallow.

Claire's own gown was of a more modest style. Gwendolen had sent it as a gift from London. Aware of her sister's simpler tastes, she had chosen a gown that was understated yet elegant—a diaphanous sapphire muslin with a thick gold silk sash that emphasized Claire's willowy waist.

"Oh, look! There are our hosts. Are they not fine-looking men?" Harriet observed, determined to steer the conversation. "The elder Mr. Campbell has such a pleasant manner. Why, when he called upon us to deliver the invitation—by his own hand, he charmed our Mama completely. I do not think his features are so handsome as his younger brother's. But what do you think, Miss Gardner?"

Claire tried to balance tact with truthfulness.

"Both of the Mr. Campbells are fine-looking gentlemen."

"But which do you prefer?" Harriet pushed.

Claire glanced over at where the two men stood on the opposite side of the room, ostensibly to greet their guests. William smiled at all he met, offering welcoming words, bowing courteously, and generally radiating a happy demeanor. He would not be described as exceptionally handsome, but he was not unattractive. His complexion was lighter than his brother and his features less striking.

The younger Mr. Campbell had adopted an off-putting stance and had his arms crossed solidly over his chest. He looked bored and arrogant. Claire knew she should be put off rather than attracted. And yet... those dark curls lent him a mysterious romantic air. He was tall and broad, his strong arms tugging against the fabric of his overcoat.

Thomas was more effortlessly masculine than any other man in the room. His demeanor spoke to a self-assurance which was compelling, even magnetic. While William was the quintessential English country squire, Claire had never imagined let alone seen a man quite like Thomas Campbell before.

She knew which of the two men she could not help but find more attractive. But she had no plans to admit it to Harriet. To acknowledge that a licentious rake held any appeal for her would be completely mortifying.

"Mr. William Campbell has an exceptionally pleasant demeanor." Well, that could not be denied, Claire thought. She hoped it would satisfy Harriet.

"Yes, he has a very kind smile," Fanny mused. "And as a pleasant nature is more valuable than a handsome face, I think he is by far the more attractive of the two."

Miss Morton shot Fanny a look as if she had forgotten the girl was there. She glanced at her brother, a smirk on her face, and caught his eye.

"Would you care to dance, Miss Rutledge?"

Mr. Morton held out a hand to Fanny. He had what appeared to be a genuine smile on his face.

A quadrille set was about to begin. As Fanny gave her assent and turned away from the group, Claire caught a glance pass between brother and sister which put her back up.

Harriet seemed pleased to have been left alone with Claire.

"Miss Gardner, I hope you will not mind my sharing something which quite stunned Charles and I."

She lowered her voice and leaned closer.

"I believe we mentioned to you when we last met that Mr. Thomas Campbell keeps an *actress*—" She hissed the last word. "—in London. Now Charles has heard from some of the servants that he has a mistress here, too. Quite close to Northwood somewhere. It is why he moved to the neighbourhood with his brother, to be nearer his second... paramour."

Harriet was doing her best to look scandalized rather than titillated.

"My goodness! How very shocking!" Claire parroted the words she knew Harriet expected her to say.

Secretly, she wondered why Charles had been conversing with Northwood servants. Surely, he knew better than to interfere with any of Mr. Campbell's maids. She felt confident the new master of Northwood would not stand for such things, guest or not.

"Indeed. *Two* women! As women of the world, you and I are aware that these kinds of courtesans are common among men of our sphere. But *two*!"

Claire bit her lip, afraid that if Harriet said the word "two" with such shocked emphasis again, she was going to burst out laughing.

"Well, it speaks to appetites I find very alarming, Miss Gardner. I do not know when I have been more shocked."

Claire eyed her with amusement. She was fairly certain Harriet was enjoying imagining Mr. Thomas Campbell and his two paramours more than was proper but would not begrudge her that.

An image came unbidden of Thomas lying between two beautiful women on a bed of red satin (she was not sure why she thought of red satin, but it seemed the most decadent choice), his muscular chest bare as they stroked him, his eyes closed with carnal pleasure.

She had seen his chest rather closely when he had held her in the rain the other day. A pleasing golden brown from days spent on horseback with a shirt open to the sun. A few curling hairs had been noticeable—dark as the ones on his head.

Abruptly, Claire realized with horror that she had been staring across the room at Thomas for some time. He was returning her gaze.

Claire blushed to the roots and swiftly turned her back to him.

Harriet had caught the exchange and looked like the cat that had eaten the canary.

A second later she peered excitedly over Claire's head.

"Miss Gardner," she hissed. "I believe Mr. Thomas Campbell is coming over here. What do you suppose he could want with us?" She smoothed her skirts and donned a charming smile.

"Perhaps he wishes to add us to his collection of concubines," Claire suggested. This time Harriet appeared genuinely scandalized.

Before Thomas could reach them, Claire put a hand on Harriet's arm.

"I believe I shall go and find Fanny. I will leave Mr. Thomas Campbell to you, Miss Morton. I feel sure you will be quite safe in such a crowd."

She walked away feeling as if she had escaped a lion's den.

"Did you enjoy your dance with Mr. Morton?" Claire asked as she crossed the room and reached Fanny's side.

"Oh, yes! He was a very good dancer. I have never thought he and Miss Morton gave me much notice. It was kind of him to ask me." Fanny's eyes sparkled.

"It was indeed," Claire murmured. "But no more than you deserve, dear Fanny." She squeezed her friend's hand gently.

If only Claire was a man. She would have Fanny up on her feet the entire evening. What fools men were to look only for diamonds when a precious pearl stood right before them.

"If you could dance with any man in the room, Claire, who would you choose?" Fanny gave her an impish look.

Claire pretended to glance around. "Oh, I'm not sure... Perhaps... Sir Bartimaeus Kingsley?" She grinned as Fanny looked towards the white-haired gentleman talking to Mrs. Gardner.

"He must be at least seventy, Claire!" Fanny whispered. Then she saw her friend's face and giggled. "Oh! Claire, that is not fair."

"And what about you, Fanny? Who would you choose? Another dance with Mr. Morton perhaps?" Though it pained her to suggest it.

Fanny contemplated the room carefully before answering with great seriousness.

"I know it is silly, but..." Claire made an encouraging gesture. "Mr. William Campbell."

Fanny blushed a little.

"It is not silly at all. He does have a very kind manner. I much prefer him to that coxcomb Mr. Morton who..." She did not finish for Fanny trod on her foot rather hard. "Ow!"

"May I request another dance, Miss Rutledge?" Mr. Morton stood before them grinning vapidly.

As she watched Fanny return to the dance floor on Charles' arm for the second time, Claire felt a qualm of misgiving. But after all, what were two dances? It was not as if Fanny were seriously interested in Charles Morton, or vice versa. She was simply happy to be given a little attention.

Claire could not help but notice that Thomas Campbell had not yet danced with any of the ladies in the room—young or old. Which was a shame as there was a shortage of male partners.

Claire did not suffer from that shortage, however. She scarcely had a chance to sit down over the next few hours. The Gardner girls had a reputation for being lively dancers and kind conversationalists, so she and Rosalind were rarely unpartnered at events such as this.

She wondered what Rosalind would have to say when she returned from London and met their two new neighbours.

Besides her two dances with Charles, Fanny was mostly neglected. Wistfully, she watched the dancers from the sidelines.

At the completion of the next set, Claire was breathless and ready to rest. Determined to lighten her friend's mood if she could, she looked for Fanny. With a little surprise, she saw her being led onto the dance floor by the elder Mr. Campbell, a sweet smile on her face. Claire could not imagine a better partner for Fanny, nor a young lady more deserving of William's consideration.

The room was warm on the July evening, even with the windows open to the night breeze. Claire made her way to the refreshment table for a glass of lemonade. Seeing the table where her mother sat surrounded by laughing matrons, she decided to join them for a rest.

Moving across the room she passed near where the Morton siblings stood talking to Thomas Campbell. Charles and Harriet were laughing uproariously over something as she neared.

She kept her eyes downwards, hoping her passage would go unnoticed by the trio. She need not have been concerned. The group was oblivious of their surroundings and seemed to have lost all sense of decorum. For the next thing she knew Charles Morton's voice was carrying over loudly.

"Rutledge! Rut-ledge! Name couldn't be more comical for such a sow of a girl. Man would rather fall off a ledge than rut with her."

He guffawed heartily.

"Now, now, Charles—" Claire overheard Harriet say primly. "—It is not poor Miss Rutledge's fault that her family name is so unsuitable for a woman of her physique. Do you not agree, Mr. Campbell? That it is an unsuitable name?"

Claire heard her snicker.

She did not wait to hear more but increased her step and soon sank into a chair next to her mother, a distracted expression on her face.

Was it possible that Thomas Campbell could fall even lower in her esteem that evening? Apparently so.

She expected no better from the Mortons. She had known them since childhood and had seen enough of their snideness to know it was both habitual and incurable.

But for Thomas to stand by while vulgar mockery was made of a guest in his home was unforgiveable. Slighting a sweet girl like Fanny so cruelly and so publicly was unconscionable in Claire's view.

She looked over as Fanny continued to dance with Mr. Campbell, happily ignorant of the unkind words and traitorous tongues surrounding her.

As the set ended, William brought Fanny over to the Gardners' table.

With a bow, he announced, "You may be shocked, Miss Gardner, but there will be waltzing at Northwood this evening." His eyes danced with mischievousness. Fanny was right, he really was a charming man, Claire thought, returning his smile easily.

"Shocking, indeed, Mr. Campbell. After this evening, you will be considered the most daring man in the neighbourhood."

William looked pleased.

He shot her an appraising glance. "As long as I continue to keep your good opinion, Miss Gardner, I shall not mind what the neighbours think." As he spoke, the music changed. Claire heard the notes of a waltz begin.

Mr. Campbell held out a hand. "It may also shock you, Miss Gardner, to learn that I have already taken the liberty of asking your mother if she will permit you to waltz. She has given her consent. Will you dance if it pleases you?"

Now Claire was surprised. Mrs. Gardner sat nearby, engrossed in her conversation with a neighbour, but Claire was certain what William said was true.

She could do nothing but take his hand, glancing back at Fanny who looked diverted by the exchange.

Claire had never waltzed before, but Mr. Campbell was a confident dancer and smoothly took the lead.

After a few minutes, she found herself becoming accustomed to the nearness the dance required. Usually, she was at ease, regardless of her partner. Mr. Campbell had thrown her off course.

Other couples had joined them, but nevertheless, she felt rattled, knowing that most of the room was watching as she waltzed with their host, and perhaps wondering why she had been singled out for this particular attention.

She looked up at William. Kind brown eyes gazed back at her calmly. His trademark smile had not wavered, but it was relaxed rather than exuberant. He was a confident man, but not arrogantly so like his younger brother.

William seemed accustomed to being able to put others at ease and arranging things the way he wished them to be. Being the focal point of an entire roomful of people, most of them near strangers, did not appear to bother him. But then, he had been used to London society. To her chagrin, Claire wondered if she was more of a country mouse than she thought.

"Is the waltz to your liking, Miss Gardner?"

Claire tried to form a response. "It is a different dance than I am used to, Mr. Campbell. But I do find it enjoyable, yes."

"Sometimes differences can be pleasing, can they not? You are different from many young women I have encountered, Miss Gardner. But it is a difference which stimulates and inspires. I enjoy your company very much."

Claire was stunned. She was not sure what to say. They had spent so little time together and yet there was a new warmth to his tone which made her wonder.

William did not seem put off by her silence. Perhaps he assumed she was merely flattered by his frankness.

"I hope we will have an opportunity to become better acquainted soon, Miss Gardner," he continued. "May I have your—"

He did not have the chance to finish, for at this point, an odd thing occurred. A footman approached Mr. Campbell, interrupting their dance to whisper a message.

William withdrew, startled. "I beg your pardon most sincerely, Miss Gardner. I must attend to an urgent matter. Please, pause here a moment."

With that he was gone. She stood alone in the middle of the ballroom floor.

If the attention of the room had been on her before, it certainly was now. Claire was not sure whether to stay or to go as the other couples whirled around her casting curious glances.

She had decided to move aside when the last man she would ever have wished to waltz with appeared before her.

"My brother has requested I take his place, Miss Gardner. I hope you do not object."

Thomas did not wait for a reply but took her hand as he spoke and clasped her waist.

Claire drew in a sharp breath. It was too late for her to object. Yet if she could have done so, she would have, for already she felt disoriented.

What was it about this man and his presence?

When Thomas touched her, the dance took on a new quality it had not had with William.

While she had been nervous at the closeness between their bodies when his brother led the waltz, Thomas provoked other sensations entirely. William exuded a sense of safety. His presence was unfamiliar, but stolid. Even comforting.

But Thomas... Everything about Thomas screamed danger to Claire. Yet she was mesmerized. Without him saying a word, she was spellbound in his arms. Incapable of speech—which, for Claire, was an uncommon thing.

The room around them faded away. The other guests became as static as the furnishings. The only thing that was real was him. The way he looked down at her, with his dark and brooding eyes. His strong mouth firmly set.

No smile lurked on Thomas's face. He might easily be described as cold by anyone.

But to Claire, he was anything but. The space around him felt charged, like the air before a storm. He radiated heat and energy. His touch was like a brand on her skin, and she felt flushed from head to toe as if a current of flame ran through his skin to hers.

Worse, she felt as if he could see right through her, as if she had been stripped bare of pretense—a mortal under the eyes of some strange and seductive god.

Even worse, she liked the feeling.

Part of her wanted to run, knew she should run. But to step out of his encircling arms? To lose this feeling?

She stayed put.

"You are awfully quiet, Miss Gardner. Have I given you cause for offence?"

Yes, actually, Claire almost opened her mouth to say. Not only have you been unkind to my friend, not only are you a debauched rogue, but you have enthralled me, and I wish to be *un*enthralled, if you please.

Before she could say anything, it happened a second time. The footman reappeared to whisper a message. At the same time, the dance ended.

Instead of waiting for her reply, she was left alone again as Thomas swept from the room like a haughty prince.

And worst of all, instead of relief, she felt disappointment.

Thomas strode down the hall, pulling on his cloak as he went.

The message was urgent and had to be answered.

William would return to their guests, while Thomas would go out into the dark summer night. Each man to his own responsibilities.

It was no loss as far as he was concerned. He would rather be with her than in a room crowded with strangers.

Although those last few moments spent holding Miss Claire Gardner in his arms had not been unendurable. From the way she had looked up at him, he might almost be forgiven for believing she may not dislike him quite as much as he had thought.

Chapter 5

The next day was damp and cold for July. As Thomas entered the foyer, William was pulling on a coat.

"Where are you off to?"

"I am on my way to the Gardners. Would you care to join me?"

"It has already come to that, has it?" Thomas kept his tone casual.

"Do not speak in circles, Thomas. Say what you mean."

"I simply mean... Well, are you courting her?"

"Am I courting *her* whom?"

"Now who is speaking in circles. I speak of Miss Claire Gardner, as you well know. Are you? Courting her?"

William looked amused. Thomas resisted the urge to grind his teeth. It would give his brother too much satisfaction.

"A waltz is quite intimate, Thomas, but few would assume courtship must by necessity follow."

"But yes. I am hoping to court Miss Gardner," William added, before his brother could retort. "If I have measured her correctly, then I believe she returns my interest."

Thomas was thrown off guard. He struggled not to show it.

"I hear church bells, William. If her mother has any say in it, I suppose she will be dragging you to the altar soon." He tried to keep his voice light, teasing, anything but what he really felt. Which was a difficult to describe sensation. An unwanted one.

"A lovely young woman like Miss Gardner would be welcome to. I am determined to know her better. Not all of us are as averse to marriage as you, Thomas."

Thomas was speechless. William turned as if to go, then hesitated.

"Did all go well last night? I should have thanked you before now for leaving the dance last night."

"It was my responsibility to manage," Thomas replied, somewhat surprised. He smirked. "Besides, it is not as if it was a great sacrifice on my part."

"Yes, yes, you need not lambast the night's entertainment again. I am well aware of your view. But... Doctor Greyson? You spoke with him when you arrived?"

"I did. To tell the truth, I believe it was an overreaction to summon him. If I had been present, I should not have done so." He looked at William who still seemed ill at ease.

"Truly, William. You know I would not discount a genuine concern. Visit later, if it will put your mind at rest."

William nodded, appearing relieved. He turned back towards the door.

"Wait. I shall join you. I should like to better know my future sister-in-law," Thomas decided.

At least he had finally made William blush.

He was truly taken with her then? Thomas could not say why this bothered him so much. What was Miss Gardner to him? A country chit, unrefined, with little elegance. She was nothing like the women he generally admired. Yet, silently he agreed with his brother. There was something there.

When the two men arrived at Orchard Hill, a carriage was already in the yard. Entering the house, they found Harriet and Charles Morton in the sitting room with Claire and Mrs. Gardner.

Thomas was not thrilled to see the siblings.

The other night, he had formed the opinion that they were the worst sort of people—shallow and spiteful; the kind he and William would do well to avoid.

Miss Morton had barraged him with questions about his elder brother at the dance, rather indiscreetly, making no attempt to veil her interest in the Campbell family's finances or any plans William might have to wed.

On top of that, the crassness of their comments about one of the guests at Northwood, a Miss Fanny Rutledge who William had singled out for a dance, had lowered them in Thomas's esteem irredeemably. When Charles had remarked on Miss Rutledge in vulgar terms, Thomas could not help asking the young man why on earth he had asked her to dance more than once that evening. The sputtering response and exchange of glances between siblings was answer enough. It was easy to see the two enjoyed making cruel sport of those they thought beneath them.

Thomas was no angel, but neither was he the misanthrope William liked to pretend he was. Miss Rutledge had seemed a shy, unassuming girl. Her demure manner reminded him of his own younger sister,

Elizabeth. He would not wish to see her treated so carelessly by any man. In fact, he would trounce any man who he learned had done so.

Miss Rutledge did not have the advantage of an older brother, which was unfortunate.

Privately, Thomas had been pleased by his brother's kindness in singling out the young lady. Although he was all too well-aware his brother was the better man, William's consideration for others could still surprise him sometimes.

Miss Morton looked thrilled by the arrival of the two Campbells. Thomas was already regretting his decision to join William on this visit.

As Thomas had previously observed, the sitting room of Orchard House was a small one. With four visitors as well as the ladies of the house, it was cramped. William had managed to seat himself next to Miss Gardner, while Thomas was left to share a settee with Miss Morton.

He took pleasure in noting Miss Morton's pinched expression. She appeared just as annoyed to be sitting by him as he was by. A second son would evidently not do for Harriet.

With a sigh, he settled himself beside her. Although he had no fear William would ever be interested in a young woman of Miss Morton's calibre, at least his brother would be spared her irritating company.

Thomas felt quite altruistic.

Then Miss Morton opened her mouth. As she babbled nonsense which seemed to be mostly local gossip, Thomas did his best to keep his face blank and his responses as brief as possible. After a few minutes, he looked over to see how things were going with William and Miss Gardner.

A little pang went through him as he saw their two heads inclined towards each other, one fair, one dark—making a perfect contrast. They were both smiling, obviously entertained by one another's conversation. Miss Gardner looked even prettier than she had at the dance.

On a less attractive woman, the plain white gown she wore might have been unbecoming. On Miss Gardner, the dress flattered her soft curves, while the vestal white highlighted the red of her cheeks and rosy tint of her lips. Was it his imagination or did she seem to be glowing as she spoke to William?

He supposed it was to be expected. What woman would be able to resist a man like William? He was everything to be hoped for in a husband—wealthy, handsome, gentle, and kind.

Miss Gardner could not possibly hope for better.

He turned back to Miss Morton. He had lost track of their conversation, but she had drawn Mrs. Gardner and her brother in to take his place.

Now she was saying something so inane it caught his attention.

"...have heard it said that Miss Rutledge is his natural daughter..."

It might have been a question directed towards Mrs. Gardner, but if it was, Harriet did not wait for a reply.

"I, for one, cannot imagine keeping a by-blow in my own house. Sharing a home with offspring who could be the product of... well, an ill-bred woman with no respectability at the very least. And the product of such a distasteful liaison. Men are, of course, entitled to their indiscretions. But the issue that come of it should never be raised to believe they are in any way equal..."

Mrs. Gardner cut her off.

"I am not certain about the suitability of this topic, Miss Morton." Mrs. Gardner's tone was mildly reproving.

Claire Gardner interjected before her mother could continue.

"What was that you were saying just now, Miss Morton? Are you speaking of my family's dear friend, Miss Rutledge?"

Miss Morton smiled as if her mouth were full of sugar. Though Thomas rather thought it to be full of something much nastier.

"Such a sweet girl..." she began.

But Miss Gardner was disinclined to let her go on.

"Yes," she interrupted emphatically. "Miss Rutledge is a sweet girl. A gentle girl. A lovely girl who would never say an unkind word about anyone no matter how much they might deserve it."

"However, what she is *not* is Mr. Rutledge's natural daughter as you have so crassly implied. She is as legitimate as you. Or your brother."

Miss Morton's eyes narrowed. Charles Morton seemed to have found something fascinating about his fingernails and was looking at them intently.

Apparently, Miss Gardner shared Miss Morton's disdain for bastard children.

Thomas supposed it was expected she would but was still disappointed by her prejudice.

He saw William glance at him, as if preparing to speak up. Thomas shot him a quelling look.

"However, even if she were a 'natural child' as you put it," Miss Gardner continued. "How dare you dismiss an innocent soul as if they were worthless merely because they were born on the wrong side of the blanket?"

It was not a phrase one often heard coming from an unmarried young lady's mouth, but then, Miss Morton had set quite a precedent for indelicacy today.

Miss Morton looked revolted.

"You cannot really mean to say though, Miss Gardner, that you would *welcome* such a child into your home and allow them to mix with your own sons and daughters."

"If the child had no other caregiver, or if their mother were deceased. Or if their father wished it so—which I would hope would be the case, as such would only be natural—I would do my best to welcome them, yes." Miss Gardner's chin was high and her face flushed from this passionate speech.

William stared at Miss Gardner with appreciation. Thomas felt much the same way. As Claire sat with her back straight, her eyes hard grey steel, obviously prepared to continue to do battle if necessary, Miss Morton could do nothing but close her mouth.

In Thomas's experience, Miss Gardner's unconventional speech was a rarity in a sheltered young lady. As was the generous belief that a husband's bastards should be welcomed into one's home.

He wondered whether she really meant the words, or simply enjoyed contradicting Miss Morton.

William would likely say Miss Gardner was incapable of insincerity and he might very well be right. Perhaps Miss Gardner had heart as well as beauty.

With a pang, Thomas suddenly wished he had noticed some of her finer qualities from the start. Which was absurd. She was William's, clearly.

Besides, he had no wish to take a wife. Although were he to do so, a compassionate woman like Claire might be the very person to fit his circumstances.

He wondered if this was what William had in mind. Chastened by his brother's thoughtfulness in considering his younger brother's predicament, even when it came to selecting a bride, he abruptly spoke up.

"In my experience, Miss Gardner, such liberal-mindedness is rare among gently-reared young women who have a tendency towards naïve and narrowminded preconceptions. If you truly are sincere in your declaration then I admire your spirit."

William shot him a quizzical look. Miss Gardner stared as if she were not sure if she had received a compliment or an insult. She was just opening her mouth to reply when the Mortons stood in unison.

"We really must be going. We have many other calls to pay."

After the Mortons had shown themselves out, William stood as well. He said something to Miss Gardner in a low voice before thanking her mother for the pleasant visit.

What had he said? What had they spoken of?

Thomas longed to know, filled with a bizarre envy over the time William had spent next to Claire, learning more of her thoughts, her mind.

It was foolishness, he knew. Worse, such thoughts could lead to others and damage the very foundation of his relationship with his brother. One which, since the loss of their parents, was especially precious to him.

The brothers were quiet as they drove. Thomas assumed William's head was full of thoughts of Miss Gardner. He determined to push all similar thoughts from his mind once and for all. She was not for him. Ironic that he had at first believed her unsuited for William when it seemed the opposite might be true. They shared a strength of character which could make for an ideal partnership.

Whereas he could never hope to deserve a woman like Miss Gardner.

At William's suggestion, they made one other visit nearby upon leaving Orchard Hill. It was late in the afternoon when they returned to Northwood and their hearts were heavy with worry.

Chapter 6

*W*hen seeking a husband, good sense and good-nature are requisite

Mutual esteem is as essential to happiness as affection in the married state. Repeated quarrels which youths believe indicative of an admirable passion will settle into irreconcilable aversion and you will not only become each other's torment but the object of contempt to your family and acquaintance. The incitement of uncontrollable passion is the domain of the rakehell rather than the good husband, and thus must not be foolishly esteemed.

The Beauford Chronicle, July 1818

Claire was brooding. Sitting at a window in the front parlor, she looked out on the tree-covered yard. The one which William had admired so much on his first visit to Orchard Hill. But it was not William who was on her mind. It would almost have been a relief if he had.

Thomas Campbell was a mess of contradictions and Claire did not know what to make of them.

She thought back over everything she knew or had been told.

He was a rake. That much she had surmised as soon as she saw him.

He kept a mistress. Two mistresses if Harriet was to be believed. As being the first to spread juicy tidbits of gossip was her lifeblood after all, there was no reason to think the information incorrect.

He was capable of rudeness and snide cruelty. He had stood by and allowed cruelty towards Fanny. Not to mention, the way he generally spoke to her so brusquely she felt as if had mistaken her for a horse and not a woman.

Yet he was capable of courtesy, too. The carriage ride in the rain may not have been ideal, but he did stop to help her. What constituted helping to a man like Thomas, anyways.

He seemed to have favored her defense of Fanny. Adding to his contradictory nature.

He was an excellent dancer.

He was dark, brooding, indescribably handsome (it pained her to admit this), and could set her heart racing with a glance.

He had moved into the area to be closer to his mistress.

One of his mistresses. The other must be pining away in London. How sad.

Well, there was no getting away from that last one.

How often did he visit the women in his harem?

She tried not to imagine it, but failed miserably. Thomas arriving outside a house on horseback, racing eagerly inside, into the arms of one of his beautiful courtesans who lay surrounded by soft pillows, scantily clad in scarlet silks, waiting to be kissed. Her lovely arms raised to throw about his neck and pull him down next to her. She must be a very skillful lover, if she could keep the attention of a worldly man like Thomas.

How had he selected them for their contrasts? Was one woman dark and the other fair? Or did one have skills the other did not? Claire reddened thinking of what those talents might entail.

With a groan of frustration, she rose. It was time for a long, head-clearing walk.

"Gracie!" she called. She had heard heavy thuds coming from above, then silence—which was never a good sign with a child. She hoped Gracie was not building a castle using all of their dressers and wardrobes as walls again. Time to get her little sister out of doors where she could do less damage.

By the time they were walking down the road, the sun was high in the sky. The castle had taken some heavy pushing to dismantle, Gracie grumbling all the while over it's tragic destruction. Claire had only been able to placate her by telling her about the little girl she had met, who lived nearby. Gracie's eyes had lit up at the prospect of sharing her special hideaways with a new friend who seemed in need of some adventure.

As they walked along the dusty road, Claire hoped Isabel Notley would be at home when they called.

When they reached the house, she saw with relief that the little girl was enjoying the fine day out on the lawn. A handsome-looking, middle-aged woman sat smiling beside her, reading out loud. This must be the beloved Mrs. Mowbray.

Pleasantries and introductions were exchanged and soon Gracie and Claire had joined the ladies on their picnic blanket to share some make-believe tea.

Make-believe tea could not keep Gracie still for long and soon she was clamoring with excitement to show Isabel the brook behind her new home. Appearing both nervous and thrilled at the idea, Isabel looked up at her governess.

"Well..." Mrs. Mowbray sounded uncertain. She cleared her throat. "I would not normally deny any child the benefit of fresh air and exercise. However, Miss Notley is quite delicate. Her recent illness has left her in a weakened condition. I am not sure her doctor would want her to risk her overexerting herself, especially on such a warm day."

Isabel looked crestfallen, then perked up again. "Papa did say he wanted me to take in the fresh air as much as possible, so I could grow healthy and strong again. Perhaps... being outside for a little longer, and just for a very small walk..."

Mrs. Mowbray smiled fondly at her charge.

"If Miss Gardner and I may accompany you both, then you may go," she answered gently.

Gracie flew to her feet, grabbing hold of Isabel's hands to pull her up. Claire watched her sister take off at a sprint across the lawn, Isabel walking quickly to catch up.

"Slow down and wait for Miss Notley, Gracie!" For once, Gracie did as she was told and waited for Isabel, taking her hand and proceeding at a more moderate pace towards the back of the house and into the woods where the brook lay.

As the two women walked behind the girls at a discreet distance, Claire noted the differences. Gracie was a sturdy, strong girl with long legs and tanned skin. She was as comfortable climbing trees as stairs – something Mrs. Gardner believed was as much a girl's birthright as boys. While close in age, Isabel was pale, slight, and petite. The word "delicate" was apt. She was mature for her age, however, and seemed older than an eight-year-old in some ways.

"Has Miss Notley been in poor health for long, Mrs. Mowbray?"

"I cannot say with certainty, for she has not been in my charge more than two months." Mrs. Mowbray caught Claire's look of surprise.

"She seems so attached to you. When we first met, she could speak of nothing but you and Matilda," Claire explained.

"Oh, yes, Matilda. I am surprised she was not brought along on this adventure." Mrs. Mowbray kept a watchful eye on where the girls walked ahead through the shady woods.

"Miss Notley lived with her mother, until recently. In conditions which, I have been led to understand, were quite unsuitable for a little girl. As was her former caretaker." Mrs. Mowbray paused as if not sure how much to share.

The opportunity to have another woman, even a much younger one, commiserate was too great for her.

"She was living in squalor, Miss Gardner. Utterly neglected. Even thinner than she is now, the poor mite. The woman who was supposed to be her caretaker had been misusing the funds meant for Miss Notley's upkeep – on spirits no less! Apparently, she was falling-down drunk much of the time."

Claire was shocked. "But what of Miss Notley's mother? Surely she could not have known..."

"Oh, she knew," Mrs. Mowbray snapped. "She knew and she did not care. Not for anything but own vanity and pleasures. Miss Notley's mother is an actress, but could not act as a mother. She did not even have Miss Notley in the same house, nor did she visit – or if so, rarely."

Her expression softened a little. "Miss Notley has never spoken ill of her mother. She loves her. What child does not? It is very difficult for a child to understand the rejection and abuse of a parent. And yet, Miss Gardner, the poor little girl had been rejected. Completely."

"What occurred to change Miss Notley's plight?" Claire wondered, thoroughly saddened by the idea of a child living so isolated and unloved.

There was a particular reason the topic of illegitimate children was one which was close to Claire's heart. But that was a family matter which she was not about to publicize, even with a caring woman like Mrs. Mowbray.

"Her father. It was he who hired me and made arrangements to immediately move us here. If it is to be believed and I think I do believe it, Miss Gardner, naïve though it may sound, he did not know the circumstances in which his daughter lived. He believed her mother saw her much more frequently than she did and that the money he provided went towards a higher quality of care and sustenance than she was receiving."

She looked ahead at the children. They had reached the little brook. The water was shallow and the girls had already pulled off their shoes and stockings and were wading in the cool water, their shrieks carrying through the trees.

"Miss Notley told me—" Mrs. Mowbray lowered her voice. "—that when her father appeared one day to see her, he quite exploded with rage. I am assuming he was rightly angered at seeing his child's living conditions. He took her from that place the same day. From what I can determine, from speaking to Miss Notley's maid, his relationship with the mother ended recently when she spurned him for some other wealthy benefactor. Only then did he think to check on his daughter." She shook her head with a frown.

"Could he really not have known how his child was living, so neglected?"

Mrs. Mowbray shook her head. "It is difficult to understand, I know. My children are older and grown now, but even when they were young... well, I could never imagine having so little care for one's own flesh and blood. That being said, men do not always have the same sense for these things as we women."

Claire, who had had an excellent father, could not quite fathom this but said nothing. It could be very true, what Mrs. Mowbray claimed, about the majority of men.

"I will say, Miss Notley's father has done his best to make amends. She is being given excellent care, the best of everything – from clothing to food to dolls. A physician calls upon her almost daily. Her father visits far more frequently than her mother ever did. There is a long road ahead of him, for Miss Notley finds him quite fierce and she can be a timid little thing. But... in time, I think she will come to know him better and grow to love him, I hope... Well, that is, if there is time for that."

"Why would there not be?" Claire's curiosity was piqued. Little Isabel's story seemed like something out of a book of fairy stories. The neglected princess rescued by her knight.

The governess looked at her sadly. "Miss Gardner, I could not help overhearing the physician when he last spoke with Miss Notley's father. There is a lung condition of some kind. The doctor believes Miss Notley may be..." The governess dropped her voice to a whisper. "...dying."

Claire covered her mouth in horror. She looked to where Isabel and Gracie played, kicking up water at each other and running back and forth over the rocks. Isabel's face was flushed and rosy. She looked more robust than Claire had seen her. Could it be true of such a little girl? Her heart tightened in her chest as she thought of a child dying without ever feeling safe and loved, without having had a true family life.

"It seems impossible, does it not?" Mrs. Mowbray sighed looking at the girls playing. "She has her good days and her bad days. This is a good one. She is the most active I have ever seen her. I hope we do not pay a price for it tomorrow. I thought it a risk worth taking as her father refuses to accept the doctor's diagnosis and insists Isabel will mend. She does have a lovely color in her cheeks now."

She clapped her hands and called in the girls' direction. "We must return home now, Miss Notley. You will be weary if we are not careful! Miss Gardner and her sister may visit you another day if they like."

Isabel turned with a look of disappointment, but collected her footwear and came towards them. Compared to Gracie, who was still jumping from rock to rock, Isabel did seem tired. She followed Mrs. Mowbray back to the house without complaint, while Claire went to collect Gracie.

As they walked down the lawn towards the lane, Gracie skipped and twirled happily, mindless of her sodden shoes and stockings. She would probably have blisters in the morning, Clare reflected, but she would not ruin her sister's enjoyment of the sunny day by mentioning it.

"Did you enjoy Miss Notley's company, Gracie?"

"Very much! She has an excellent imagination. We have named the brook 'Isabel's Delight.' The woods are now to be known as 'Grove of Grace.' Isn't that a beautiful name?"

Gracie did not usually go in for imaginative play, preferring to be as active as possible. Miss Notley might balance her out very well. Claire wondered if Mrs. Mowbray and her mother might approve of the girls sharing some of their lessons.

"And what of the house? Has Miss Notley named that as well?"

"Of course. At first, we thought of calling it 'Rose Cottage' because there are roses in the garden and along the walls. But it is not really a cottage, is it? It is larger than Orchard Hill. Isabel says there are eight bedrooms! Besides Mrs. Mowbray, she has two maids—just for her!"

After Gracie finished being impressed by such grandeur, she continued. "Then we thought of 'Notley Manor.' That sounds grand and imposing, does it not?" Claire nodded agreement. "But we decided it was not a very welcoming sounding name, and Stoneybrook would be best. The stones in the brook and the stones on the roof..." Gracie waved a hand back towards the stream.

"Stoneybrook. Yes, I see what you mean. Very pretty. Every house should have a name. It will make it much homier for Miss Notley." Gracie nodded her agreement.

The sisters had just reached the road when the sound of horse hooves made them step to the edge. As the noise grew closer, they saw a single rider coming towards them at a trot.

"Oh, Mr. Campbell!" Gracie exclaimed, excited to have more company.

The sun was a smoky orange, nearing the horizon. Claire put a hand to her brow and squinted. "So it is. I wonder why he has ridden so far out this late in the day."

As William neared them, Gracie called out and waved. The gestures were returned and Mr. Campbell dismounted and came over.

"We have just come from Stoneybrook, Mr. Campbell." Gracie said with a secretive smile.

"I do not believe I have heard that name before. Is it a large estate?"

"Oh, no. Quite small." She spun with her arms out, enjoying herself immensely. Claire and William exchanged amused glances, stepping out of the way of Gracie's rotations.

"Is it near or is it far?" William asked, obviously enjoying the banter.

Gracie paused her twirling. "Very near. Very near indeed."

Mr. Campbell put a finger to his lips and looked all about.

"Do you give up?" Gracie cried.

"I do indeed. I am new to the neighbourhood, after all. You must have pity on me. This Stoneybrook is a mystery to me."

"That is because it did not exist until an hour ago. Miss Notley and I named it ourselves."

Mr. Campbell's expression changed as Gracie finished but Claire could not pinpoint what it conveyed.

"Miss Notley is the little girl who lives in the house there," Claire explained, pointing towards Stoneybrook. "She and her governess are our new neighbours."

"Ah, yes! It is a pretty storybook kind of a house, I've always thought. When riding on our way to Orchard Hill the other day, I mean." William seemed a little flustered.

"I was on my way to... Well, it does not matter. I am here now. May I escort you home, fair damsels?" He gave an exaggerated knightly bow that sent Gracie into cackles.

Claire was glad Gracie was there with her, a tiny chaperone, and a buffer between herself and Mr. Campbell.

However, any hope she had of Gracie's presence preventing awkwardness disappeared as her sister raced ahead. Claire followed behind at a more moderate pace, with Mr. Campbell beside her, reins in hand.

"Thomas and I enjoyed our visit to Orchard Hill the other day, Miss Gardner. As well as the stimulating conversation."

He shot Claire a grin which she ruefully returned.

"Yes, the Mortons have a way of bringing out the stimulating conversation in me, although I am sorry for the indelicacy of the topic."

"Not at all. I enjoyed your frankness. It was refreshing to speak of something other than tea or the weather. Moreover, I agree with you and Thomas on the subject. Children should not be held accountable for their parents' faults and all should be given the opportunity to thrive, regardless of their descent. It is a moral imperative. I have no patience for the small-mindedness of people like the Mortons." There was a pause. "I thought you showed remarkable restraint, in fact, considering it was your friend Miss Morton intended to slight."

"Miss Rutledge is such a sweet girl that I am not sure why the Mortons seem to have her in their sights of late."

"Some people enjoy making mischief. Perhaps due to a lack of happiness with their own lot in life."

They walked on in companionable silence.

Claire felt Mr. Campbell's gaze as he glanced over from time to time. She made sure to keep her eyes on the road.

Mr. Campbell was a charming man. He was handsome. He was well-to-do and could easily provide for Claire and her family, if it came to it. He would probably make an excellent husband and an affectionate father. Clearly, he had a kind and generous heart.

But she felt nothing when she saw him. He might as well have been the farmer across the lane or the postmaster.

She could admire his character and rationally know that he would be a wise match, but... The truth was that she had felt a spark between herself and Thomas and while she knew it was utterly foolish to envision any kind of a life with a rake, if she ever did decide to marry, could she not at least hold out the hope of perhaps feeling such a thing again in the future with someone else?

Someone who did not already have at least one woman in his life and in his bed.

"Did you enjoy the dance at Northwood, Miss Gardner? I hope the waltz was to your liking despite our interruption. I was sorry to leave. You were an enjoyable partner."

"I did, thank you. After hosting such a lovely evening, I believe you will find yourself a most popular man in Beauford, Mr. Campbell."

She spoke lightly, determined not to discuss the waltz.

Or what she felt during the waltz. Or most importantly, with whom she had felt it.

"I hope that you will visit Northwood again soon, Miss Gardner. I would be happy to show you the grounds. Although I am sure you are more familiar with them than I am. Perhaps you and your mother would like to come one afternoon. With Gracie, too, of course." He looked at her with a charming smile. "I am eager to spend more time with you, Miss Gardner, as you may have already perceived."

While the idea of roaming Northwood's parklands again was appealing, Claire was not inclined to accept an invitation into which Mr. Campbell might read more than she intended.

"Perhaps, one day." Claire said lamely. She smiled to soften the words, but William's eyes widened a little. If he had been expecting a more enthusiastic acceptance, it would be better to make things clearer now. "I have heard you are becoming a favorite with Beauford's young ladies, Mr. Campbell. I am sure you will have no trouble finding a more suitable walking companion soon."

Was she being too subtle? Bluntness was generally her forte, but she had no wish to injure William's feelings when he had striven to be so kind.

"You mentioned your sister was still in London, Mr. Campbell. Perhaps I will meet her there next spring. My mother insists I must have at least one season and while I have managed to put her off this year, I do not think she will relent again." She hoped the choice of subject would provide a hint.

Mr. Campbell gave her a considering look before responding.

"Yes, Elizabeth remains in London with our aunt. I am sure she would be glad to make your acquaintance." He smiled at Claire. "I do not envy the pressure a young woman must face when coming out in

London. As you do not seem to be relishing your upcoming time amidst the *ton*, I hope it will be your first and last."

He seemed to understand. Claire felt herself relax a little.

They were coming up to Orchard Hill. As they walked through the yard, the front door opened and Mrs. Gardner came out, accompanied by Fanny Rutledge.

Gracie had arrived ahead of them. Her golden head popped out from behind the women, her fists stuffed with tarts she had evidently pillaged from the kitchen, a grin on her jam-smeared face.

Fanny's mouth formed a pretty "O" as she saw who accompanied Claire. William's presence immediately threw her into a shy silence.

"Fanny!" Claire greeted her friend warmly. "Have I missed your visit? I hope you have not been waiting long for us to return. Not that my mother is not excellent company."

"We had a very pleasant afternoon together," Mrs. Gardner assured her daughter. "Good afternoon, Mr. Campbell. Or rather, good evening, I suppose I should say."

William greeted the ladies. "While it is delightful to see you all, I must be on my way. When I encountered Miss Gardner and Gracie I took a pleasant detour from my intended destination, but I think I will still be able to reach it before suppertime if I hurry. I bid you all a good evening."

As he mounted and rode out of the yard, Fanny grabbed her hand with a squeal.

"Were you walking out with Mr. Campbell, Claire? He seems to be paying you special attention."

Claire looked at her affectionately. While she knew Fanny found Mr. Campbell attractive, there was not an envious bone in her friend's body. Claire knew she would only wish her well if she learned she was to marry William the very next day. However, it was not going to come to that.

"I think that Mr. Campbell and I will merely be good friends."

Fanny's expression of concern made her smile.

"That is my choice, Fanny," she said gently. "Mr. Campbell is a delightful man, but I do not feel any particular..."

"Connection?"

"Yes. There is not a connection. Beyond friendship, that is." Claire shot her a grateful look.

"Perhaps Mr. Thomas Campbell will have better luck with you, Claire." Fanny smiled playfully.

Sometimes Fanny was rather too astute. "Fanny!"

"Do not think I missed the exchange of glances between you and the younger Mr. Campbell at the dance the other night, Claire. I am quite sure Harriet did not. Did you notice that neither of the two Mr. Campbells asked her to dance the entire evening? She was practically shooting daggers as you waltzed with them both!"

"She has nothing to be envious of. Mr. William Campbell is free to pursue any woman, including Harriet if he likes—" Fanny looked as if she did not think that was probable. "—while Mr. Thomas Campbell is..."

"Tall? Dashing? Handsome as sin?" Fanny supplied helpfully, with a grin.

"I thought it was William you found the more well-favoured of the two." Claire glared.

"Well, I do. But I am not blind. Mr. Thomas Campbell has a certain rakish and romantic air to him. I am sure we are not the only ones to have noticed it. I do not think there was a single woman in the room who could keep their eyes off of him when you were waltzing. Well, maybe Mrs. Gardner." She smiled impishly.

"Yes, well, I am sure he is quite aware of his own charms. Sin is the perfect word to describe a man who has not one but two mistresses."

Claire hoped her friend would not notice the hint of resentment in her tone.

"Two mistresses!" Fanny looked fascinated. "Did he tell you that as you waltzed?"

Claire rolled her eyes. Why on earth were women so intrigued by womanizing men? Was it the allure of knowing a man like Thomas was highly desirable to other women?

"No! Fanny, really? Is that what you think we discussed? He has better manners than to raise topics that are so..."

"Sinful? Wicked? Seductive?"

"I was going to say highly inappropriate. You are quite the thesaurus this evening, aren't you? Will you please stop waggling your eyebrows at me like that? You look ridiculous. Like a caterpillar."

Fanny continued to smirk but had the decency to look a little chastened. Like a dog with a bone, she would not let go completely though.

"Who told you then? About his two mistresses? Was it... the older Mr. Campbell?" Her eyes went round.

Claire groaned and pulled her friend towards the house. "If we are going to discuss such *sinful* subjects, may we at least do it over some of the tarts Gracie was clutching a moment ago? I have been walking for hours and am famished."

"Very well. But do not think I am going to simply forget about this, Claire. I want all the details you have concerning this seductive libertine in our midst. You know, that reminds me—the *Chronicle* has been publishing a series of articles you might find extremely enlightening. I shall have to bring some along the next time I visit."

Fanny shook her head in feigned concern, barely hiding a smirk.

"Grant me patience," Claire grumbled as they entered the house arm in arm.

Chapter 7

William wandered into the drawing room where Thomas sat, smoking and reading. Thomas glanced up. His brother had a distracted expression, his brows furrowed.

Thomas supposed he had been out with Miss Gardner.

He had been preparing himself for William to share some good news about his courtship. He wanted to be sincerely glad for his brother's happiness. If Miss Gardner was to be his sister-in-law in the not-so-distant future, he was determined that neither William nor Claire would ever suspect he felt anything else.

"How is Miss Gardner, William?" He put down his book to give his brother his full attention.

"Hmmm?"

"How is Miss Gardner? Based on the distracted look on your face, I assume you have just come from seeing her? Is she well?" A pause. "William...?

Was it possible things had moved even faster than he had expected? Could it be that they were engaged?

It would explain William's state of total preoccupation.

Thomas cleared his throat and prepared to offer felicitations. Benedictions. Congratulations. Whatever one was supposed to do for one's brother upon finding out he was engaged, that was what he wanted to do for William. Whatever was right.

What did it matter that the dreams he had been having of Miss Gardner of late had been so very, very wrong. That day in the rain... The peculiar combination Miss Gardner had embodied. Half bedraggled kitten he wanted to scoop into his arms and protect. Half succulent minx, soaked to the skin, with a dress so transparent that it made a man want to peel it off and run his hands over... Oh, God. It was happening again.

At least at night, he could awake in the morning and feel blameless. One could not control one's dreams. Not for lack of trying on his part.

He supposed he should be grateful to at last be dreaming of someone other than Serafina. Even if this new nighttime muse was even more unsuitable.

He cleared his throat. "Do you have some news to share, William? Concerning you and Miss Gardner?"

William crossed over and took a seat, slouching into the leather chair.

"I was mistaken. About Miss Gardner." He put a hand to his chin absent-mindedly.

He did not seem particularly put out, simply confused, as if he had made a wrong move in a chess game.

"What do you mean? What are you saying?" This time Thomas's reaction was genuine. "Have you learned something to alter your opinion of Miss Gardner's character?"

William gestured dismissively. "Nothing like that. Merely that today, I realized I was incorrect. My perceptions of her interest were mistaken."

Thomas wondered if his bafflement was showing plainly enough.

"She does not return my interest, Thomas," William explained as he looked at his brother's expression. He spoke slowly, as if to an infant.

Thomas did not particularly appreciate being condescended to, but if William had just been roundly rejected by a woman, he would grant some leeway.

"What? Of course, she does!" Thomas drew a deep breath. "Of course, she does. Of course, she must, William. Why wouldn't she?"

He could not help adding, "She is a single female, is she not? And you a single man with a fortune who is—" He looked his brother up and down. "—not ugly."

William glared. "Thank you, brother. Your kindness warms the heart."

"Very well, you are moderately well-favoured," Thomas amended. "And perhaps not every woman, but I firmly believe the vast majority of females in the country of England would find you to be a more than acceptable suitor."

"Oh, Thomas." William sounded cross. He really had been rebuffed then. Thomas's heart was a Judas for it sped up as he realized he might not have to welcome Miss Gardner as a sister after all.

Good Lord, that could have been awkward.

He changed his tone. "Miss Gardner is young. Perhaps she simply does not know her own mind yet. I am sure you have misconstrued her somehow."

"And Miss Gardner seems to you to be a woman who would not know her own mind, does she, Thomas?" William asked wryly.

He sighed and looked into the fire. "No, Miss Gardner is a forthright girl. I appreciate that. I believe she made herself clear. I am not sure how enthused she is about the prospect of matrimony in general—to anyone. Not that many women have the privilege of being against it. Regardless, she made it evident that she is not interested in me, in that way."

"I... am sorry, William." Thomas tried to gauge how much he should say.

William rubbed his forehead. For the first time, Thomas noticed how tired he looked.

"To be honest—" He glanced at Thomas. "—I discover it is not myself I feel the most disappointed for."

"Whatever do you mean?"

"Can you really be so dense, Thomas?"

Thomas glared. "It would appear that I can."

"You have a daughter who is desperately in need of a mother." He raised a hand. "And before you continue to open your mouth to say she has one, let us not bother with pretense— that unfortunate excuse of a woman has proven herself to be incapable of properly caring for a delicate girl like Isabel."

"You wanted Claire to be Isabel's mother." Comprehension dawned on Thomas's face.

"Well... someone should be. Someone needs to be. She deserves that, Thomas. After how she has been treated by her own. Abandoned. Mistreated."

"And ignored and forgotten by her own father." Thomas spoke quietly.

"I do not say you mistreated her, Thomas. You are not capable of such a thing. You simply did not know how dire her circumstances were until things with Serafina were at an end."

"Because I did not care enough to inquire."

"You were... distracted. As many men would have been. Most are content to pay for their by-blow's upkeep and nothing more. But Isabel..." William rested his head in his hands for a moment, before looking up again, and directly into Thomas's eyes. "I do not say I agree with the physician. But if he is correct, if she truly is consumptive, Thomas, I would wish her to know the love of a family. Not only because I believe it is our Christian duty, but we owe her that much."

Thomas's throat tightened.

Perhaps William could tell for he sighed and looked away.

"I did not expect you to be the one to marry, of course. I know you are still... recovering."

"Yes," Thomas said bitterly. "Convalescing. From a broken heart. Broken by a worthless woman, too self-absorbed and vain to care for her own child. Yes, I pine, like a fool. While my child perishes. Self-absorbed, narcissistic Thomas, as always. My brother must put my child's interests ahead of his own, since I do not even think to do so."

William let him finish his rant. "Somewhat melodramatic, even for you, Thomas. But a fairly accurate summary." He sighed. "Well, we are all fools in love, are we not? Did not Shakespeare say that? I know I have read it somewhere, and it rings true. That is not to say the object of your affection was a deserving one. While I know she was the most notable of your loves, she was not your first misstep." He paused, lips twitching a little. "You truly have terrible taste in women, Thomas."

Now it was Thomas's turn to slouch down in his chair with a groan.

"I do, don't I? How much more of a cliché can a man be? To fall in love with an actress, a renowned courtesan. But in my defense, William, it was nearly a decade ago that I met Serafina. I was young, woefully raw. Incredibly naïve and stupid. Have I missed anything? You may say I got what I deserved. Go ahead and say it, William."

"I will not say it for I do not believe any man or woman deserves to have their love betrayed when it was given openly," William said levelly. "Certainly not for such mercenary motives."

There was silence as both men recalled a time they had decided was best forgotten. A period involving a great deal of whisky on Thomas's part, a considerable amount of debauchery, and not a few gutters.

Finally, his older sibling had persuaded him to accept the truth about his ladylove and Thomas had begun to recall his responsibilities as if emerging from a fog.

"I fell for it, bag and baggage. But finding Isabel a mother... William, do not be so gullible as I was. Regardless of what Miss Gardner espoused, few wives would be willing to accept their husband's—or their husband's brother's, for that matter—bastard into their home. Let alone *love* such a child. I think you put too much faith in Miss Gardner's words the other day. They were admirably said, but she is idealistic, nothing more."

"Besides," he added, "this is not your affair."

"On that first point, I believe you are wrong. But I will not argue. It is true what you say about most women. However—" William looked surprisingly stern. "—a husband may decide such things in his own household. I do not doubt it might cause some tension between husband and wife, but I am resolved to have Isabel a part of our family. Concern over the tittering of our new neighbours will not put me off much longer. She belongs with us. And if she continues so ill, then she belongs here, at Northwood. I know our sister will feel the same way."

Thomas's throat constricted again. "You are a far better brother than I deserve, you know, William. Have I told you that lately?"

William waved his hand dismissively, but smiled a little.

Almost inaudibly Thomas spoke again, "Please, do not mistake me. I do care a great deal for her, you know."

He cleared his throat quickly. "However, William, you cannot take all of the wrongs of the world on your shoulders, much as I know how you would like to. She is my daughter. I must be the one to manage these arrangements. I will consider your idea. It does seem a fine one. I know Isabel would be excessively happy with the prospect of being closer to us both."

William nodded. As he stood, he placed a hand on his brother's shoulder. "I know you care for her, Thomas. But does she? It would be a—" He cleared his throat and lowered his voice. "—great tragedy, would it not, if she did not know how loved she truly was."

If she died, he meant. Thomas could not even think it.

William did not wait for a reply. "I must go. Please promise me you will continue to be civil to Miss Gardner, Thomas. For my sake if nothing else. She has done nothing to deserve otherwise."

"I do not say she was the wrong choice, William. She is a—" Thomas stumbled on the words a little. "—pleasant young woman. You were right about her from the start. She would have suited you well."

"Well. She would suit some man very well." He shot an odd look at Thomas. "But it is not me."

Chapter 8

A *void foolish adventures*

Neither knowledge nor pleasure can accrue from indiscreet attempts by youth to seek out adventurous undertakings. Rather commit yourselves to more useful employments and do not devote excessive hours to leisure or dangerous recreation. We refer, of course, to the pastime of excessive walks and the seeking out of unusual locales for picnics and the like, for during such foolhardy and even dangerous excursions young women may find themselves alone and in perilous situations which the libertine or rake may use to their favor.

The Beauford Chronicle, July 1818

Claire ducked her head to avoid a tree branch and pulled her skirt from a snagging twig. The day was proving as changeable as a young man's heart. When she and Fanny had set out on their walking expedition, the morning had revealed gentle sunshine in a cloudless sky. Now gusts of winds and a stinging rain foretold an imminent deluge.

The two girls had planned for an entire day outdoors, walking through the extensive park. The Rutledges' estate, Hillcrest Hall, shared a border with neighbouring Northwood and when the Darbys had been in residence, the girls would often walk the grounds together.

Hillcrest was fittingly named for it perched on a high hill overlooking a rugged valley carved by a narrow winding river. The girls had followed the river's path all morning, pausing to pick wildflowers or rest or read at their leisure, before continuing.

Now Fanny was lagging behind Claire in a worrisome way that did not bode well for reaching Hillcrest before the storm broke. Claire prayed the temperamental summer weather would somehow hold in their favor and was wishing the dark clouds away.

Only an hour earlier, the woods had been a place of restful beauty. Now the wind whistled through the leaves as tree trunks creaked ominously. Claire feared it would be a furious storm. They were still at least a mile out from any shelter. They had packed cloaks, aware of how changeable the weather could be—Claire's lack of proper attire on her walk home a few weeks previously had been an exception to her otherwise practical nature—but even warm clothing would not be enough in a severe storm.

"Shall we stop for a rest, Fanny?" She paused as Fanny reached her side, panting a little. They were pushing themselves, but as the storm clouds continued to gather it did not seem as if it would be enough.

Fanny looked about, reorienting herself. "You will not wish to hear this, Claire, but Northwood is closer than Hillcrest now. If we crossed through the valley, we might reach it within the hour."

Claire peered ahead to where the trees ended and the land dropped to the valley below. More of a ravine really, with large rocky outcrops and tangled brush—both of which might prove useful. The rocks tempered the steep drop and the low bush could provide them with handholds as they went down.

"We must cross before the rain becomes too heavy and the river begins to swell." Fanny followed Claire's gaze.

"And before the ravine turns to mud." Claire grimaced. If they moved quickly, they could at least reach one of the tenant cottages on the outskirts of Northwood land.

A crack of thunder in the distance spurred them to action. Moving hurriedly, they reached the ridge and looked down.

"It does seem rather more daunting from above." Fanny took a step back nervously.

"Follow where I lead. My footwear is more suited to this than yours." Claire eyed Fanny's impractical slippers, which, though comfortable on a warm summer day, were not as sturdy as the low leather boots Claire wore.

The rocks were damp and cold, their slick sides difficult to grasp. Full of sharp barbs, the brush was not much better and soon Claire's hands were covered with scratches. It would only get worse, however, she thought grimly, once heavier rain made the rocks more treacherous.

She gasped as her foot slid on the slippery shale.

"Are you all right, Claire?" Fanny came more slowly behind her, watching her step carefully.

So far, so good. They were about halfway down.

Going up the other side would be another matter.

As they reached the valley floor, the water, which had been a river so narrow at this part of its passage that it might have been called a brook, was quickly expanding.

Though quick-moving, the water was still shallow enough to cross, but any low rocks that might have served as steps were now nearly covered. Their feet were soaked.

Fanny noticed Claire staring and glanced down. Her slippers were nearly in tatters.

"I might as well be barefoot," Fanny said ruefully.

"Shall we trade?" Fanny was a shorter girl than Claire whose boots were considerably larger. Claire was not sure the trade would be an improvement, for either of them, but then, she was also not sure how Fanny was going to walk all the way in such bedraggled footwear.

"No." Fanny was emphatic.

The girls paused only briefly to catch their breaths, before starting up the opposite cliff.

The wind was picking up as they began their trek up the other side of the ravine. The cloaks they had carried with them that morning had already been donned. They provided some protection, but soon the gusts blew Claire's hood down so frequently that she gave up trying to keep it on.

About halfway up, the deluge came.

Heavy drops barraged them, blurring their vision. Claire slowed her pace, checking on Fanny frequently to make sure she was close.

Although they were nearing the clifftop, she was cursing the decision to come this way. If they had sheltered in the woods, it would have been cold but they could have huddled together. At least they would not now be meters above the earth being pummeled by a storm which threatened to dislodge them at any moment.

Despite imagining the worse, Claire felt a jolt of shock when Fanny's cry came. She heard the clatter of sliding shale behind her, turned, and Fanny was gone. Her heart leaped as she saw a crumpled figure on the ground below.

Going down was quicker than going up. Claire gave barely a thought to her handholds, sliding down in places, desperate to reach the bottom, fearing for the worst.

"Fanny!" In relief she saw her friend trying to sit upright, wincing as she did. Claire crouched next to her, helping her sit, before running hands gently over Fanny's legs. The girl let out a cry of pain as Claire touched her left leg. Her ankle was already beginning to swell.

"It hurts, Claire. Is it broken?"

Claire shook her head. "I cannot say. Perhaps broken, perhaps sprained. Either way we are in quite the predicament."

Putting an arm around her friend's waist to lift her, Claire helped Fanny hobble over to the side of some large rocks. The rock face provided at least a modicum of shelter from the wind. Both girls were already beginning to shiver, wet to the bone, and no longer warmed by the climb.

"Go on without me," Fanny said stalwartly. "It is the only thing to do. You can bring back help once you have reached a farmer's cottage. I will be fine here." She tugged her cloak closer.

Claire bit her lip. It seemed a reasonable suggestion, but the thought of leaving Fanny alone did not sit well. While wolves were uncommon, there was always the chance. Claire envisioned the worst, then looked at her friend with her lips tightly set.

"No. I will stay with you, Fanny." She looked about. "Perhaps with my help, we could try walking out of the ravine, following the brook. There may be a more passable way further ahead."

"The water is rising, Claire."

Claire's eyes darted to the water. The river was starting to swell with rain, covering the pebbled bed they had walked across only a few minutes before.

"The rain will stop soon. Your father will have people looking for us, if he does not already." Claire spoke with more confidence than she felt. They were now a ways off-course from where Fanny's father would assume the girls to be.

"Someone may still come along. Farmers. Or hunters returning..." Claire trailed off.

Fanny's silence told Claire she was in considerable pain. She certainly would be in more if they tried to continue walking.

"At least we are together." She huddled down beside her friend, wrapping her arms around her as best she could, trying not to notice Fanny's shivering had increased. Fanny rested her head on her shoulder, closing her eyes. The rain water trickled down her face.

"At least we will be very, very clean after this." Fanny opened her eyes and looked up at Claire with a grimace.

"Indeed. We will not need baths for months," Claire agreed, trying to match Fanny's lightness. She managed a smile.

They were silent after that. Claire watched the brook, now more a small river. It was a wide valley. The water was still at least twenty feet away. But it was creeping closer.

With any luck, the rain would stop.

Of course, their luck had not been particularly good so far.

"Do you hear something?" Fanny sat up straighter.

Claire started to shake her head, then heard it too—the pounding of hoofs.

"A horse!" she exclaimed, rising to her feet swiftly. She scanned for the source, finally spotting it at the top of the cliff they had just come from. A single rider on horseback.

"Heigh!" A man's voice called.

"Help! Down here!" Claire shouted as loudly as she could over the rain, waving her arms frantically.

"The wind is too loud." Claire looked at her friend, twisting her hands together.

"It shall not matter. He can easily see we are in need of aid," Fanny said optimistically. She was right. The horse was pacing back and forth. The man shouted something, but they could not make out the words. Then he turned his mount away.

Fanny grasped Claire's hand, pulling her back down to her side.

"Whatever he is doing, I hope he does it quickly. I am beginning to freeze."

Claire looked worriedly at her. Fanny's face was pale and her teeth were chattering. Resolutely, she stood and pulled off her cloak, wrapping it around Fanny and ignoring her weak protests, before sitting back down and pressing up close against her again, trying to give her as much heat from her body as she could.

Minutes went by. Or were they hours? Claire was losing all sense of time. There was only the wet and the wind.

Horse hoofs clattered over rocks.

The girls looked at each other. Claire jumped up.

The rider was back, coming along the valley floor. He must have found a way down further along.

Claire was soaked to the skin, but determined that Fanny would not stay in this place one minute more than she had to.

The man drew near, urging his horse forward at a canter.

Claire could make out his face. Her heart leaped for the second time that hour. It was Thomas Campbell.

Of course, it was. Of course, on this day of all days, the last person on earth she would wish to have see her in this predicament had appeared as their saviour.

Thomas dismounted, wiping the water from his brow as he came towards them. He did not look much drier, but he was dressed more warmly than they were, with his high Wellington boots and thick wool coat.

"Miss Gardner!" He seemed truly surprised.

"Miss Rutledge has been injured in a fall, Mr. Campbell." It was all she could do to point towards Fanny. Now that help had arrived her energy was fading fast.

Thomas knelt by Fanny, quickly inspecting her leg. Then he looked at his horse. "You will both ride. The mare can take two. I will stay here."

Two girls on a horse they were unaccustomed to riding, over difficult ground. Claire shook her head. Thomas saw and continued.

"Or, you will both ride and I will lead the horse."

"No." Claire put her hands on her hips. "We do not even know where you managed to ride down, let alone how to get from here to the nearest shelter. The ground is rough and with Fanny in front of me, I do not trust myself with a horse I have not ridden before, especially on such treacherous ground. It is your mare; you are familiar with the area. I will not risk Fanny with more recklessness." She bit her lip, hoping he would not notice she had essentially admitted to some recklessness.

They looked one another in the eye. Thomas's face was set stubbornly. She hoped this would not take long. There was no time to waste.

"It is not open for discussion. I will remain. You will take Fanny, as quickly as you can. Once you have taken care of her, you may send someone for me."

Seeing the doubt in his eyes, she added: "I will be fine. Really."

As his eyes narrowed, she thought it best to make herself clear.

"There is absolutely no way you will get me on that horse unless you are prepared to drag and tie me."

Thomas's eyes narrowed further, as if he were considering the prospect.

"Mr. Campbell, you have no rope, and believe me I will not make it easy. Now please, let us have no more of this. Take Miss Rutledge quickly and go. Now."

He nodded slowly, displeasure marking his face. He was as stubborn as she was, but she had won this round.

Within moments, Fanny was settled on the sturdy mare, Thomas behind. Claire feared Fanny's injury would not be improved by a jolting ride over rocks and moor. But Fanny's leg was not Claire's only concern. The smaller girl was nearly blue with cold and shaking hard. The sooner Thomas could get her to warmth and shelter and, moreover, a physician the better.

As they rode away, Claire realized Thomas had not noticed the swelling brook. That was to her benefit, or else their dispute would have lasted much longer.

Fanny still had her cloak. Claire wished she could exchange her wet muslin dress for a thick, wool winter one. She closed her eyes to think.

She could shelter by the rocks, fearfully watching the water come closer and closer, or she could take her chances out in the open and try to find safe passage on her own. Wrapping her arms around herself, she began to walk.

Chapter 9

*M*odesty and silence are a woman's best weapons against the rakes and libertines who hide among us

We wish to warn young women of taking indiscreet freedoms, particularly in conversation with men. Many are of opinion that a very young woman can hardly be too silent and reserved in male company, but we recommend even more strongly that young women avoid the majority of such company altogether for fear their ears be insulted by the words of the unprincipled and their minds contaminated beyond repair.

The Beauford Chronicle, July 1818

As they rode, Thomas thought of more and more reasons why this was a ridiculous plan. Why the devil had he agreed to it. Miss Gardner alone... and with not even a cloak to cover her, he realized, noticing Fanny's layers.

Miss Rutledge leaned against him limply, holding onto the pommel with one hand. She had not spoken since they left. Thomas hoped she was not about to faint. Having her sit behind him would have been more proper, but with the slickness of the horse's back in the rain, he was not about to risk it.

He spurred the horse onwards. The closest tenant was Bill Evans. He had a small cottage no more than a mile away. Thomas prayed he would be home.

The rain was unrelenting. He was glad he had taken the hunter that morning rather than the Arabian he often rode. The mare was plodding forward as best it could on such soft ground. Would she be able to make the journey back to Miss Gardner again, was the question? She would have to, although the beast would be exhausted.

He thought of the brook and gnashed his teeth. He had not taken it into account. The water would be rising. Miss Gardner was in a terrible spot. Somehow, he knew she had been well aware of this when she made him leave with Fanny.

He calmed himself. Miss Gardner was no fool, no matter how pigheaded she may be. Nor was she injured. She would remove herself from danger before it got that far.

Nevertheless, there was an added urgency he could not displace.

As they came up to the cottage, no smoke rose from the chimney despite the cold. Thomas held out hope as he lifted Fanny gently down and carried her to the door, but looking inside confirmed it was empty.

He placed Miss Rutledge as carefully as he could manage in a chair near the cold hearth. She was a dead weight in his arms, still and silent. He grabbed a thick blanket off the bed and, quickly tucking it around her, crouched to make a fire.

As the flames began to crackle, Miss Rutledge stirred. Thomas reached out a restraining hand, worried she might try to rise and do herself greater injury. The last thing he needed was an unconscious woman on his hands.

"Shhh..." He spoke softly, as if calming a horse. "Miss Rutledge, we have reached a cottage. But as you can see, the owner is not at home."

Miss Rutledge glanced around slowly, making an effort to wake. As understanding returned, she stuck out her chin purposefully.

"You must go back for Claire, Mr. Campbell. I will be all right here. This tenant—"

"Ned Evans," he supplied.

"Mr. Evans may return soon. In the meantime, I am warm and safe. Claire is not. The water was rising, Mr. Campbell. You must go." She shifted in her chair and he saw her wince. Still in pain. She had grit though. She was not afraid of being alone, nor was she complaining.

Thomas nodded his head. He was not about to disagree. He shared her concern. Could hardly keep Miss Gardner from his mind, in fact. He would not be satisfied until he knew she was out of the ravine.

As he stood to go, Miss Rutledge grabbed his sleeve. "Bring Claire back, Mr. Campbell."

He looked into her eyes and saw the fear. Again, he nodded.

The mare had been given a small reprieve. Now Thomas pressed her hard, hoping they would meet no delay as they rode back across the windswept moor.

When they reached the ravine and started down the part of the cliffside he had found passable, his heart began to pound. If she had fallen asleep, if she had slipped and fallen in the deepening water, if she had...

But there she was. Walking slowly alongside the brook, her head down to watch her footing. She had discarded her bonnet. She had no cloak and her slender figure trembled like a willow tree—slight but unbreakable. Her long dark hair fell in wet ribbons around her face. Her arms were wrapped around herself tightly overtop the soaked dress.

She must be freezing and frightened.

An unexpected feeling of anger welled up in Thomas's chest as he thought of what she had put them both through.

It was intolerable to feel so strongly about someone he hardly knew. Especially an infuriating woman whose presence he could scarcely stand.

Glowering, he jumped down and waited for her to notice him.

But when she finally looked up, she did not detect his exasperation. He saw naught but wholehearted relief.

"Fanny?" Her eyes were alight.

Thomas's scowl dissipated.

"She is fine," he answered shortly, then softened. "She is indoors, warm, with a fire."

"There was no one there? To call a physician? To take her to Northwood?"

"The tenant was out. I had to return here for you."

"I could have made my own way," came her maddening reply. "I was nearly out of the ravine, as you can plainly see. You should have remained with Miss Rutledge. She is the injured one!"

Thomas gritted his teeth—a mannerism that seemed to be habitual around Miss Gardner. How unsurprising that Miss Gardner would prefer to criticize her rescuer rather than thank him.

He had a strong impulse to swing her up over the saddle and onto his lap without another word.

Unclenching his hands at his side, he took a deep breath.

"Am I to take it you believe you would have reached the cottage on your own with no need of anyone else's assistance?"

"Without a doubt." She lifted her chin.

"In that case, I shall leave you to it." He moved towards the horse.

He had the satisfaction of hearing her gasp with indignation.

He turned back with a witty quip on his lips but found himself drawing in his breath sharply instead.

Miss Gardner had placed a hand on one slender curving hip, while raising her other to push the wet hair off her face. Her soaked gown clung to her curves and he was reminded of the last time he saw her similarly attired. Was he to forever be tantalized by the spectacle of this untouchable woman in the rain?

Annoyance had brought a lovely blush to her face. Her eyes flashed with irritation. Her nose crinkled with frustration.

And Thomas found himself thinking the picture she made was enchantingly attractive.

A choked cry came from his throat. He must be possessed. This woman was a menace.

His day was ruined, his body soaked with sweat and rain, his stomach empty, and now, if the state of his trousers were any indication, his own flesh was betraying him.

He closed his eyes, willing his body to release him from its state of temporary insanity.

He opened them. She was still there and was now gazing at him with perplexity.

He took hold of himself. "Yes, Miss Gardner? Was there something you wanted? A message to pass on to Miss Rutledge?"

There went the flashing of eyes again. "You really are the most—" She ground her teeth. "—despicable, exasperating man."

"You would so slander your rescuer? Oh, I am sorry. I forgot. As you would have it, you were rescuing yourself." He could not help goading her.

There was something intoxicating about feeling as if he held the power to drive this woman mad. He would quite prefer to drive her mad in a different way, but as that was unthinkable verbal combat would have to suffice.

Miss Gardner glared and marched over to the horse. Seeing she was preparing to attempt to mount unaided, he quickly grasped her waist and boosted her up. He had the pleasure of hearing her yelp with outrage.

He mounted behind her, turning the mare back up the slope.

The ride was silent. Miss Gardner was seething.

Thomas decided the wisest course was to allow her to continue to seethe uninterrupted for fear she would throw herself off the horse if provoked any further.

Such a rash act did not seem so unlikely with such an insufferably headstrong woman.

Miss Gardner rode side-saddle as Miss Rutledge had, one side leaned against him, the other pressed up on the pommel—which he assumed could not be comfortable.

"Leaned" was too strong a word, however, for Miss Gardner was endeavouring to hold herself as far away from him as she could. To sit so rigidly must have required a fair amount of energy at their present pace. He found himself appreciating her considerable willpower.

Despite the similarities in the women's positions, Thomas was experiencing things in a very different way than he had with Miss Rutledge.

With Claire Gardner in front of him, every sensation was heightened. He was minutely aware of every movement she made, no matter how small. The smell of her damp hair mixed with the sweet scent of her skin. She had been walking and naturally had perspired a little, but it was not an unappealing scent, quite the opposite. It made him think of other pleasurable activities which might bring a sheen of perspiration to Miss Gardner's body.

And with such thoughts, the feel of her thigh pressed up between his legs was an exquisite torment.

As they reached a rockier stretch of terrain, Miss Gardner could no longer hold herself as upright. They cantered over a rough patch of ground and with a jolt, she lost her grip on the pommel and gasped reaching out to brace herself.

Her free hand found Thomas's thigh and clutched it firmly. Although she hurriedly removed her hand from that indelicate location, a moment later he felt her sigh with exhaustion.

Soon Thomas saw her eyes close, and finally, she gave in and allowed her body to relax against him. Her warm, rounded shape fitting snugly along his chest. Her head rested under his chin. She was a taller woman, but they fit together well.

On a horse, at least. Thomas could easily imagine other ways in which they could fit together. He shifted a little in the saddle as he tried to clear away the image of Miss Gardner sprawled on her back in a bed, her face an expression of ecstasy, her wet dress around her waist, the bare damp skin of her breasts exposed to his lips.

Thomas suddenly understood why it was considered indecent for women to ride astride. There was something about females on horseback that made a man's mind go to lewd places.

And there was an intimacy to sharing a horse with Miss Gardner, in particular, which quickened his pulse. He had not felt himself on such tenterhooks in a very long time. It was unsettling.

His shoulders relaxed as they neared Evans' cottage. Soon this exquisite torment would be ended, and he and Miss Gardner could return to their respective positions of mutual hostility.

He noted the absence of any horse or cart in the yard. Evans had not returned then.

Looking down at his companion, he saw her eyes remained closed. Was she asleep or simply pretending, so as to avoid acknowledging their closeness?

The wind and rain were battering the small cottage, but Thomas could see smoke still rising. He hoped Miss Rutledge was no worse than when he had left her.

A crack of thunder made Miss Gardner jump. Her eyes popped open and she looked about. Comprehending they had reached their destination, she moved as if to slide off. Thomas quickly dismounted before she could do so and turned back to help her down.

The woman was obstinate as a mule. He could see what was unfolding but could not move fast enough to prevent it. As Miss Gardner once again tried to resist his help, she began to slide too quickly. Indecorously he reached for her waist, trying to prevent her from falling into the muck.

Seconds later he was lying on his back in the very same, the wind knocked out of him, a furious-looking young woman towering over a few inches away from his face.

On the downside, he was now wet and filthy; at least on one side. But the feeling of Miss Gardner's breasts pressed up against his chest was providing some consolation. He had an excellent vantage as Miss Gardner raised herself half-off him, her sodden bodice gaping and revealing two lovely round mounds.

He raised his hands to help her push herself off.

Sourly, Thomas noticed she did not offer him a similar hand up, but rather stood distractedly trying to brush the mud from her hands before giving up and striding to the cottage door.

When no one answered her rap, she peered inside.

"This cannot be the right cottage, Mr. Campbell. There is no one here!" She folded her arms over her chest and glared.

"What the devil do you mean..." he began, pushing past her. The fire was still crackling in the hearth, but Miss Rutledge was no longer inside.

Quickly putting two and two together, he reassured her. "Ned must have come back and taken her up to the house. William will be summoning Dr. Greyson as we speak."

Of course, that did nothing for their own quandary. The mare was quite spent, her flanks frothy with sweat.

"Ned will return for us soon. In the meantime," he gestured towards the cottage interior, "we must wait. The mare is spent, she cannot take us further. Unless you would prefer to walk on by yourself?"

The accusatory look he received for delivering this insight made him wonder if Miss Gardner suspected him of violating virgins or practicing human sacrifice.

A loud crack of thunder added perfect emphasis. The rain chose that moment to increase its intensity. Still, Miss Gardner stood in the yard, as if patiently waiting to be struck by lightning.

Ignoring her, he brushed past to warm himself at the fire. After a moment, he heard the door close.

As his hands began to warm, he peered over to where Miss Gardner had seated herself nearby. She had settled in the same chair by the fire Miss Rutledge had used.

Her chin rested on her hand, as she stared into the flames gloomily.

"You should try to dry yourself. Perhaps lay out your wet clothes, wrap yourself in a blanket from Ned's chest. I'm sure he will not mind in the least." He had meant the words as a peace offering, but instead she crossed her arms over her breasts protectively.

"Oh, I am sure you would like that, wouldn't you?" she snapped.

Thomas had the grace to blush. He could not remember the last time he had felt his cheeks redden so embarrassingly.

"You are the one covered in muck. Perhaps it is you who should disrobe, Mr. Campbell." She spoke smugly, but a matching redness crept over her cheeks as she thought through the implications of her suggestion.

She looked away quickly, muttering something under her breath.

"What was that, Miss Gardner?"

She glared fiercely.

"I *said* it is just my luck to be trapped here alone, with a rogue, a scoundrel, a man with a notorious reputation, rather than a... a..." she sputtered, searching for the word.

"A true gentleman?" he offered helpfully.

"Indeed! A gentleman." She sat back with a huff.

He was fairly certain that was much longer than what she had initially muttered.

Sitting back on his heels, he pondered for a moment, looking at her.

"What kind of a reputation did you say?"

She gave him a dirty look. "Notorious. As I am sure you are well aware. Do not try to deny it."

"On my honor, I would fain dispute the word of a lady." He grinned. "Even a lady covered in mud."

He was pleased to see her put a hand to her face before she could help herself.

"A notorious reputation, you say..." He rolled the words on his tongue. "Surely I should be aware of such a thing. Would you care to elaborate, Miss Gardner?"

She glared, then lifted her chin. "It is common knowledge, Mr. Campbell, that the true reason you have moved to Beauford is a—" She could not seem to bring herself to say it. "—a dishonorable one," she finished.

He raised his eyebrows.

"Your other mistress!"

He choked.

"My *other* mistress?"

The little minx had the nerve to look delighted. "Yes, Mr. Campbell. Apparently, one is not enough for such a proliferate wastrel as yourself." It was clear she believed this to be a grievous insult. Thomas had been called much worse.

"Two mistresses..." he mused. He supposed he should be flattered. Did his neighbours truly believe him so virile?

This would not do much for his family's reputation about town, however. He supposed he had best clear up the matter.

"It will shock you to learn, Miss Gardner—" he began. "—that I have not *two*..." He paused cruelly on the word.

Miss Gardner leaned forward eagerly. He was enjoying this far too much.

"Yes?" she encouraged.

He stopped. "You must promise me, Miss Gardner. This cannot go further than this cottage. For my brother's sake, if nothing else."

Miss Gardner looked solemn. "I promise you, the reputation of an honorable man such as your brother is not something I would ever take lightly. No matter what you are about to say, you may be certain I shall not share it."

Thomas smirked. "Very well."

He cleared his throat.

"Well, then, Miss Gardner. I have not two mistresses. Nor one mistress. In fact, the truth of the matter is—" he met her eyes directly. She seemed fully prepared for him to say three, four, or perhaps even five. "—I am such a poor rake that I do not have even a single mistress to my name."

Miss Gardner looked as if she would like to slap him.

The silence was deafening.

Feeling a little sorry for her, he eventually allowed, "I did have."

"Of course, you did," she scoffed.

"But not two. What is that supposed to mean?"

"Only that I find it unlikely a man like yourself is capable of valuing the deeper and more lasting affection that comes from a union of mutual respect between a man and wife."

Thomas opened his mouth and closed it. He wanted to tell her that he knew quite a bit about faithfulness and lasting affection. But he feared she would find the idea of a man being faithful to a mistress ludicrous.

"I did not realize you had such a high opinion of the married state, Miss Gardner. If that is the case, I am greatly surprised you remain single. Or are not in London seeking a husband, as I suggested when first we met, as you will perhaps recall."

He had struck true. She gave a huff of exasperation and looked away.

"Or perhaps it is simply that you feel no man could ever be worthy of the inestimable Miss Claire Gardner. Do you hold yourself in such high regard then?"

Miss Gardner met his gaze steadily. Her expression had changed. She no longer looked furious. Merely a little sad.

She bit her lip as if debating whether to speak.

When she did, her voice was low.

"My parents had a very happy marriage. When my father passed away, they had been together almost twenty years."

He stared, confused a little. "As did my own. I would have thought such an example would be more likely to lead one into early matrimony, not the opposite."

"When my older sister went to London for her season, Mr. Campbell—which you seem to hold in such profound esteem as the best method for a young woman to find a suitable husband, though it is often simply lambs to the slaughter—she did not find a worthy man. Rather, unworthy men found her."

She paused. He found himself wishing for her to continue but feared saying so would ensure she did not.

"I am very sorry," he said softly.

She nodded. "I do not wish to put my fate in any man's hands. As I am a woman, my choices are fewer than yours. I may gamble my liberty through marriage or remain single but never enjoy the—" She searched for the phrase. "—pursuit of pleasures which seems the birthright of every man."

He appraised her. "I would not argue with you there. But if you are saying you would prefer to remain unwed, a spinster, aging alone..."

"Please refrain from speaking as if you had any concern for my well-being or future, Mr. Campbell," she snapped. "We both know that you speak merely to irk me, to satisfy your own pride in some ill-natured way. Besides, I did not say I would never marry. Merely that I have no desire to seek out a husband when I am happy and content as I am."

Thomas stared. The idea of Miss Gardner remaining happy and content as an eternal vestal virgin did not sit well with him. Not well at all.

Why on earth should it matter to him what this irksome snip of a girl did or did not do?

It would be a waste, that was why. A woman as passionate and provoking as this one... There was much one could teach her about desire. So much about her he found himself admiring despite his best intentions. So much about her that a man might spend his whole life yearning for.

When had she become so very tempting?

It was unnerving. One moment, he wanted to be as far away from Miss Gardner as he could. The next he could hardly hold back from reaching out to her.

She had no idea what he was thinking, however. He could see it on her face. She thought he would open his mouth and prod her yet again.

Let her be surprised.

"That is a shame."

Her eyebrows raised. "Excuse me?"

"I mean that it would be a shame if you did not marry."

"Yes, I grasped that, Mr. Campbell. What I am trying to understand is why you feel it would be a shame and why you believe you have any right to care what I do or do not do."

He stared. She was right. Why did he care?

The fire had waned yet gave off enough of a glow to light Miss Gardner's features. Tendrils of rich auburn hair fell around her face. Her lips were flushed, full and rosy. Her wet dress clung alluringly to all of her womanly softness. Her back was straight, her chin high. She was proud and beautiful. And he wanted her. Most desperately.

"It is unfair. That the pursuit of pleasure, as you put it, is such a male prerogative. Particularly when the pleasures men seek are equally as pleasing to women, perhaps even more so. I am simply sorry you will never know them. That you will tarry away, losing your bloom, never knowing..." Should he say the words?

"Passion. Desire." He paused. "You say your parents had a happy marriage. At one point, they must have felt those things for one another. Are you not curious? About what it must be like? How it would feel?"

Miss Gardner blinked, opened her lips to speak, closed them again.

He shrugged and stood, as if prepared to let the topic go. An idea had come to him and, roguishly, he decided to go along with it.

"You suggested I remove my wet clothing earlier, Miss Gardner. I believe I shall follow your advice. I find I am quite uncomfortable. If you will, pray, turn aside..."

He waited modestly, giving her a chance to look away. After a moment, he turned his back, faced the fire, and shrugged out of his shirt.

He knew from experience that women were no less susceptible to the sight of an attractive man than a man was to an attractive woman.

He knew his form was not unseemly. His chest was broad and strong, his muscles hardened and taut as he stretched his arms and lifted the shirt over his head and hung it on a rack near the fire. Even then he did not turn back to her, but crouched before the flames rubbing his hands together. Close enough to where she sat that she could reach out a finger and touch him if she wished. Mere inches away.

He waited a minute before turning his head and looking at her from under his dark lashes. Miss Gardner had not turned away in disgust or modesty.

Rather she was biting her lip so hard he feared it would bleed. Her hands were tightly clenched on the armrests of the chair.

But it was her eyes he was most interested in. They would tell him what he wanted to know. When he met them with his own, he saw the hunger there. She was young, she may have been content. But she yearned, even if she did not know what for.

Abruptly, she stood up.

"It is cold..." She faltered, glancing across the room at the chest he had mentioned earlier. She crossed to it, bent and rifled through, pulled out a thick wool blanket.

"You will have need of this, I think." She held it out, almost appealingly.

He stood and moved across to her slowly, letting her look her fill. Her hand that held the blanket towards him was trembling.

Should he do this thing? There would be no going back once he did.

Temptation won out.

He grasped her hand instead of the blanket, and as it fell, pulled her to his chest in a single fluid motion. Her other hand stretched up as he had known it would and touched his bare skin, just below his breast. They stood like that for a moment. Her hand on his warm skin. The thin damp piece of muslin she wore the only armor between them. The heat of their bodies mingling.

He could feel her heart pounding and wondered if she could feel how fast his beat in turn.

She was looking up at him, eyes wide. A beautiful doe trapped by an experienced hunter. He could release her, could go back to being only the despicable rake she believed him to be and nothing more.

He could see the spark in her without having to be the one to light it. He was not the man for her, and perhaps there would be no such man.

Above all, he should not kiss her. It was not too late to stop.

But then it was.

With a surge of desire too strong to repress, his hands cupped her face, tilting it up to meet his own, and then his lips settled on hers. She froze, and for a split second he wondered if he was about to receive the well-deserved slap he had seen her long to give earlier. Then her lips opened to him and she met his movements stroke for stroke, plundering in return. Her hands tentatively came to rest on the sides of his arms, the skin bare under her fingertips. He wanted her to touch him, along his arms, his shoulders, everywhere. He wanted her hands running over his chest. He pulled her closer against him, his hands encircling her waist, running them up and down her hips, as his lips continued to play upon hers.

When he began to stroke her bottom lip with his tongue, darting into her luscious mouth once, then twice, then again, she let out a gasp that became a moan and her hands were tentative no more. She raised them to the back of his neck, tangling fingers in his thick hair, tugging his mouth closer to hers. The feel of her soft breasts pressed against his chest was driving him wild. It was taking all he had to resist pulling the wet dress from her shoulders, and pushing it down to her waist. He would not risk it. Yet.

He moved his hands up and down her body over her dress instead, along her back, the curves of her hips, then lower, pulling her flush against him and letting her feel how much he wanted her. She might have stepped back then. Instead, she gave a small moan and began returning the kiss with greater fervor.

There was something so pure about her kiss, so passionate, so honest. Her innocence was intoxicating. Despite what she might believe him to be, seducing virgins was not, in fact, his pleasure.

But now that she was in his arms, he wanted her to know where he could take her. She was infuriating, brash, overconfident. Incapable of manipulation, of pretense; the opposite of the woman he had believed he loved for so many years.

She was his younger self all over again.

An irresistibly, utterly feminine one. She was different from any other woman he had known—and entirely different from the one he had thought he would always want. He wanted to know her.

More than that, he wanted her to want him.

Claire's head was swimming. She was drowning. Was it possible to drown in another person? For them to dive so deep within you that you felt lost? If so, she was. But she did not wished to be saved.

Thomas was everything she had been terrified he would be. Now that he had touched her, she could not let him go. His spell-like presence wound around her like a twisting vine. She no longer cared to be unenthralled. Only to continue like this, for the sensation to never stop.

She met the caress of his lips, of his tongue, with her own, drowning in his heady tide of pleasure. When she ran her own tongue over the edge of his lips, he let out a groan that sent a thrill through her body. Was this why women became mistresses? She felt filled with a seductive power.

Yet there was an unwanted tug behind the thought.

She pushed it away, ignoring a sense of foreboding.

She should not touch him. She knew that much. She should step back, step back before it was too late. She put her hands on his chest, willing herself to push. Instead, they took on a will of their own, betraying her. Her hands ran up along his chest, trailing over his shoulders, back behind his neck, tangling in his thick curling hair. She gave a gentle tug as she wound her fingers through, teasingly, playfully pulling, drawing him ever closer down to her.

She wanted more and knew without a doubt that so did he. His hands caressed her body, moving up to her shoulders to the edges of her damp dress. She shifted slightly to let the tips of her breasts brush against his chest. As he let out a gasp at the touch, his fingers were moving steadily, looking for a way to pull her dress down.

And she wanted him to. She didn't know what would happen next, where this would lead, and moreover, she knew it was wrong, very wrong, but oh, God, she wanted his touch and in this moment all she could do was follow her desire.

The door opened with a bang.

Chapter 10

A chill gust of wind sped through the cottage and roused Thomas to a state of more rational thought. He stepped away from Miss Gardner.

Two men and a woman stood framed in the doorway.

The woman was in front, standing uncertainly on the threshold. Her wide blue eyes were widened incredulously.

"Claire?"

"Rosalind!" Thomas saw Miss Gardner's eyes dart about the room, as if searching for some other exit besides the cottage door.

"I came back from London on the coach. We arrived this morning. When Miss Rutledge's father sent word you had not returned, I insisted Arthur let me come along with him to search—" She gestured to the grey-haired groom on her left whom Thomas had met once before. "—We met Mr. Evans on his way out from Northwood and he kindly brought us here, assuming this was where you would return with Mr. Campbell..." Her voice trailed off.

Thomas tried to make sense of the two women. They were sisters, but in appearance were more different than alike. Rosalind was shorter than Claire by far. Soft blonde curls framed a heart-shaped face with a full rosebud mouth. This younger Gardner sister was more rounded, from her fuller cheeks to her curvier figure. Her pert snub nose was the opposite of Miss Gardner's straight and delicate one.

But their cadence of voice was remarkably similar. As well as their facial expressions, which right now were nearly perfect reflections of one another, both mouths open in shock.

Miss Gardner looked as though she might faint. All color had drained from her face.

Rosalind glared at Thomas, obviously concluding he was the source of her sister's distress—which he could not fault her for.

He was not sure he had ever been in such an awkward position in his life.

The thoughtful Mr. Evans who had arranged this pleasant gathering stood to Rosalind's right. To his credit, he had remained speechless so far.

Miss Gardner raised her chin. Thomas could see her lips were trembling.

"Thank you, Rosalind. I wish to go home. Immediately if you please." She walked quickly to the door, catching hold of her sister's arm as she pushed between the two men, and pulling her out with her.

Arthur shot Thomas a grim look before following.

A fine mess this was. Thomas rubbed his hands over his face. Looking down, he noticed the rough wool blanket pooled on the floor at his feet where Miss Gardner had dropped it. Could it really have been only a few minutes ago?

He strode to the rack where his dirty shirt hung and snatched it up.

"Is Miss Rutledge at Northwood, Ned?"

Evans nodded. "When I came home and found her, Sir, I thought that was the best thing to do with her..." He faltered. "I hope I did right..."

Thomas nodded curtly. He donned the mask of the formidable gentleman.

"Take me to the house." His tone was terse.

Let the man understand his place was to listen and obey. What he thought he had seen was of no concern.

In the cart, on the way back up to the manor, Thomas spoke up, his voice stern as a parson preaching a Judgement Day sermon.

"When you and Miss Gardner's sister came into the cottage, Evans, she had been passing me the blanket which you saw on the floor. She tripped carrying it over and I caught her. Our... proximity... was happenstance, nothing more. In fact, I owe the lady an apology. After being out in the storm, the hard ride—well, she was quite..." Thomas reached for a word that seemed closest to the truth. "...unsteady."

"Indeed, sir." Ned kept his eyes on the road as he drove. "Looked as if she were to faint, she did. White as ash."

"A dreadful thing for two young ladies to find themselves lost on a day like this," he added.

"Quite so." Thomas thought the conversation had reached its natural conclusion.

He decided the man was likely to be discreet. He was their tenant after all, on an estate which, under William's direction, was making rapid improvements to enhance the quality of life for all inhabitants. Surely, Evans understood he owed the family a little loyalty.

The rain had slowed, and the wind was letting up. The summer day was giving up what little light it had left as darkness fell.

For Thomas, the day had taken on an air of total gloom. As they drove, rainwater dripped from his hair, into his eyes. He brushed it away. He was giving up hope of ever being dry again when he saw the lights of Northwood through the trees ahead.

A carriage was out front. It must be the surgeon's. With a last nod to Ned, he entered the house.

Their butler was not near the door, so he flagged down a passing footman.

"Is Miss Rutledge still here?"

The footman looked at Thomas's dishevelled state, then at the puddle that was forming on the floor before stuttering out his answer.

"Yes-s-s, sir. Miss Rutledge is upstairs with the doctor and her father. And your brother," he added.

There was no reason to add to the crowd around Miss Rutledge's bedside. Besides, he was not precisely eager for his next encounter with William.

He dressed alone, peeling off his wet clothes and exchanging them for dry, warm ones. The rain had chilled him to the bone, but it was nothing that a hot meal, a stiff drink, and a chair close to a fire could not sort out.

Only after his stomach was full, his body warm, and a whisky was in his hand did Thomas begin to allow himself to think on what had passed.

He had ruined Miss Gardner.

Compromised her reputation.

Destroyed her prospects of marriage.

She had spoken of limited choices for women. Well, now her own were even more limited.

Though only twenty-eight years old, Thomas had made some fairly stupid decisions in his brief lifetime.

This one put them all to shame.

Now there was a word—shame. It hung much more on women than on men, which was, indeed, unfair.

If Thomas chose, he could continue with his life, go about his business. For him, nothing would change.

Except perhaps the loss of the Campbell brothers' good name in the neighbourhood. As outsiders, William had been cultivating good will since they arrived. Now Thomas may have destroyed that all in the span of fifteen minutes.

Was it fifteen minutes? Or five? Or could it have been an hour? Time had seemed to stand still. It had been a perfect moment in some ways, completely outside of time. Outside of the normal world.

Her lips had been his only world and somehow it had felt as if that was the way it was supposed to be.

Until the normal world intruded with a bang and blast of cold air.

He brushed the memory away. Ridiculous romanticism—no, be honest, and call it what it was—impulsive lust was how he got here in the first place.

Perhaps shame was what he should be feeling right now. He was sure that William would be, in his place. But he simply felt numb and tired.

The kiss had been...enjoyable.

Very well. More than enjoyable.

But was a kiss worth giving up his freedom for?

He wondered what answer Miss Gardner would give.

She was probably at home right now, trying to explain things to her mother and sister. Would she be expecting him to call, to set things right that very same night?

He had no doubt that were William in his position, his brother would be out on the road to Orchard Hill already, riding hard.

But then, William would never be in such a position. He was far too noble, too honorable to ever compromise a woman.

He slunk further down in the leather seat. He was an utter rogue.

They had moved Isabel here, to a rather remote part of the country, certainly a dull one by Thomas's standards, in order to give her a fresh start. William had even had the daft idea that they could somehow move her into Northwood, be her proper family, to the neighbourhood and to the world.

Certainly, they had at least been able to see her frequently. Allowing Thomas to finally establish a true relationship with his child.

Now he had done something that would draw the worst kind of attention to them all.

He was finally meeting his responsibilities when it came to Isabel. She should be his one focus now, after all that she had endured.

There was no room for further complications. Certainly not a wife. No matter how tempting the woman.

What kind of a husband would he make, anyways? A terrible one. Miss Gardner would be miserable. She would be better off living alone with her mother the rest of her days than tied to a man like Thomas.

Especially as she seemed determined to despise him. She was probably at home right now, rueing the day she had met him.

All he had done was prove her preconceptions of him correct. He was a libertine, a vile seducer, a rake who could not keep his hands off vulnerable young women.

What had she called him? A rogue, a scoundrel. Ungentlemanly. She had all but said he was not worth the ground she walked on.

He had not even been able to keep a mistress happy, let alone a woman like Miss Gardner who had much higher expectations of men. Albeit, less mercenary ones.

Thomas rubbed a hand over his face.

And yet he knew it was absurd that he was still talking to himself as if there were a true choice in the matter.

William entered, looking surprisingly cheerful for someone who had just come from a sickbed.

Thomas raised his eyebrows questioningly. Suddenly he felt too tired to move, let alone speak.

"Miss Rutledge is a stoic young woman, Thomas," William began, as he poured himself a drink at the side table. "Dr. Greyson is certain she will recover with rest and care. Her ankle is sprained, not broken. Nevertheless, she must have been in considerable pain. Especially on that lengthy ride. She is determined not to show it, however. She was quite sweet and merry with us, trying to put her poor father at ease. He was in a terrible state when he first arrived." William took a sip and went on, not waiting for a reply.

"It has been decided that Miss Rutledge will remain at Northwood until it is safe to have her moved. Doctor Greyson is concerned that the cold and damp may be more cause for concern than the ankle. When she arrived, she was blue with cold, shaking so hard she could not stand." He shook his head.

"Thank God, you found her in time. Her father would like to thank you as well, I'm sure." He took another sip, then sat down opposite Thomas.

"Ned brought her inside right away, good man, and then I carried her up to a room. She was so exhausted, she felt as small and soft as a broken-winged bird in my arms." He cleared his throat.

"Miss Rutledge's father is having her maid brought over as we speak. She will stay with Miss Rutledge so she is not alone in the house with two young rogues." He grinned playfully at Thomas, then saw his grim expression.

"What is it, Thomas? Did Miss Gardner make it home safely?" His face was all concern.

Thomas stood. He could not face William right now, or risk his brother seeing through his barely maintained façade of normalcy.

"She is well. We reached the cottage just as her sister and their groom arrived to take her home again." He took a deep swig and set down his glass. "Perfect timing."

Well, it probably was. Who knows what might have happened next? He had a feeling that was something he would be wondering about a lot that night.

"I am sure she will be pleased to hear her friend is safe. We must extend an invitation to visit Miss Rutledge while she convalesces..." William trailed off as Thomas rose and walked to the door, heedless of his brother's chatter.

"Are you going to bed so soon?"

"It has been a long day. I find I am more fatigued than I thought." He spoke shortly, hoping William would put it down to exhaustion.

Upstairs, he lay in bed, exhausted but restless. He could not help permitting himself a moment to reminisce. As soon as he allowed one recollection, the others flooded in like a torrent.

The feel of her, the taste of her, the smell of her. Her eagerness, her passion. The suppleness of her body as she pressed against him.

He put his arms behind his head and tried to think clearly.

There were worse things in the world than having to marry an enticingly attractive woman.

Even if she were as stubborn as the Devil himself.

Worse things than having to *bed* a beautiful young woman.

And she was quick-witted and intelligent, he'd give her that.

Well-read, too, perhaps.

He was not a man prone to labeling a woman a "blue-stocking" simply because she was able to participate in animated, intellectual conversation—which had been the purpose of the blue-stockings in the first place, though soon forgotten.

He had scoffed at her novel, but in truth Mrs. Radcliffe could be found in the library at Northwood as well. There had been an ample arrangement of books lining the walls of Orchard Hill, and Mrs. Gardner seemed the kind of woman who would encourage her daughters' education rather than repress it.

But it was not her reading ability which, in the end, was Miss Gardner's greatest attraction.

He imagined her standing at the foot of his bed and could suddenly see her clear as day.

Her long dark hair loose around her shoulders, as she disrobed slowly before him, her dress falling into a pool at her feet as she stepped forwards, arms demurely at her side, her body lovely and bare.

Good God, he was going soft in his old age.

Hard would also be an accurate adjective, he conceded.

With a groan, he accepted his fate.

Whether she despised him or not, whether he wished to take a wife or not, both of them had little choice in the matter at this junction.

They would simply have to make the best of it.

The lucky Miss Gardner was going to be a bride.

Chapter 11

C laire decided she would join a nunnery.

Except there were no nunneries in England. Henry VIII had seen to that.

Very well. She would travel to Italy, convert to Catholicism, and then find a small nunnery that would accept a penitent young woman. One who could not speak a word of Italian.

Rosalind could accompany her on the journey. She had always wanted to travel. Well, this would be her chance to see the world.

She imagined the tears as Rosalind embraced her and left the nunnery to return to England.

"Farewell forever, dear sister. Do not worry yourself over me. This is my life's true calling. Give our mother my love."

Then the convent gate would close and... what then? Claire was not sure what exactly happened in a nunnery. A lot of praying and kneeling. She would need to refresh her Latin.

Guinevere had entered a convent. Then she had died. Or had Lancelot died first?

Rain was pouring down her face, but she did not bother to wipe it away. She stared unseeing into the darkening yard.

"Claire? Are you coming?" Rosalind stood on the steps of Orchard Hill.

She was home, but she had never felt so much less at home than she did right now.

Still, it *was* her home. Perhaps she could cloister herself there for the rest of her days. Was that not what she had told Thomas? That she would not mind living the life of a spinster? She would read many books. Tend the garden. Learn to sew properly. Learn to read while sewing above all.

And while she was at it, why not commit to helping the poor and the downtrodden. She could live a life of sacrifice without having to step foot in a nunnery.

Though it certainly sounded like a silly fantasy when put that way.

Rosalind was tapping her foot with exasperation.

"Are you going to stand there daydreaming all night, Claire? In case you had not noticed, it is pouring rain and you have taken on the appearance of a drowned cat."

Claire glanced down at her soggy clothing, then brushed past her sister, head down. She embraced her mother hastily, provided a brief explanation of the day, assured her she was well, only tired, and then escaped upstairs before the flabbergasted Mrs. Gardner could ask any more questions of her prodigal daughter.

It was not that her mother would not understand. Claire feared her mother would understand only too well. The ability to understand her children, to love them despite any failing, was one of her best qualities. But right now, if her mother offered her tenderness, acceptance, or understanding Claire thought she would break. And she was only holding on by a thread as it was.

The door to her room banged open. Rosalind stood there, hands on her hips.

"Oh, no, you don't," she announced. "I shall let you get away with not telling Mother yet, but you *will* talk to me." She shut the door behind her firmly and marched over to the bed.

"Nothing happened. Everything is fine," Claire's voice came out sounding as weak as a kitten's. She cleared her throat. "Mr. Campbell was merely... You see, his shirt was dirty and wet. He had fallen into the mud, you see... We were... And then, I was passing him a blanket and..."

"You were kissing him. That is what you were doing! A blanket? Ha! Wrapping yourself around him like a blanket is more like it." Rosalind had a wicked grin on her face.

Claire stared, unable to return her mirth.

"How can you find this funny?"

"How can you possibly not? If it were not funny, I expect you should be weeping instead."

Claire looked bleak. The tears were there already, she had simply not allowed them to fall. Yet.

"I'm ruined, Rosalind," she whispered.

"Somewhat melodramatic, but yes, perhaps you are." Rosalind put a finger to her lips thoughtfully.

"There are worse men to be ruined by, I suppose. The one you were kissing looked rather dashing. Was he a good kisser? I think that should be a prerequisite for husbands. Gwendolen says her husband is an excellent kisser."

Claire stared. "I do not think you fully understand the implications of the situation."

"Of course, I do." Rosalind said brightly. "You are getting married. Sooner than expected, and I shall miss you very much now that I think on it. Which is odd as we argue so often. Your room gets better light. Would you mind if I switched? Once you have gone, I mean. You may use my room when you visit, of course."

"I am not going anywhere," Claire said between gritted teeth.

"Mother will be shocked but happy, I expect." Rosalind rolled on relentlessly.

"I think part of her worried you would never marry. Of course, you are saving her the cost of a season in London so I expect that will be a relief. You would probably not have had a very good time anyhow. I wonder if Mother would let me use some of what will be saved for a voyage. I should like to travel before I settle down. Young men have their universities and their Grand Tour, but what do we women get? A season of husband hunting in London— as if that were any real education! It's absurd. Utterly absurd."

"*You* are absurd," Claire muttered.

"Rosalind..." She took a deep breath. "Rosalind, there will be no wedding. Thomas Campbell is not going to ask me to marry him. For him to do so would go against everything I know about his character. He is the worst sort of rake. Nothing like his brother. There will be. No. Wedding."

She flung herself back onto the bed with a moan.

"Moreover, I would not marry Thomas Campbell were he the last man on earth." Her throat felt choked. The tears were beginning to flow.

Rosalind stood over her for a moment.

"What do you mean?" she said softly. "Is he really such a terrible man, Claire? You truly do not think he may be counted on to do what is honorable?"

Claire shook her head. She did not want to say the words. To tell her sister she had ruined herself with a man she was now even more certain had no concept of honor.

"Please. Believe me when I say there will be no wedding. Now please, go away, Rosalind." She closed her eyes.

Claire heard the door shut and turned to face the wall. What an ill-fated day.

A few moments of pleasure, now a lifetime of penance.

Her heart leapt. She was certain he would never ask her to be his wife. But what if he asked her to become his mistress? He had said he did not have one. Could it be true? Was there a vacancy to be filled?

She would slap him in the face if he tried to propose such a thing.

She imagined her mother chasing him out with a broomstick. Rosalind would rain down verbal fire and Gracie would throw frogs and other reptiles.

She sniffed, wiping some of the wetness off her face.

Better to think of scorning the man than of doing other things with him.

Such as having his lips on hers. Or the way his warm strong hands had felt as they roamed her body as if she was his to plunder. She gave a shiver.

Perhaps being a mistress was not altogether terrible for the woman, a small voice inside of her said.

How much did a man settle on a mistress, anyway? Enough to fill a library with an excellent collection and have enough to live on besides?

It was an idiotic thought. She might be ruined, but she would never consider such a thing. She would not destroy her family's reputation by sinking even lower than she had.

Besides, there were decided negatives to being merely the plaything of a man.

For one, she could not imagine the pain of bearing a child out of wedlock.

Sweet little Isabel Notley was not only facing a life-threatening illness but would also grow up with society's judgement upon her all her life, if she lived that long. It was a heavy burden for a child, even with the support of her father.

She sighed and covered her face with her hands. Sleep was beckoning. She could only torment herself for so long tonight.

She suddenly wondered if the whole thing might be simply covered over.

Was it too much to hope that a girl could make one mistake and get on with her life?

Tomorrow she would talk to Arthur. He had been with the family for many years. If gossip was to spread, it would not come from him.

Mr. Evans was another matter.

Chapter 12

A *void the fantasies of a weak mind*
       But surely, Dear Reader, one of the most insidious practices
of the libertine and rake is to stimulate those young women of weak
mind with idle fantasies and thoughts which are ignorant of truth or
goodness. Devoting the mind, even in sleep or imagination, to conduct
improper in the daylight leads to a disturbed mind and unhappy
conscience.

The Beauford Chronicle, July 1818

In the morning, when he rose, everything seemed much, much worse.

The whisky must have gone to his head.

How could he have forgotten that William had tried to court this woman?

How on earth could he possibly explain himself and expect to be forgiven?

William had already rescued his prodigal brother more than he deserved, extricated him from financial and romantic woes, and forgiven much.

Would he forgive Thomas for seducing a woman he had considered asking to become his wife?

There was also the matter of Isabel. Miss Gardner had no knowledge of the girl.

Thomas could not even begin to imagine how to explain Isabel to Miss Gardner or Miss Gardner to Isabel. As he had told William, he doubted Miss Gardner would actually stand by the opinions she had espoused before the Mortons.

No, Miss Gardner seemed attached to her stubborn prejudgements of people. She already had a low opinion of Thomas. Finding out he had brought his illegitimate child to be her neighbour would surely only add to it.

Wouldn't it?

He ran a hand over his stubbled face, and stumbled out of bed. As his valet prepared him for the day, he wracked his brain for alternatives to matrimony. None seemed feasible. None that would avoid the ruin of an innocent young woman.

He was damned if he did and damned if he didn't, that much was clear. William would be furious either way.

But if he were to ask himself what William would tell him to do in the end...

Well, then the path was clear.

And it led straight to Orchard Hill.

Claire awoke to the persistent drizzle of rain on the window. The greyness of the day perfectly matched her state of mind. She went through the motions of her morning routine—dressing, eating, conversing with her mother and Gracie, avoiding conversing with Rosalind, avoiding eye contact with Rosalind. When her mother and Gracie had finally departed to pay some calls and Rosalind had given up and left her blessedly alone, she curled up on the window seat and pressed her forehead to the cool glass.

If she pretended nothing was wrong, perhaps nothing would be wrong and it would all just go away.

She hunched there forlornly for a while, uncertain of how much time was passing, until the sound of a carriage pulling into the yard made her sit up.

Drat! If it was the Mortons she would pretend she was not at home. Let Rosalind deal with their pleasantness today, she could not manage it.

Her fickle heart betrayed her with a lurch when she saw Thomas Campbell step out.

He stood in the yard for a minute, looking at the house, turning his hat over in his hands, before slowly walking towards the door.

Whatever the purpose of his visit, he did not look particularly pleased to be there.

Upstairs, Rosalind was tidying her room while singing a sea shanty extremely cheerily and extremely loudly. Claire prayed she would not hear the door.

There was a loud rap, followed by a clatter as Rosalind dropped whatever she had been holding, and bounded down the stairs two at a time in her rush for the door.

Claire tried to beat her there but uncertainty over whether or not she ultimately wished it to remain open or closed slowed her pace, and it was too late.

There he was. Looking as handsome as he had the day before. Just as imposing, too.

Was it possible he had grown taller overnight? Claire felt small and mouselike. She wished she were wearing a less wrinkled morning dress. One that did not have a tea stain on it.

She stood up straighter and tried to rally herself.

"Why, good day, Mr. Campbell! What brings you to Orchard Hill this fine afternoon?" Rosalind smiled brightly. She was enjoying this far too much. Claire made a mental note to strangle her later.

"Good day, Miss Gardner. I do not believe we formally met yesterday…" He hesitated.

"Very pleased to meet you indeed, Mr. Campbell. I am Claire's younger sister, Rosalind."

Claire gritted her teeth. She would not have been surprised if Rosalind had added "Welcome to the family!"

Fortunately, she did not, thus sparing the trouble of bloodshed.

"Delighted. And may I take this opportunity to compliment your singing. I have never heard Spanish Ladies sung with those lyrics before." His lips twitched.

"Yes, well, I like to improvise," Rosalind explained.

Thomas smiled, then glanced at Claire. "I wonder if I might have a word with your older sister."

"But of course." Rosalind stood aside to let him enter.

Thomas stood awkwardly in the small space between the hall and the front sitting room looking at them both.

"Well, I shall leave you two alone shall I?" Rosalind looked back and forth between them, a smirk playing on her lips.

"I mean, not completely alone," she added hastily. "I will be upstairs." She glanced at Claire and wriggled her eyebrows suggestively in an infuriating "I-told-you-so" manner.

"Will you sit down, Mr. Campbell?" Claire did not wait for a reply but took a seat as soon as Rosalind left.

She did not meet his eye. She felt timid and restrained. It was not like her. She did not like it.

Thomas remained standing.

She stole a quick glance upwards. Now that Rosalind had taken her sunshiny self away, he looked rather cross.

He did not want to be here. He did not want to do this. Her stomach plummeted sickeningly.

"Miss Gardner, I am sure my presence is no surprise. You must know why I am here."

Her eyes narrowed a little. He thought she had been expecting him, that she would demand this of him?

"I am certain I do not. Please do take a seat, Mr. Campbell. It is very uncomfortable craning my neck to peer up as you tower above me like a giant."

There. That was more like herself.

He sat stiffly, looking even less pleased than before.

"Miss Gardner, the events of yesterday afternoon..." He cleared his throat. "I have come to beg your most humble apology. My conduct was exceedingly improper as well as ungentlemanly. As you have so kindly pointed out before, it is a flaw in my character. One which I see I must strive to work upon."

He had left himself wide open to a sarcastic response, but Claire found she was not up to witty repartee today.

He waited for her to accept his apology. At least, that is what she assumed he was waiting for.

The moment stretched.

He shifted in his seat.

"I find it difficult to believe you do not understand the reason for this visit, Miss Gardner. Surely you understand we have no choice but to marry."

He cleared his throat. "I am here to ask you to become my wife."

The last line was said so arrogantly, so coldly that even if Claire had wanted to accept—which she did not, of course—there was no way she could do so now.

He clearly did not want her.

Moreover, it sounded as if he believed she should be flattered to even be asked.

Her hackles went up.

Did he expect her to fall on her knees and thank him for coming to save her? He had all but said, "I am here to bestow upon you the illustrious opportunity to marry the one and only Thomas Campbell."

He was continuing. "I will speak to your mother and discuss the reading of the bans. The sooner we are able to arrange…"

She interrupted.

"I see nothing of the sort."

"Excuse me?"

"I see no reason why we must wed."

A stifled gasp came from somewhere in the vicinity of the kitchen. Evidently Rosalind had not gone upstairs.

"Miss Gardner, you do understand that two men and a woman saw us in what the vast majority of polite society would consider to be an extremely compromising position yesterday afternoon, do you not?"

Was this the same man she had kissed? This irritating, infuriating, horrid man? He spoke so heartlessly. He offered marriage as if it were his duty, a drudgery he must fulfill.

No inkling of the emotion he had shown yesterday. No sign of warmth or tenderness. No sign of the passion or desire he had claimed were so essential to a fulfilling life.

Claire felt a stabbing pain in the vicinity of her heart.

For a brief moment, she had hoped she might see a different Thomas. The man who had revealed himself to her yesterday, who had seemed to want her, desire her, burn for her.

And who had kindled those things in her in turn—things she had not even known she had wanted.

She did not know who the man in front of her was. He could not be the same person.

She levelled her eyes.

"You told me yesterday…" she started slowly. Oh, Rosalind was going to enjoy this. "…that you agreed it was unfair women could not so easily access the world of pleasure as men. And you offered me a taste of such pleasures.

"Out of the kindness of your heart, I suppose," she could not help adding scathingly. "What were your words exactly? Oh, yes, you worried I would 'tarry away,' 'lose my bloom.'"

Thomas was narrowing his eyes. She drew a deep breath.

"It is equally unfair that such a fleeting and meaningless—" She made a point of emphasizing the word. "—moment, which left us no more altered than before—"

That was a lie but he would not know it.

"—should cost us both our freedoms. And so, I politely decline."

"What?"

"I decline your proposal."

"Yes, I heard that part, Miss Gardner…" He rubbed a hand over his face, before adopting the tone one might use when speaking to a young child. "But it is not really a question, is it? Nor a choice either of us have the luxury of making. You have been compromised. Your reputation besmirched. Your family's honor is on the line. As well as mine…"

"You do this for honor then? You do not believe you have a choice?" She interrupted. This was important.

He stared. "I do it because it is the right thing to do. But yes, if not for me, then for my...brother... who wishes to remain in this neighbourhood. A scandal would destroy that prospect for our family."

"Well, I appreciate your nobility in doing the honorable thing, Mr. Campbell. However, I will not marry you. I cannot."

Thomas glared.

"Is the state of singlehood truly so much more appealing than marriage, Miss Gardner? Can you truly say you have no wish to ever be a wife? A mother? To have a home of your own?"

"You do not love me." She stated it simply. "And furthermore, I do not love you. You believe we have no choice in this. I believe we do."

Thomas smiled cruelly, and her heart broke a little.

Howsoever these feelings had arisen she wished them gone. If this was romance (she would not even think of another word), then it was much too painful a thing for everyday life.

"Love?" He said the word so scornfully that she coloured, knowing he was about to mock her.

"Love is not a basis for a marriage, Miss Gardner. Marriage is an arrangement of convenience between two parties for the begetting of children. Nothing more. Now, I am more than equipped to care for a wife if that is a concern. I can assure your mother of that fact. I shall endeavour to maintain you in the manner to which you have been accustomed..."

Claire tuned out after that, closing her eyes so she would not have to see his face as he spoke.

He may have been sweeping his eyes over the room, turning his nose down at her family home for all she knew. Indeed, he likely was.

It was like their first meeting all over again. She had told him only the day before that her parents' marriage had been a love match, but apparently nothing she had said had been remembered or interpreted as she intended.

And he thought she would accept him as her husband? She could hardly stand to be in the same room as this man, let alone share a house, a table. A bed.

She shut out the part of her that said the sharing of a bed might be the only enjoyable part of marriage to Mr. Campbell. He had already shown himself adept at those pleasures of the flesh which he evidently held in such high regard.

Somehow, she knew there was much more to his knowledge than had been shared yesterday. More than kissing, more than embracing through wet garments. The begetting of children, as he put it so delicately, might not be so terrible if that had been only a brief introduction on how to achieve it.

"Your eyes are closed, Miss Gardner," he broke in. She opened them. He looked annoyed. "Am I boring you with the details of our marriage?"

"You have no money," she blurted out. Now where had that come from. As if his money or lack thereof was of any concern to her. "You are reliant on your brother. I do not wish to be supported by your family or to be a draw upon your brother's resources."

His expression soured. "Once again, I must wonder where you receive acquire your information, Miss Gardner. I had not taken you for a gossip—"

"I am not one!" She exclaimed, astonished. Yet, here she was quoting Miss Morton as if her word was gospel. She pursed her lips together. "I believe this is common knowledge."

It was an exaggeration, but she was not about to admit it. If that was low of her, so be it.

The look on his face was frosty.

"Very well. Regardless of where you heard such stories, your information is false. Our parents left us, their three children, well-provided for. While yes, I did for a time—" He paused. "—make many unwise choices, I assure you that they did not extend to running through my entire fortune. Nor am I dependent on my brother."

He looked at her coldly.

"Not that any of this is any of your concern, Miss Gardner, particularly as you have said you will not be my wife."

Claire realized she had embarrassed him. She felt a twinge of shame, which she quickly suppressed. Why should she be the one to feel ashamed when he had led them to his juncture in the first place?

"I have no doubt you still believe me to be a vile rake, Miss Gardner, and nothing I say may make you believe otherwise. But I am not the man you seem to think I am."

"Merely the man who claimed *not* to be a seducer of innocents and then..." She stopped herself. These were unworthy words. It was unfair to cast all of the blame on him.

But it was too late. He was looking at her contemptuously.

She cleared her throat. "In any case, it does not matter, Mr. Campbell. The point is moot, for we shall not wed."

He stood up.

"You are speaking incredibly foolishly, Miss Gardner. I can only assume the effects of the cold and the rain have addled your brain. I see I must discuss this with your mother. I take it she is not in? I will return tomorrow."

"My mother?" Now it was Claire's turn to scoff. "My mother will not make me marry you, Mr. Campbell. Regardless of what has happened to my reputation, you have mistaken her character if you believe that she would. She may be disappointed in me and I may have brought her unhappiness, but she would not wish for me to be miserable for what could be a very, very long time."

A shadow crossed Thomas's face. He was angry, that much was clear. But there was something else she could not pinpoint. Wounded pride most likely.

She had no doubt that mere minutes after he left Orchard Hill, he would realize that she had given him the out he must be silently longing for.

"Have you spoken with Mr. Evans?"

"What?"

"I asked if you had spoken to Ned Evans. Your tenant, the man who was at the cottage yesterday. Have you spoken to him, asked him not to mention this matter to anyone?"

Thomas hesitated. "Not in those precise terms."

"Might I suggest you do so? My sister may be many things—" A shameless eavesdropper for one; she hoped Rosalind was enjoying the show. "—but she is not a gossip. Furthermore, Mr. Arthur Beckett has worked for my family since Gracie was an infant. I feel sure that when I speak with him, he will understand this is a matter best forgotten."

And she would speak with him as soon as Thomas left, she decided.

He was looking at her as if he did not recognize her. No, as if he despised her.

She was making the right choice then. She swallowed hard.

"You really are the most obstinate mule of a woman I have ever met, Miss Gardner," Mr. Campbell said derisively. "Do you really believe you may manipulate the world as you see fit? You have absolutely no idea who Mr. Beckett or Mr. Evans may have already spoken to..."

"Then I suggest you speak to him soon. Immediately. Upon returning to Northwood," she interrupted again.

He set his mouth in a hard line.

"This is not the reaction I was expecting, Miss Gardner."

"No, I do not suppose it was. Presumably, you expected me to kiss your feet or faint with gratitude at receiving your generous offer."

His face was turning an unflattering shade of red.

"But you see, Mr. Campbell," she said quietly, "you cannot save me when you were my undoing in the first place. Trusting you for a moment was my great mistake. Marriage to you would be a catastrophic blunder for us both."

"And I think you know that as well," she added, trying to soften her words a trifle, though not knowing why she bothered.

The sounds of a commotion in the yard brought their dialogue to a close. A moment later the door opened and Gracie and Mrs. Gardner entered, talking and laughing. As they noticed Mr. Campbell and his angry expression, the noise died down.

"Good day, Mr. Campbell..." Mrs. Gardner began. She glanced at Claire, trying to understand what they had walked in on.

Thomas threw a last brief glance at Claire, before sweeping past her mother and sister without a word, leaving the door open to the rain.

Mrs. Gardner pulled off her gloves. Claire saw pity in her eyes. "I think it is time you told me what is going on, my darling."

Thomas ground his teeth as he sat in the carriage. Had he actually proposed marriage to that woman? The idea was insanity.

No, the true madness was that she had refused.

What kind of young woman cared so little for her reputation that she would refuse a respectable offer of marriage?

He may not be as decent a man as William, but it was certainly a better offer than she would have received otherwise.

Was she holding out for a man with greater fortune? A noble title?

Or did she simply loathe him so much that social ostracism or spinsterhood was a better alternative to sharing his table and his bed?

Clearly, she would rather believe the lies her neighbours told her than accept the truth from his own lips. To her, he was a monster. Or if not a monster, something relatively close to one. A rake.

Of course, he did not *want* to marry Miss Gardner. The idea was ludicrous. He knew that from the start. He was endeavouring to do the honorable thing for once in his life, of his own volition. Nothing more.

But he had wanted her to want to marry him.

She could forgo the kissing of the feet, but confound it, yes, she should have been grateful.

Did she not appreciate what it took for a man like Thomas to even contemplate the prospect of shackling himself for life?

Especially after what he had already been through at the hands of a faithless female.

But she did not know, and he could not tell her. Could not say that the love of his life had been his mistress—a word Miss Gardner tossed about with such disdain and so little understanding.

Did she realize some men genuinely loved their mistresses? Those women who shared their beds and their lives, but whom they could never—or very rarely—call wife?

He could never have hoped to call Serafina his wife. Thinking back, she would likely have laughed at the idea. The experience of motherhood had clipped her wings enough, and she had been eager to escape it as quickly as she could. She would never have wished to give up her freedom for him. Or her career.

She was an actress. An artist so talented, so lovely, so charismatic that men flocked to her. Men of all sorts. The rich, the powerful, the handsome, the hideous. Married or unmarried—it made no difference to Serafina. She would accept whatever tribute they wished to bestow upon her.

Like a statue of an ancient goddess, they would bring precious gifts, do obeisance. Kneeling before her on a London stage.

And for a while, nearly a decade in fact, that goddess had chosen him.

He had thought she had chosen only him.

For a while, perhaps she had. He did not know what to believe anymore. Did not know how soon it had started—her lies and his blindness.

Although he had given her everything he had and more, it had not been enough. Love was an empty word in her mouth. She was incapable of it.

He had been young and stupid and, most importantly, somewhat rich. She had taken what she could get before casting him out in exchange for a wealthier and more influential patron.

She had done the same to their daughter. If not worse, and for much longer.

Since the moment of Isabel's birth, really.

The lurching of the carriage brought him out of his reverie. He peered out. They were nearly at Northwood.

Though it pained him to admit it, Miss Gardner was probably right. They would have made one another miserable.

He supposed he should count himself lucky to have been given such an easy way out of the entire mess.

He would not think about how the prospect of holding her in his arms again had been the one bright side in all of this.

Bedding her would not have been intolerable, but it was more than that. The embrace they had shared in the cottage—he found he could not put it out of his mind. The urgency of the kiss, her ardency.

She had been unlike any woman he had ever known, and one he had not known could exist.

Marriage to that woman—the one who could let go of herself, surrender to her passions—well, it might not have been such a hardship after all.

For a brief moment, he had considered saying just that to Miss Gardner.

Then he had seen the coldness in her eyes. She had not felt the same way. Her talk of love made that quite clear.

She was not the woman he had mistaken her for.

He had deluded himself into thinking she might have felt more for him than fleeting desire. But, no, Miss Gardner had everything planned out from the moment he arrived at her home.

He would talk to Ned Evans as she had asked. Nay, commanded.

Anything to settle the matter once and for all.

Chapter 13

D iscern between the rake and the common man

Young women may do well to ask, how then can we, O Wise Counselor, discern between the licentious libertine and the truly virtuous man. Remember, Dear Reader, that even the best of men are sometimes liable to be inconsistent with themselves, prone to sudden starts of passion, hurried into expressions and actions which their cooler reason may condemn. They may have some peculiarities of temper, be subject to accidental ill-humour, but they are never destructive of mutual felicity. Infallibility is not the property of man so you must not expect what is never to be found, but rather through force of observation and silent reason pick out the despised from the deserved.

The Beauford Chronicle, August 1818

When Thomas returned to Northwood from a morning ride two weeks later, William was coming down the main staircase. His hand slid lightly along the carved mahogany bannister. A smile danced upon his face.

"You look unusually cheerful," Thomas observed, as he discarded his wet coat. August was proving to be an even wetter month than July this year.

"Miss Rutledge and I have been reading *Waverley*. You know, I had never noticed how humorous a book it was before. Miss Rutledge has been reading aloud. She has an uncanny knack for dramatization, in fact—" William broke off as he saw Thomas's face. He cleared his throat.

"Yes, well, Doctor Greyson visited this morning. He says Miss Rutledge should be able to return home by the end of the week."

"Will you be sorry to lose the 'empress of your affections'?" Thomas asked wryly, loosely quoting the novel. He had not realized William had been visiting Miss Rutledge so often. It was kind of him to try to occupy her. He could not imagine the tedium of remaining in bed for days on end.

William blushed a little. "Miss Rutledge has been excellent company. I can only hope I have been as much of a diversion to her as she has to me, particularly as she is the one who has been ill."

"Has she walked on the ankle at all since she arrived?" Thomas asked, only slightly curious, as he went towards the stairs. The ride had been a long one on a hot day, and he needed a change of clothes.

"Yes, we took a short turn around the garden earlier, in fact. Before the rain returned. She seems much stronger, although she did require some assistance, particularly on the stairs. She is excited to share her progress with her father when he visits today."

"How kind of you to lend your arm to a 'female form of exquisite grace and beauty.'" Thomas quoted with flare.

William frowned, evidently unsure of whether he was being sarcastic or not.

"You always were better at recalling your lessons than I, Thomas. Not that *Waverley* was ever prescribed reading. As you remember it so vividly, I take it the book made quite the impression and you remain more of a youthful romantic than I have given you credit for lately."

Thomas shrugged. "I merely recall what I read more easily than you do, and always have. I see you did not disagree." He raised his eyebrows teasingly, trying to get a rise out of his brother.

William looked serious. "I do think her to be a pretty girl, and moreover she is a very kind one. I should not like to think you were mocking Miss Rutledge, Thomas. After that incident with the Mortons... Well, I fear she is not as valued by her neighbours as she should be."

"And you have discovered her true value, I take it?"

William's expression became reflective. Thomas decided the topic of Miss Rutledge had been exhausted.

"Speaking of physicians," he said. "Isabel's doctor from London paid a visit this morning while I was there."

He caught William's worried look. "It is not bad news. Doctor Amherst believes there has been substantial improvement. He suggests that Isabel's frail physical condition may have been brought on by her malnourishment as well as a state of intense anxiety and fear which was the by-product of her...neglect."

"Which is what I have been saying all along, as you will recall," he added, seeing William's eyes brighten.

"How is her cough? Is she as pale as when I last saw her?" William asked anxiously. Thomas felt warmed with affection towards his brother. Not for the first time he wished he were as naturally paternal.

Isabel may not have had the most dutiful parents, but she was fortunate to have William as her uncle.

"There was color in her cheeks, yes, if that is what you mean. Although do not forget that Doctor Amherst said that a blush is meaningless if it is truly consumption. The redness could be caused by that and nothing more. However," he continued hastily, seeing William's face change, "do not mistake me. Doctor Amherst appears to be stepping back from that diagnosis. He was impressed by her energy and appetite. He left me with a great deal of hope."

"We have young Gracie Gardner to thank in part for that," William said. "She has been a frequent visitor to Stoneybrook since meeting Isabel."

He smiled. "She is such a rough-and-tumble girl that I think her company has been stimulating for Isabel, who is inclined to be more sedate."

"Yes, well, you may thank her for me the next time you see her. She was not there today." Thomas felt cross at the mention of any Gardner woman, even the smallest of them.

As he prepared to go up, William seized a paper off the table in the hall and held it out.

"I am not sure if you have already seen this, Thomas. It arrived this morning."

It was a letter. Could it be from Miss Gardner? Thomas's heart sped up a little.

He tore it open and recognized the handwriting. Serafina. He tossed it back on the table in disgust.

"You should read it, Thomas. You would not want her showing up here unannounced one day because you had ignored her." He hesitated. "Could it be she wishes to see Isabel?"

"Wishes for us to fill her coffers again is more like. She had no interest in Isabel until we wanted to take her away. Essentially forcing me to purchase my own daughter before she would withdraw her talons. She is a harpy, not a mother. Ours, rest her soul, would have put her to shame."

"I should have liked to have seen that," William said softly, looking saddened.

Thomas felt sorry for having mentioned it.

Their parents had both passed almost a decade ago. Isabel had never met them. Thomas sometimes wondered whether they would have liked to see his child, their grandchild. Even an illegitimate one.

"What of Elizabeth? Has she written? Does she still wish to join us in Bath in October?" Changing the subject, he clasped his brother's shoulder and steered him towards the drawing room.

Claire had been correct about her mother. Mrs. Gardner understood. What was more she sympathized—more generously than Claire felt she had any right to. She had not chided nor scolded. She had not insisted Claire accept Mr. Campbell's tepid offer. Claire was not even sure she was altogether upset or disappointed.

Instead, a faraway look had come into Caroline Gardner's eyes as Claire briefly but poignantly described the kiss which had led to this mess.

Then she had patted Claire's hair gently, until she had fallen asleep, lying with her head on her mother's lap, as if she were a little girl again.

Mrs. Gardner had insisted on talking to Arthur herself. After that, nothing more had been said about the matter.

That was nearly two weeks ago.

This afternoon Claire was venturing out from Orchard Hill for the first time since Mr. Campbell's visit. She had remained close to home, unwilling to risk encountering neighbours, even though she knew how very unlikely it was that anyone had learned of her indiscretion. Or ever would.

She knew and that was bad enough.

When Mrs. Gardner absent-mindedly asked Claire to go and retrieve Gracie from Stoneybrook, where she had been since early that morning, Claire had started to object and was about to suggest Rosalind go instead. But then she saw her mother had forgotten her desire to stay out of view, including her reason for doing so, and she swallowed her excuses.

A horse was in the yard as she approached Stoneybrook. For a moment she stood motionless, frozen on the outskirts of the yard. It was absurd.

The thought occurred to her that it was probably Doctor Grayson's horse, come to check on Isabel. Feeling relieved, she continued her march up the drive and was reaching out to knock on the door when it swung open revealing Thomas Campbell.

He looked as shocked to see her as she was to see him. Stoneybrook had no butler, being a smaller household like Orchard Hill. Claire at least had the consolation of knowing a servant was not standing nearby watching the ridiculous facial expressions passing over Thomas's face. She had no doubt her own would have been cause for equal amusement.

How many times would she be forced to encounter this wretched man? Was there no hope at all that he would decide Beauford was not to his liking and return to London? Ideally, forever.

Why on earth was he at Stoneybrook?

"What are you doing here?" Thomas demanded.

Claire's hands had moved to her hips instinctively. A defensive position.

"I might ask the same of you, Mr. Campbell. I have more reason to be here than I would have thought you had. My sister is visiting Miss

Notley—the young mistress of Stoneybrook."

"Yes, I know who Miss Notley is," he said impatiently. "I did not realize you were a frequent visitor here as well as your sister. If I had known I might have to encounter an entire gang of Gardner women..." He stopped abruptly, scowling.

A dark curling lock had fallen across his face as he spoke. It was preposterous, but Claire had the urge to push that stray curl off his face and tuck it gently back into place. She clenched her hands tightly in case her body had any plans to betray her. Once had been enough.

"I do not see how it is any concern of yours who visits Miss Notley. But as my sister is currently one of her guests, I believe it is my right to ask what you are doing here, Mr. Campbell. Visiting a house of unmarried women."

She had a wild thought. "Were you..." She stopped.

"...liaising with a maid?" he supplied. "Or perhaps you think I have just come from a tryst with Mrs. Mowbray. The cook is also quite a fetching woman despite being a grandmother of twenty. Shall I summon her for you, Miss Gardner, so you may ask if she is my mistress?"

He looked entertained with himself.

Claire no longer wished to tuck away that stray curl. A strong tug would be too gentle a gesture.

"As you are clearly only interested in spouting nonsense, Mr. Campbell, please step aside. I am here for my sister."

His expression changed.

"Your sister..." He cleared his throat awkwardly. "Yes. About that. I have been meaning to thank your mother."

Claire furrowed her brow.

"For allowing your sister to call on Miss Notley," he explained. "Her doctor tells us that Gracie's visits may be just the thing Isabel needs to encourage and energize her spirits."

Claire began to ask why Miss Notley's physician would be sharing personal details of her health with Thomas Campbell before realizing she already knew the answer.

Those beautiful black curls, the dark wide eyes.

Miss Notley's features were merely a more delicate and feminine version of Thomas's.

"You are her father," she said slowly. It was not a question.

"I am."

"You did not move to Beauford to be near your mistress."

"I did not."

"You moved here... to live nearer your daughter? For her health?"

He nodded.

This would not do. It would not do at all.

A Thomas Campbell who had altruistic motives, who considered the welfare of someone other than himself...? Who wished to thank her mother for allowing her child to visit...?

In a flash, the image she had fixed in her mind of Thomas Campbell's self-absorption, his arrogance, and most importantly, his licentiousness, burst like a bubble in the sun. He had already adamantly denied all of the claims Harriet had made regarding him.

But if he was not that man, who was he?

He was looking at her oddly. "Does this shock you?"

She refused to say it did.

"Not at all." The words came out stiffly.

"I can see from your face that it does. You would prefer to think of me as a villain, Miss Gardner. I assure you I am a man with many faults, but flesh-and-blood like yourself."

She knew that already. It was his flesh which was so enticing. That irritating smirk on his face. She had let those lips touch her own. She started to blush. It would never do to give a hint of the truth, to let him suspect for a moment that the sensations he had stirred in her that day were never far from her mind, asleep or awake.

She dwelled on them much more than she liked or would ever admit.

She bit her lip.

Thomas was struck by the picture Miss Gardner made standing on the doorstep of his daughter's house. The sunlight reflecting off her auburn hair gave it a splendid ruby hue. Her hands were on her hips —a posture which she likely intended to convey exasperation. But it also emphasized her shapeliness and caused her beautifully rounded breasts to press tantalizingly against the blue muslin dress which constrained them.

And she was biting her lip, bringing an even rosier flush to that lush mouth.

The end effect was that rather than being put-off, he was having the urge to part those soft lips with the tip of his tongue, as he had done once before.

He gave himself a shake and took a breath. "This may surprise you, Miss Gardner, but I do not sacrifice small children, attack the elderly, or even defile virgins on a regular basis."

He wanted to add "you would have been the first" but wisely held back.

"I suppose I would have been the first," she replied tartly. She blushed and quickly looked away.

All of a sudden, the urge struck him again.

He wanted to say he regretted nothing. That the memory of that day had become a kind of jewel he held and treasured, against his better judgement, against his will. He wanted to say that he wished nearly every day that he could repeat their mistake. Wished with an almost painful yearning that her sister had not walked in, that the afternoon had continued uninterrupted, that she had compromised herself with him so thoroughly there would have been no going back.

That she had continued to reveal to him who and what she truly was, and allowed him to do the same.

He wanted to say that lately he woke up in the night and looked at the place in bed beside him and imagined her lying there. Her lovely rich hair spread across the pillow; her eyes closed peacefully as she dreamed. Of course, she was devoid of all clothing in these fantasies. As her bare breasts gleamed enticingly in the moonlight, he would reach one hand out...

He was doing it again. It was pathetic.

Before he could stop himself, a sigh escaped.

What had begun as genuine dislike and then evolved into a stimulating battle of wits had turned tedious.

Could she not accept that there was more to him than she had judged? He was no longer the rake he once was.

He would not go on trying to convince her, however.

"I will stand aside, Miss Gardner," he said quietly, moving out of her way. "I apologize for my rudeness."

You bring out something wild in me, he wanted to add—or would she somehow anticipate that, too?

She gazed at him for a second, pressing her lips together.

"Misunderstanding one another seems to be what we do best, Mr. Campbell." She moved to go, then stopped and looked up at him.

"Miss Notley is a very charming and bright little girl. Gracie enjoys her friendship very much. You have a lovely daughter."

Thomas stared.

He did, didn't he? It was the first time he could remember anyone besides William ever saying so.

Fatherhood had not come naturally to him. Sometimes he still could not believe he had a child. Before he and William took over her care, Isabel had not seemed real most of the time. He had known she existed, of course; had visited her from time to time, albeit briefly.

But Serafina had been so very averse to the idea of motherhood that it had been easy to pretend there was no child.

Only their love—or his self-centered idea of what love was.

All the adoration, obsession, and infatuation had left no room for the mess and chaos a child brought. Even a child born supposedly from love.

How differently he felt now. How ashamed of that former, foolish man.

Isabel was a person to him. He was learning her thoughts, her opinions, her favorite stories, the names of her dolls. Matilda was her favorite, he remembered with a jolt. He knew that. He knew her.

As did Miss Gardner. She knew his daughter and cared for her enough to bestow what unexpectedly felt like the highest compliment anyone could give.

He swallowed hard.

Suddenly he understood why William had sought a mother for Isabel, and why he had thought Miss Gardner might be such a one.

An image came into his mind, unbidden, of what it might look like to be a family of three.

He pictured a beautiful summer day, a country road, and Miss Gardner and Isabel walking together hand-in-hand, laughing and talking to one another, as he walked behind.

Separate but connected to them by invisible threads. Looking ahead at the pair with pride, knowing that they were his.

Except it was a dream that Miss Gardner had made clear she did not share.

"Thank you, Miss Gardner. That is..." He stopped. He had a thought. "I hope that your mother... Now that you know about Isabel, I hope that Mrs. Gardner will still permit..."

"Knowing that she is your child will not change a thing," she said quietly, looking back with a steady gaze. "My mother will still allow Gracie to visit, I promise you. Isabel is not the only natural child in Beauford, you know. Besides, it is a person's character my mother considers, not their birth. Miss Notley is a sweet girl. She is probably a better influence on Gracie than Gracie is on her."

"Well then..." Thomas was not sure how one concluded such a conversation when it had touched on a topic most young ladies would consider unseemly.

"Thank you," he said again, lamely.

She looked straight into his eyes. "Of course."

Something fluttered in his chest. If a man's chest could be said to flutter. It seemed a ridiculous description. But certainly, his heart felt oddly detached from the rest of him.

And as Miss Gardner stepped past him and entered the house, he knew with a sharp pang that it was no longer attached to him at all but had joined itself to that slim, feminine figure who had just gone inside.

Claire walked home alone slowly. Gracie had begged for one more hour at Stoneybrook and Claire had not thought her mother would object. Mrs. Mowbray had gladly given her assent.

Seeing Thomas Campbell had thrown Claire into a whirlwind of confusion.

She was not used to being wrong. Especially not this wrong.

She felt she had made a grave error in judgement.

It was tempting to lay all of the blame for this at Harriet Morton's feet.

But the truth was that it was entirely her own fault for being so ready to believe that her first impression of Thomas had been the correct one. He had wounded her pride and given her offense. To be told by Harriet that he was their moral inferior had been all too easy to believe.

But she had been led by pride, not virtue.

She should have known better than to trust anything a Morton said, especially after her last two encounters with them.

When it came to a single, handsome men with adequate fortunes, Harriet had probably been hoping to eliminate any feminine competition that lay between the Gardner girls and the Campbells.

Two mistresses! To think she had thrown the accusation in his face. Claire felt like such a fool now. How he must have laughed at her expense afterwards.

Claire had brought along a book to read while she walked, but now she was nearly at Orchard Hill and it rested untouched in one of the deep pockets she had sewn for just such a purpose.

As she walked up the slope and through the orchard, where a few uncollected apples still littered the grass, she saw a petite figure coming towards her with hands outstretched.

"Fanny!"

Her friend appeared the picture of perfect good health.

Fanny's face was an image of pure happiness, the emotion lending a radiance to her features and elevating them from pretty to beautiful.

"Whatever has happened to make you smile so?"

Fanny blushed. "It is merely the consequence of an enjoyable two weeks in good company."

Claire looked at her curiously.

"Few would call convalescing in bed 'enjoyable.' The company must have been excellent indeed. I take it you refer to one of the Campbell brothers—unless they have an exceptionally charming housekeeper who visited you with stories and sweets?" Claire's eyes danced.

The blush deepened. The smile widened.

"It was not the housekeeper. William... Mr. Campbell, I mean, was kind enough to visit me from time to time."

Claire deduced the visits had been frequent.

"He really is a charming man, Claire. We read aloud together, played chess. Conversed on many topics. Walked in the garden as I became stronger."

"You must have been sorry to leave Northwood after such good company."

Claire was exceedingly pleased by what she was hearing. These new developments seemed so opposite from what she had experienced since she and Fanny separated. Her friend's interactions with the older Mr. Campbell seemed everything that was fitting and agreeable.

"I would have been very sorry... if Mr. Campbell had not told me more than once that he hoped to call upon Papa and I when I returned home."

Fanny's eyes sparkled.

"And he has done so, Claire. Twice already!"

"I am so happy for you, Fanny. How flattering! It is high time a man of quality recognized the jewel in front of him." She poked Fanny playfully. "Certainly, such regard is nothing but what you deserve. Do you believe he is..." She tried to phrase it delicately.

"He has asked Papa for permission to court me, Claire. Only yesterday afternoon." Fanny looked down modestly.

"That is splendid news!" Claire exclaimed. She smiled slyly.

"If I had known our misadventure would lead to your being romanced by such an agreeable, good-humoured, and most of all, handsome man, I would have insisted we visit the ravine during a storm long ago." She would not mention the other unintended consequences that had come of the adventure.

Fanny giggled. "It was rather worth the pain of the fall, to make his closer acquaintance. I am happier than I can express. But what of you, Claire? I have not seen you in over two weeks. Tell me all your news. I insist, or else I will be unable to cease singing Mr. Campbell's praises."

Claire forced a smile, her mind racing. She had not given any thought to what she would tell Fanny, and now that she was here she did not want to discuss the brother of the man her friend was now courting.

A part of her whispered that she was afraid of being lowered in Fanny's esteem. Would her friend be shocked? Horrified? Would she think her a fallen woman?

Fanny was waiting. Claire mustered a smile.

"The younger Mr. Campbell transported me to the cottage. It was empty when we arrived—you must have left shortly before. We were there only a few minutes when Rosalind and Arthur appeared, accompanied by Mr. Evans. It was all quite dull compared to your trysts with Mr. Campbell." She tried to speak lightly. If only Fanny knew.

Fanny looked as if she wished to ask more.

"Think of Miss Morton's face when she finds out Mr. Campbell is courting you, Fanny," Claire said quickly. "I wish we could be there to see it. I admit I am only a little sorry for Mr. Morton. At the dance at Northwood, he seemed quite intent on winning your affections." How grateful she was that would never come to be.

"I enjoyed dancing with Mr. Morton, but he was being neighbourly, nothing more. I could never have considered him in such a way anyhow. He does not have Mr. Campbell's strength of character, for one. Not that he is not a nice young man in his own way," Fanny added.

"You think too well of everyone you meet, Fanny. I think it is a characteristic you share with Mr. Campbell. I would not be able to say anything pleasant about a Morton these days, not even about their dancing."

"He is an extremely amiable man," Fanny reflected. "Mr. Campbell, I mean. But he is wise and intelligent, too, Claire. I respect him greatly."

"Exactly as you should your future husband," Claire said playfully as they walked towards the house.

Chapter 14

The Bear and Bull was the most frequented public house in Beauford.

This was due to its status as Beauford's *only* public house.

Thomas had been inside a handful of times. Today his visit was a matter of necessity.

It was a scorching August day. He had ridden to town to the stationers' shop only to find himself parched and famished by the time he came out.

He had nursed a drink and a bowl of mutton stew in brooding silence for almost an hour, appreciating the cool shady gloom of the tavern's interior. The proprietor did not seem to appreciate Thomas taking up a table on his own for so long. But it was not Thomas's fault if his perpetual glower had the unintentional effect of dissuading would-be companions. Although it had been two weeks since his failed proposal and he had seen Miss Gardner in more pleasant circumstances since then, a dark cloud lingered. He was in no mood to break bread with his fellow man.

As he finished his meal and rose to leave, he noticed Ned Evans off in one corner, a cup in hand. The table at which he sat was full and the men were talking loudly. Evans noticed Thomas and tipped his hat before quickly looking back down into his glass.

Thomas had heard Evans was a drinking man. Perhaps he did not wish for his landlord to invade his comfortable watering hole.

Or perhaps Evans had lost some respect for Thomas after the events at his cottage. As long as that was all it was. The man was entitled to his opinions. So long as he did not share them.

As Thomas walked out into the street the sun's heat was beginning to diminish. He was preparing to mount when the sound of raised voices drew his eye to a closed landau across the road.

Hearing a woman's voice gave him pause and he was considering whether or not to step over when the carriage door opened and Miss Fanny Rutledge tumbled out. Her dress was ruffled and her hair unpinned.

As she stood, she caught Thomas's eye, flushed a deep red, and hurried away as quickly as she could.

It was very strange. He was contemplating following to make sure all was well when who should exit next but Charles Morton. The young man glanced about, before brushed away something on his face, and then smoothed down his lapels and adjusted his cravat.

There was no mistaking the meaning of such gestures in combination with their setting.

Thomas had made them himself more times than he could count. Just as he had seen the similarly flushed faces of dishevelled beauties on equally countless occasions. He had tumbled a woman in a carriage or two in his time.

Miss Rutledge, however, was the absolute last woman he would have expected to see emerging from one in this way.

As he reached his conclusions, a cold rage filled him and he stared across at Charles Morton waiting for the man to notice him.

But when he did, the dandy merely smirked and nodded before crossing the street, giving a wide berth to Thomas, and entering the tavern.

Thomas was tempted to step back inside and call him out, there and then, but decided the best course of action was to return home.

Truth be told, he felt more anger towards Miss Rutledge than Morton. The behavior was unsurprising in the young man, but in her it was beyond the pale.

But why should it be? Was this not exactly the same way he had acted towards Miss Gardner? Taking liberties with her person—one might even say seducing. Yet he did not look down upon Miss Gardner for being a willing party. Far from it. Her responsiveness had impressed him. She was not the prudish, missish type he had taken her for. Indeed, his mind was still coming to terms with the fact that he had misjudged her in many ways.

Besides, the rules for women were far too stringent—what was good for the gander, was not good for the goose; the hypocrisy was evident to anyone with eyes, as Miss Gardner had rightly pointed out herself.

No, it was not any lack of virtue which bothered him but the lack of loyalty.

William had always held a more favorable view of human nature. While Thomas enjoyed scoffing at him for his tender-heartedness, even calling it naivety, the truth was that deep down Thomas knew it was one of William's finest qualities.

Furthermore, it was what set them apart. He did not relish the idea of William becoming more like himself—pessimistic, distrusting, and worse, forced to carry a scar on his heart.

Thomas knew what it was like to be betrayed by a woman one truly loved, and he would not wish the pain of the experience on his worst enemy, let alone his dearest relative.

If there had been no third party to be injured by their actions, Thomas might easily have walked on and never given Morton and Miss Rutledge a second thought.

But William was about to propose marriage to this girl. His heart was already entangled.

Thomas did not know Miss Rutledge well—truly, they had not exchanged more than twenty words. Most of the courtship had been conducted at Hillcrest.

All he knew was that William had quickly come to hold her in the highest esteem.

She made him happy.

That was enough for Thomas. He had been fully prepared to welcome her as a sister.

But now...Now he was to be forced into the role of messenger of doom, an unwanted Hermes delivering a harsh missive that would wound William to the core.

He would not forgive Miss Rutledge for that.

Her life was her own to lead, but taking advantage of William's open-heartedness, his eagerness to love, misleading him into believing she returned his love—that was inexcusable.

He should have known William would not believe him. Anticipated it. But to actually ball up his fists as if he would like to strike him? Thomas would never have expected that.

"I would not have shared this with you if I had not seen it with my own eyes. You must believe that. I hold no grudge against Miss Rutledge. Till now, I shared your belief that she was a gentle-spirited, amiable young woman. Certainly I did not think there was any love lost between her and the Mortons. But Miss Rutledge must not have felt so herself, or she would not have chosen to share such an... intimate arrangement... with Mr. Morton."

William exhaled slowly, struggling for control.

"I believe that you believe what you saw," he said slowly. "As for my believing it. Well, that is another matter, Thomas. There must be another explanation."

"What other explanation could there be for a man and woman to emerge from a carriage in such equally dishevelled states?" Thomas asked in disbelief. "Clearly they had arranged a liaison. I was infuriated on your behalf, William. I still am. I nearly called Mr. Morton out, right there in the street. And am still tempted to do so. Only concern for our family's reputation prevented it."

He paused. "One good thing has come of this. There is still little knowledge of your connection to Miss Rutledge. Now we can make sure that it stays that way. She has played you false, William. It sickens me to the heart to have to say so. Please believe me when I say I would prefer you not share the same experience I suffered with a woman. But..." The look on his brother's face made him trail off.

"I will have to speak to Miss Rutledge, Thomas," William said quietly. "How unfair we are being to discuss her in such a way and to make such judgements concerning her nature when we do not have the full account."

Thomas knew his brother was being generous in including himself in that statement. It was Thomas who was urging for judgement to be passed.

"Of course. Speak with her if you must. See if her version of today's events aligns."

He threw up his hands.

"Although I cannot help but worry that a woman who could so easily practice such a deception will be able to easily come up with some sincere-sounding explanation."

"If it is a convincing one, I will see no reason not to believe it, Thomas."

"Of course, you won't." Thomas snorted in frustration. "In fact, you will probably be so moved by her story that you will propose on the spot. If that is the case, why don't I invite Serafina to live here as well? We may as well have two false women under one roof..."

"Stop." William's voice was cold. "No more, Thomas. We will not speak of this again until I have met with Miss Rutledge. Until then, you will keep your altered opinion of her to yourself. Or risk my wrath."

He strode from the room.

Thomas stared after. So much for brotherly trust and gratitude. He supposed he should be grateful William was not weeping on the floor.

But it seemed he was merely postponing the inevitable. When the betrayal had been confirmed, the real pain would arrive.

William had seen Thomas through such pain. It had not been a pretty spectacle, nor had it passed swiftly.

Now it was his turn to do the same for his brother.

Chapter 15

Thomas could be idle no more. William had returned from seeing Miss Rutledge, his face an ashen mask. He had hardly spoken beyond a few words, which led Thomas to understand Miss Rutledge had been unable to provide an adequate explanation.

Although he had known it was coming, Thomas was oddly shocked. It seemed as if part of him had held out a smidgen of hope after all that he would turn out to be wrong, that it had all been a mistake.

But if Miss Rutledge herself had not denied it...

In time, perhaps William would be grateful that he had found out before it was too late. Would Miss Rutledge have accepted his proposal? Married him and continued to see Morton on the side? If so, William would have been in for a world of heartache.

Thomas could not understand the appeal of a man like Morton. William was the better of the two in every possible way.

But there was no accounting for taste, especially not where women were concerned.

He could not deny that Miss Rutledge's conduct with Mr. Morton had struck an uncomfortable chord. No matter how he wished to disregard it, the fact was Miss Gardner and Miss Rutledge would soon find themselves in remarkably similar positions.

He was not so different from Charles Morton then.

Beyond their choice of venues. A closed carriage on a public street seemed indiscreet in the extreme.

Not like a remote cottage.

Which had a bed.

Worse then.

Thomas ran his hands through his hair. What troublesome things these rules of polite society were. A man might begin to find life on a desert island tempting.

He shook his head. He had condemned Miss Rutledge without a second thought, relayed the news of her conduct to his brother unhesitatingly. There was no doubt the news would soon circulate. These things always managed to spread. Especially in small towns.

It was only a matter of time before the same thing happened to Claire Gardner.

Miss Gardner had expressed absolute confidence in her groom, but Thomas hardly knew the man. Who was to say what he might have already said in the privacy of his own home? To his wife?

No matter how roundly Miss Gardner had rejected him, Thomas found he still had no wish to see her brought down low, to be shamed by her neighbours, or have to face their silent condemnation.

He thought of the strange look on Ned Evan's face in the pub.

When he had spoken to his tenant, the man had promised the matter would stay between them.

But if there was one thing Thomas knew well, it was that liquor loosened the lips.

He sighed. In some ways, mistresses were simpler. Young ladies were so easily ruined.

The longer they delayed the inevitable, Miss Gardner risked horrendous consequences.

She was living in a fairyland if she did not recognize that.

"Come down here quickly, Claire!" Rosalind called.

Claire put away the pelisse she had been folding. Walking down the stairs she saw with surprise Fanny's father standing by the entrance. The slight grey-haired man was twisting his hat in his hands.

His face was a canvas of misery.

Mr. Rutledge looked up with relief as he heard Claire's footsteps.

"Miss Gardner, I wonder if I could impose upon your time and ask you to visit my daughter."

"I saw Fanny only a few days ago," Claire said with surprise. "Has something happened? Has she had a relapse?"

Mr. Rutledge shook his head. "I cannot say, Miss Gardner. I do not believe it is her health. She will not speak to me. But her state is so changed. She is so miserable. I must know what has happened. Please, will you come and speak with her now? I feel sure you will learn more than I have. I do not know what else to do."

Claire put a reassuring hand on his arm. "Of course. Of course, I will come," she said quickly. "Let me gather my things."

She met Rosalind's eyes as her sister passed her hat and cloak, and a quizzical look passed between them.

The journey to Hillcrest Hall was a pretty drive but today it felt interminable. A little under an hour later they arrived.

Mr. Rutledge walked the hall with her to Fanny's room. The door was closed.

She rapped once, twice, then called softly. There was no answer. Mr. Rutledge stood behind her, wringing his hands once more. This would not do.

Claire tapped on the door once more. "I am coming in, Fanny." She tried the handle. It was unlocked.

The curtains were drawn and Fanny was still abed. This was not like her. Claire walked across the room.

"I am going to draw the curtain a little, dear Fanny," she said quietly.

When the room was a little lighter, she pulled a chair up to Fanny's bed. Fanny's eyes were closed.

Claire leaned forward, resting a hand gently on the bed.

"What has happened, Fanny? Are you ill?"

She waited, then tried again.

"Your father is so worried. Will you not help me put his mind at rest?"

Her thoughts were racing. Could something have happened with William?

"No matter what has happened, your father loves you, Fanny. As do I. Nothing will change that, no matter what has occurred. I assure you of this. Will you not talk to me please?"

Fanny opened her eyes.

"Oh, Claire," she whispered. Her eyes filled immediately with tears.

Claire bit her lip. She was having a little trouble keeping her own from moistening. What could have happened to bring this good-natured girl so low?

"Talk to me, Fanny." She stroked her friend's hair gently as if she were a child.

She wondered if she should have brought her mother along. Mrs. Gardner would know just what to say, just what to do. Fanny had lost her own mother when she was just a little girl.

If Fanny would not speak to her, she would have Mr. Rutledge go back to Orchard Hill for her mother, Claire determined.

But Fanny was preparing to speak. She shifted in bed and sat up. Her face was pale and wan.

And then Fanny told her.

Told her of how she had gone into town alone the day before. She had been walking to a shop when the Mortons' carriage had pulled up alongside her. Charles had hopped out and explained Harriet wished a word with her. He had helped her up into the carriage.

Only for her to find it empty.

Before she could step out, Charles had closed the door and begun to barrage her.

At first, he did so only with words, spouting claims of adoration and love which rang so false in Fanny's ears that she was too flabbergasted to respond.

When he began to propose marriage, she could not believe what she was hearing. Not only was this the first indication she had that he thought of her in such a way, but her heart already belonged to another and she was steadfast on this.

At first, she strove to explain things gently. Then, when he would not hear, more firmly. At last, he had refused to hear at all and had thrust himself upon her.

She struggled, pushed him away, tried to call for help. When he placed a hand over her mouth, she managed to badly scratch his face and while he was still reeling, she jumped down from the carriage.

She was distraught and alone. When she spotted Thomas Campbell across the street, she had no thought of requesting aid. Only of fleeing as far from public eye as she possibly could.

Claire's facial muscles tightened as she listened. It was clear where this story was leading.

"William... Mr. Campbell came to see me yesterday. He told me his brother had seen me with Mr. Morton. He asked me to explain." Her voice choked.

"What could I say, Claire? No matter what I said, it would have been wrong." She looked at Claire helplessly. "I am ruined."

Her voice dropped to a whisper. "I have lost him."

Claire ached for her friend, but a fire of rage was also kindling.

"Did you explain to Mr. Campbell what had actually occurred? Does he know this was not your doing? That Mr. Morton coerced and confined you?" Claire took a breath and willed herself to slow down.

"I... tried. I did try." Fanny's voice faltered. "But I fear I made a very bad job of it. And Claire, the essential facts were the same as what his brother had repeated. And ...I did not know how to explain. I was afraid, Claire. I did not see how he could possibly believe me over his own brother. No matter what I said, I thought he was sure to think less of me."

She leaned back on her pillows, staring off into a corner of the room unseeing.

"I fear I did not say as much as I could. As much as I now wish I had," she said slowly.

Her eyes were swimming with tears.

"Oh, Fanny." Claire swallowed hard. What beasts these men could be. Whether a woman was willing or not made no difference to many of them. Even if she was willing, the woman always paid the price.

The most incredible part of it all was that Charles Morton had dared to propose marriage. His actions were unfathomable to her, but what was evident was Fanny's guiltlessness. He had placed her in a terrible position, and he had done so intentionally. There was no other explanation. She silently swore she would get to the bottom of it all.

"I am sure, Mr. Campbell..." She hesitated.

What did she really know of William Campbell after all? They had only known him a few brief months. He had an amiable character, this was true. But was he the kind of man inclined to believe the best or the worst? How attached to Fanny was he, if he could so easily leave her like this?

Of course, even the best natured man would be disturbed to hear the woman he was courting had been seen in such compromising circumstances. Especially when he learned of it from his trusted brother.

But there must be hope.

She squeezed Fanny's hand to regain her attention.

"I am sure Mr. Campbell was merely upset. He will have returned home to think things through, and when he does, I am sure he will come here to speak with you again. You must explain things more clearly, Fanny. Above all, remember you were faultless in this. You must make him see that."

She thought for a moment before adding, "And even if he does not see it, know that you are blameless, Fanny. Regardless of what William chooses to believe, your true friends will always know the truth."

Fanny looked at her through watery eyes.

Claire wondered what on earth they should tell Mr. Rutledge. He was not a confrontational kind of man. Quite the opposite. He shared his daughter's sweet nature and had a timid spirit.

He would be devastated to learn that one of his neighbour's sons had done such a thing.

Claire did not doubt for a moment that he would believe his daughter. But he would not have a solution to her dilemma.

She wondered if there was one.

"We must go and talk to your father," she said gently. "Do not doubt he will understand. I will be right there with you."

Fanny nodded. Claire rose and went to the door. She had at least two destinations in mind after she left Hillcrest. But first she would need to return home.

She opened the door and stepped into the hall.

Chapter 16

Pay no heed to erroneous advice
"*A reformed rake makes the best husband*" *is a common opinion oft resulting in unhappy victims of the female persuasion. A man who has long been in the company of the worst sort of women is very apt to contract a contempt for females in general. Incapable of esteeming any woman, he is suspicious of all and to him the fairer sex is a continual source of ill humour. What prospect of happiness can there be with such a companion?*

The Beauford Chronicle, August 1818

Traveling home in the Rutledge's carriage, Claire allowed her rage to simmer.

Two men were to blame for her friend's present heartache.

Mr. Morton, of course.

And Thomas Campbell.

His actions stung the most.

He had condemned Fanny without a second thought, without offering her assistance, without even bothering to speak with her first.

He had destroyed a sweet, innocent girl's prospects of happiness—when he was guilty of the very same crime.

As was she. Claire remembered that she had not bothered to share that information with Fanny. Would it have helped? To know that Claire might easily be considered just as compromised, though of her own volition.

There was quite a difference between willingly kissing a man and being attacked without any provocation as the detestable Charles Morton had done. She was not sure the knowledge would have been much comfort.

She hoped Fanny had scratched Charles hard. Left deep marks. Hopefully ones which would become scars.

He was a would-be rapist, as far as she was concerned. It horrified her to think of how much worse things could be right now.

Would Charles Morton tell others? If it was to his advantage in some way to do so, then Claire had no doubt he would not hesitate to tell his twisted version of the truth.

Not after he had shown himself to be so ruthless in other ways.

And what of the Campbells. Was it possible Thomas had already told anyone other than his brother?

Oh, that infernal man!

To think that only a few days ago she had felt her heart softening towards him. As they stood and spoke on the steps of Stoneybrook, she had seen something new in his eyes. Love. Selfless concern for another. He cared for his little daughter very much.

She wondered what had led to his sudden change of heart towards her.

Mrs. Mowbray had told her that Isabel had been neglected, but Thomas was certainly remedying that now.

Isabel was a pretty girl. She shared many of Thomas's features, but her own were delicate porcelain. She would be a beauty one day. Claire tried to picture what her mother must look like.

Thomas's mistress. Almost a wife—they had a child together.

Why had he left London? He had told Claire he had no mistress. But did he wish he still had? Did he miss Isabel's mother? Were they still in contact? Continuing to share in their daughter's upbringing?

She imagined Thomas and Isabel sitting on the lawn at Stoneybrook, a beautiful woman between them, their faces lit with happiness as they looked at her.

Why oh why had she kissed that man.

A few moments of pleasure— and admittedly, it had been an intense and deep-seated kind of pleasure which still made her flush head to toe to recall— could not possibly have been worth all this embarrassment and awkwardness.

Meanwhile Thomas Campbell could go on as if nothing had changed.

Oh, admittedly he had offered her his hand. But she had known in that moment it was a formality and nothing more. He did not wish to be tied to a woman, especially not a woman as young and inexperienced as Claire was. She must seem a raggedy country girl in comparison to the sophisticated women of London he was used to.

Claire shook herself from the unwanted reverie. The carriage had stopped. She was home. Stepping out, she saw there was another conveyance already in the yard.

Thomas was holding a teacup and talking to his future mother-in-law. She might already be, if she had not raised such an obstinate daughter.

He had not had much opportunity to converse with Mrs. Gardner before this. In contrast to Gracie and Rosalind, Caroline Gardner shared Claire's dark auburn tresses. Hers were tinged with silver now, and her waist had thickened from age and childbearing. She was still a pretty woman.

What was more, Mrs. Gardner had a kind disposition and right now, she had turned it on Thomas in full force, evidently intent on putting him at ease.

She had appeared surprised when she opened the door and found him standing there. Then a sympathetic look came into her eyes.

She knew.

He took a sip of his tea and endeavoured to focus on what Mrs. Gardner was saying.

"Claire was only fourteen when my husband passed away. She had a very close bond with her father. He was so devoted to his girls."

How had they gotten on to the topic of Mrs. Gardner's dead husband? What had he missed?

He nodded and tried to look sympathetic.

"Of course, you and your brother know what it is like to lose a parent." Mrs. Gardner took a sip from her cup and looked at him expectantly.

He cleared his throat. "Yes. William and I lost our parents nearly ten years ago. Our sister, Elizabeth, was very young then. William took on a father's role in many ways."

"It must have come very naturally to your brother. He seems a considerate and kind man."

Thomas nodded agreement.

At least there was one Campbell man who had not disgraced himself. He wondered how much Mrs. Gardner had heard about his own reputation.

Did she wish her daughter to marry a man who was thought of by at least some of her neighbours as a degenerate rake?

"...which was why we were so happy to hear of your brother's new connection with Miss Rutledge."

Thomas dropped out of his musings with a thud.

Mrs. Gardner was beaming at him.

"Miss Rutledge has been a dear friend of the family for years, you see. Such a lovely girl and so deserving of happiness. Very well-suited to a man with your brother's temperament. Fanny's mother passed when she was a little girl, not much more than Gracie's age."

In horror, Thomas saw Mrs. Gardner start to tear up.

"I cannot imagine one of my girl's growing up motherless, Mr. Campbell. My heart breaks for such ones as your sister and Miss Rutledge. Not that the devotedness of brothers and fathers is not also a comfort, but..."

"Pardon me, please." She delicately wiped her eyes with a handkerchief, and paused as if waiting for Thomas to add something to the conversation. Which he supposed he had not been doing a very good job of.

"A girl needs a mother. Yes, I quite agree, Mrs. Gardner."

He was being a craven hypocrite, but this did not seem like the right time to throw cold water on Mrs. Gardner's hopes for their family friend.

Abruptly he wondered if she knew about Isabel. Had Claire shared that, too? He could not blame her if she had.

Mrs. Gardner had been sipping her tea. Now she looked directly into Thomas's eyes.

He felt rather as if he were before his old nurse. Was he in for a scolding?

She smiled gently.

"I know she can be rather outspoken at times, but my Claire is a kind and loving girl. I know she is fond of Isabel. Gracie has been enjoying her summer with your daughter. It is nice for her to have a companion nearby."

She hesitated a moment before continuing.

"You seem to be a devoted father, Mr. Campbell. Claire tells me that you and your brother moved to the neighbourhood to be nearer Miss Notley. She seems to be receiving excellent care."

Another pause. "Not all men..."

"Would do more than provide for their bastard's basic welfare?" He gave a strained smile. "Our parents raised us to place a high value on family, Mrs. Gardner. Regardless of which side of the blanket they were born. My father's elder brother was also a natural child, you see. They were very close. William, in particular, takes this duty very seriously. He is a devout man, a good brother. More than I deserve."

She took another sip.

Thomas cleared his throat.

"I have not always been the father you think, Mrs. Gardner," he said slowly. "Isabel has not always received proper care, as your daughter may have mentioned. I am not sure..." He hesitated. "I am not sure how much she knows about Isabel's history. It was only recently that I began to... attempt to fulfill my responsibilities."

"Well," Mrs. Gardner said softly. "What matters is you are trying to do right by her now."

She placed her cup on the table.

"Shall we speak about the reason you are here to see my daughter, Mr. Campbell?"

Thomas's eyes widened.

Mrs. Gardner was a widow. He supposed she had every right to expect to discuss the matter in lieu of Claire's father.

"I..." he began. Need he begin at the beginning? Good Lord, this was going to be painful.

Mrs. Gardner raised a hand.

"Please. There is no need, Mr. Campbell. I have no wish to hear you recount what I am sure would be an awkward tale for you to tell and me to sit through. Besides, Claire has given me a rough account of what occurred."

Thomas thought he caught the hint of a smile, but then it was gone and she was looking at him calmly and directly again.

He found himself again impressed by Claire's mother. She was forthright, he would give her that. Apparently, that ran in the family.

"These things happen, Mr. Campbell. They happen more than children know and perhaps more than even young men such as yourself—" Young rakes, did she mean? "—probably realize."

She paused.

"What matters is..."

"I am here to try again, Mrs. Gardner," he interrupted. Well, dash it all, he was. Though now that he was sitting there, it was beginning to seem like more and more of an idiotic plan.

She gave him a genuine smile then, and had just started to speak again, when the front door slammed open with a bang, and Miss Gardner strode in.

She flushed red as she spotted Thomas there.

Not the pretty red shade of a maidenly blush. More of an apoplexic color.

"What are you doing here?" she demanded bluntly.

"Claire!" Mrs. Gardner sounded shocked. "I am sorry, Mr. Campbell..."

"Do you know what this man has done, Mother?"

Mrs. Gardner glanced over at Thomas nervously.

Oh, God. This was not going to go well.

Mrs. Gardner rose hurriedly. "If you will excuse me, I believe I will go and see what Gracie is doing upstairs. She has been awfully quiet the last hour."

Thomas barely stopped himself from asking her to stay.

A loving and kind girl, had she said? Miss Gardner did not look that way right now. More like an avenging angel.

She was wearing white again, reminding him of that day in the rain when her gown turned transparent. It was a lovely color on her, making the red tones of her hair even more noticeable. She was truly a beautiful girl. Terrifying at the moment—in fact, he would not have been surprised to see fire shoot from her eyes—but indisputably beautiful.

Once again, he would face the full force of Miss Gardner's wrath.

Then he remembered he was not in the wrong. Miss Gardner had simply received an inaccurate recounting of events.

"Miss Gardner, I will not apologize for informing my brother of your friend's false and improper conduct. Particularly not when he was considering proposing to the girl," he started.

The words came out a little more pompously than he had intended.

Was it just his imagination or had Miss Gardner's face turned even redder?

"Even you must admit—" He paused. That was probably not a good way to begin. "—that my brother deserves a wife whom he may trust to be loyal and chaste."

Redder and redder still.

Miss Gardner took a deep breath and pushed some fallen hair off her brow. "I have just one question for you, Mr. Campbell."

Thomas leaned forward a little before he could stop himself.

"When you saw my friend tumble from the carriage in which Charles Morton had been attempting to violently ravish her, did you stop to consider for one moment going to her assistance or pursuing her assailant, or did you simply get on your horse and gallop as fast as you could back home to share your slanderous words with your brother with absolutely no heed of the fact that you would be shattering two very deserving young persons' greatest chance of happiness with your baseless lies?"

It had all come out in a great rush. Miss Gardner paused to catch her breath.

He frowned.

"What the devil are you talking about?"

She shot him an irritable look but spoke more slowly.

"When you saw Fanny exit the Morton carriage in a state of disarray, Charles Morton had been attempting to... to..." She looked frustrated by her inability to find the word.

"Seduce her?" Thomas supplied.

Miss Gardner looked as if she were about to boil over.

"No, Mr. Campbell," she said through gritted teeth. "I do not mean 'seduce.' Although there may not be a great deal of difference to you, perhaps, between rape and seduction, what Mr. Morton had in mind was most definitely the latter."

Thomas glared at the implication.

"Now, see here," he said hotly. "How was I to know any such thing? Miss Rutledge was, as you say, in a state of disarray— to put it mildly. She saw me and she did not request my aid. Rather, quite the opposite—she fled the scene."

Miss Gardner opened her mouth to interject, but he pressed on.

"And as for Morton—he looked pleased as punch, Miss Gardner. The perfect picture of a man who..." He trailed off.

"Had just been gratified?" She supplied, giving him a look of the utmost disgust. "Yes, I believe I know the look."

Annoyance pricked at him. "I do not know what your friend has told you, Miss Gardner, but need I remind you that she has every reason to maintain a deception if it is in her benefit to do so. I had no way of knowing whether she would ever tell my brother of her conduct. Can you consider his perspective for a moment? Would you wish to find yourself partnered to a spouse who had been disloyal even before you had wed? Of course, now that she has been caught, Miss Rutledge does not want word of this to get out..."

"It sounds so familiar, Mr. Campbell," she interrupted with a sneer. "One would think you had read this book before."

Thomas clenched his jaw. What had he come here for again? Oh, yes, to save this defenseless young woman from ruination. Young vixen more like.

"It takes two to..."

"To what?" she cried, interrupting once more. "To be raped, Mr. Campbell? Are you saying that my friend deserved to be attacked?"

He gritted his teeth. "I am not saying any such thing, Miss Gardner. However, if she was indeed attacked as you claim, she is nevertheless still..."

"Ruined." Her face deflated. "Ruined, even though she fought him tooth and nail."

"Yes." He softened his tone a tad.

"It will not matter to the world whether or not she claims it was unwanted attention or not. To the majority, the truth will not matter an iota. She chose to enter that carriage, I assume, unless you also claim Mr. Morton dragged her inside in broad daylight. And based upon the expression on Morton's face, indelicate or not, he looked quite pleased with himself and headed straight into a tavern full of men, Miss Gardner. Now tell me that you believe he is a man known for his discretion rather than the type to brag about his exploits given half the chance." He exhaled.

"And so, what? You are saying there is no hope, that Miss Rutledge should do what exactly? Let her good name be smeared? Perhaps she should marry her attacker, Mr. Campbell—is that what you would recommend?"

"It is not a completely preposterous suggestion, Miss Gardner, as you must well know. Particularly if things in the carriage went as far as..." He cleared his throat.

Miss Gardner let out an outraged gasp.

"I merely mean," he added hastily, "for Miss Rutledge's protection, it might be for the best if there is any fear of..."

"Oh, yes, for her protection," Miss Gardner said bitterly. "In case of the birth of a natural child. Is that what you were about to say, Mr. Campbell? You would know all about such matters, I expect. How thoughtful of you to consider the best interests of the poor children."

Thomas had been doing his best to keep his temper in check, but now he felt his grip loosening.

"Yes, Miss Gardner, I realize I am not in any position to make such a judgement. But I do know a little of the pain that comes from fathering such a child and knowing they will be at a disadvantage all of their lives because of their parents' mistakes. Furthermore, you must realize there is a vast difference between a gentleman's mistress and a young lady bearing a child out of wedlock. You know as well as I do, that she is ruined regardless of what either of us would like to believe. Her options are severely limited."

"As are your own!" He exclaimed. "Must you really be reminded of that?"

"Your concern for Miss Rutledge is duly noted, Mr. Campbell, but fear not, there will be no child—as you so vulgarly suggest. Not that it is any of your business. And yes, thank you, for reminding me of my own tenuous situation. One which I would never have been in if you and your brother had not moved to our neighbourhood in the first place." She bit her lip so hard he wondered if it would bleed.

"What solution are you here to propose this time, Mr. Campbell? As I have already refused your offer of marriage, I suppose you will next suggest I become your mistress to spare my reputation?" She gave a bitter laugh but looked a little shocked by her own words.

Thomas was reaching his limit. He rose from the seat and walked over to stand before her.

She looked up at him, breathing heavily. He was reminded of their disparity in height. Not so great as it was with Serafina—Miss Gardner was considerably taller; but still only as high as his chin. If he tilted his head down just a little and she raised hers a few inches. Well. It had been the perfect fit.

All at once, he felt a little wicked.

"Would you like that, Miss Gardner?" He said softly, tilting his head down so that his breath warmed her face. He had the pleasure of watching her flinch slightly, but she did not step back. "What is it you think a mistress is for exactly, Miss Gardner? Do you know why a man would have such a woman? Do you have any idea why a woman might enjoy being one?"

He lowered his head just enough that his next words would warm the skin of her neck.

"Would you like me to show you?" he whispered, huskily.

He was close enough to see her shiver.

He had hoped to have that effect upon her.

He had not anticipated the powerful effect being so close to her again would have on him.

Before he could think properly, his hands were gripping her waist and pulling her towards him for a searing kiss.

It was not a gentle kiss. He kissed her roughly, savagely, stroking her hard, parting her lips and thrusting his tongue between them. Weeks of suppressed desire were in that kiss. He suddenly realized how badly he had been wanting her all this time.

Miss Gardner's hands still hung loose by her sides, but she gave a little moan against his mouth, and once stirred, her lips began to respond to his.

She took back the kiss, darting her sweet tongue into his mouth in turn, licking him softly, nibbling his lip. As with the first time, it was all happening with confusing speed. She was so responsive, reciprocating with the same desperate urgency he felt. He did not want it to stop.

The sound of footsteps upstairs, right above their heads.

Their mouths froze in place.

Was her mother about to come back? God, this was unbearable.

"Come with me," he commanded. Grabbing her hand, he pulled her towards the door. He knew this was insanity, but his body was leading the way not his brain, and he had no wish to return the reigns. As he opened the door, she stopped, covered her mouth with her hands. But he saw the spark in her eyes. She wanted this too. He tugged her hand again, gently but persistently.

"I am taking Mr. Campbell to show him the orchard, Mama!" she called quickly up the stairs.

And then they were out the door. He pulled her along, almost dragging her behind him. How far from the house should he go? What he truly wanted was to lay her down in the grass and take her there and then, but he had barely enough presence of mind to know that was too far.

He paused when they reached the outskirts of the treeline at the edge of the yard. Pulling her a few meters into the grove, he drew her up against him. Her body was yielding and pliant in his arms. Her mouth met his again eagerly, opening hungrily.

It was not enough. He wanted more. He was thirsty, desperate, like a man parched in a desert. His hands roamed her body, pulling her closer against his own, letting her feel his desire. She gasped as her body pressed up against him and let out a low moan.

With one hand, he held her waist while with the other he caressed her hip, her side, sliding his hand upwards to cup her breast through her dress. When he found her nipple under the light muslin gown and rubbed it with his thumb, he felt her shudder and tremble as if she might faint. She leaned back slightly to allow him better access.

He covertly eyed the front of her gown. It was tempting to try to remove it or to loosen it in some way. But he would not risk it. There were other ways.

When he pulled his mouth from hers, she sighed and tried to pull his head back down.

"Shhh, lovely," he whispered. "Wait." And then he lowered his mouth to her gown. As he had hoped, the fabric was fairly thin. He flicked his tongue against the muslin, feeling her nipples grow hard. He could not see them, but he knew they were perfect. Small round rosebuds. He popped one into his mouth and ran an expert tongue over the tip. Miss Gardner was making all kinds of noises which he assumed were of pleasure. Her hands were threaded through his hair, holding him in place as if afraid he would stop.

And just think, a voice inside said, it could be like this always. Better even. Much, much better. Thomas groaned at the thought. He suddenly wished they were back in the cottage, with the bed.

The cottage...

The image of Ned Evans' cottage conjured the most unwelcome image of Ned Evans himself. He frantically tried to push it away, but it was too late. He pictured the two men standing in the doorway, looking at Miss Gardner once more in shock and disapproval.

He was doing it all over again. Forcing her to put everything she had on the line for these moments of pleasure, which to him were nothing. Well, not nothing—but certainly nothing he could not come back from.

He reluctantly let the nipple slip from his mouth. Lifting his head, he saw the wet patches he had left on her dress. He could not undo what he had done, but he could stop it before it went further. Past the point of no return.

Disoriented, she mewed, almost sadly. Her hands were still clasping his shoulders.

She had not let go.

She did not want to let go of him, he realized, and was filled with unexpected happiness.

"This is not what I came here for, I..." He felt her stiffen immediately. Was he doomed to start every sentence in such a terrible fashion with her?

He tried to explain. "That is not what I meant. I mean," he bit his lip in frustration. "Miss Gardner, you must listen to me."

He had her attention. She had begun to step back but now froze and looked up at him. Beneath the overhanging branches, her face was in shadow, her expression unfathomable. Was she angry? Confused? Sad? He could not say with certainty.

He was about to say "Marry me" when she covered her mouth with both hands again.

"What have I done?" she whispered. "Fanny..." She shook her head. He saw tears trickling down her cheeks. "I..." She turned and ran back towards the house.

Thomas let out an almost beastly growl. This could not be happening again. He could not lose her a second time.

He started forward, to go after what was his. She was his. How many times must he try to claim her?

But he knew what would happen when he reached the door. It would be barred against him.

As far as Miss Gardner was concerned, it was not Miss Rutledge or even Morton himself who was to blame for her friend's loss of virtue and happiness, but Thomas himself.

A nagging feeling told Thomas her standpoint was not an altogether irrational one.

Could it be that he was in the wrong?

He replayed the events in his mind. Miss Rutledge's hasty flight, the look on Morton's face. Miss Gardner's words came back to him— Miss Rutledge had fought Morton tooth and nail.

He remembered Morton's gesture—hand to his face, he had seemed to wipe something away. Might it have been blood?

But if it had... There was an unpleasant, sinking feeling in Thomas's stomach.

If it had, then he had let Miss Rutledge go off alone after what he could only presume had been the most nightmarish experience of her life. He had let a would-be rapist prance right past him with an expression of sickening satisfaction on his face, without even trying to wipe it off with his fist.

If it had, then he had destroyed his brother's happiness and turned him against the woman he loved. He had caused William to miss the opportunity to comfort and support his future bride—for there was no doubt in Thomas's mind that this was what his brother would have done, would do, if what Miss Gardner said was true.

And he had given Miss Gardner a tangible, rational reason to hate him. To associate his touch with something despicable, rather than something pleasurable.

This was unconscionable. Something must be done.

If Thomas had indeed gotten it all wrong, then Miss Gardner was entirely in the right to feel she was betraying her friendship by being in his company.

Not for the first time, he wondered how differently things might have gone if he had talked to Miss Rutledge when he first saw her. It was too late for such regrets.

He had rushed headlong into this, now it was time to find out if he had done what was just or simply been an impetuous fool once more.

He strode back to the yard and prepared to find Charles Morton.

Chapter 17

Claire was sobbing by the time she reached the house. She quickly stepped in, closing the door behind her, before sliding down against it to the floor with her face in her hands and her knees to her chest.

She heard footsteps coming down the stairs.

"Oh, my dear." Her mother's voice spoke softly. A hand was placed upon her head.

"You did not accept him then?"

Claire smothered a sob, removed her hands from her face, and looked up.

"What do you mean?"

Mrs. Gardner's face was puzzled.

"Mr. Campbell..." She began, looking uncertain. "He came here to try again, Claire. He wished to ask you to marry him."

"For a second time." A small wry smile crossed her mother's face. She caressed Claire's hair softly. "What has happened?"

"He..." She faltered. "He did not ask me."

She had not given him an opportunity. She had barraged him with everything she had. And then... Well, there had been few words once he had touched her.

Lit her aflame more like.

Her eyes were pleading as she met her mother's.

Mrs. Gardner crouched down beside her with a sigh.

"Oh, Claire. If he did not, perhaps it was only because he did not have a chance. You seemed very cross with him when I left."

That was an understatement. But he had deserved it.

"When you left the house—well, I thought it meant you had accepted him. That you were..." Mrs. Gardner cleared her throat delicately. "Celebrating your engagement with a walk."

Claire blushed furiously and crossed her arms. Her mother was correct about that part of things.

"He has ruined Fanny's life!" She blurted out quickly, trying to cover her reaction.

Mrs. Gardner's eyes widened a little.

"Can it be as bad as that? Mr. Campbell does not seem a dreadful sort of man to me, Claire. You yourself have admitted he has good qualities, just recently..."

"I was wrong. He is an ogre. All men are ogres." She buried her head again; the last words were muffled.

"Oh, my darling." She could hear the smile in her mother's voice. "Would an ogre propose marriage to my beautiful but incredibly headstrong, outspoken daughter twice in so many weeks?"

"Or, intend to propose, at least," she amended. "If he did not propose, Claire, I truly believe it was his intention."

When there was no reply, she went on. "Claire, a man like Thomas Campbell is not used to rejection. Nor does he enjoy it. No man does. Imagine what it must have taken for a man like Thomas to come here with the intention of trying again, after you rebuffed him—none too gently either, if I know you?" She raised her eyebrows.

Claire set her lips. "He did not deserve to be rejected gently. He does not wish to marry me. He merely asked because... because he is worried about his dashed brother and my confounded reputation. He does not really care about me at all. All he cares about is my re-rep-reputation." It was humiliating but the tears were coming again. She did not wish to give her mother the wrong idea.

What was the wrong idea? That she cared for Thomas Campbell? But she did not.

She simply enjoyed kissing him. Though she knew it was very, very wrong of her to have done so a second time. And then a third.

And to some extent, she enjoyed arguing with him. It was rather stimulating.

Though she would prefer to argue about less unpleasant topics.

With a sigh, she felt her anger begin to dissipate. It was exhausting being so furious.

Her mother was waiting patiently.

"Tell me what has happened with Fanny," she said.

Claire told her everything.

She left out the worst parts of her argument with Thomas. The unseemly parts, such as when he had suggested Fanny might be increasing.

Her mother looked reflective.

"It is clear to me he acted out of loyalty to his brother, which is admirable. Yet to jump to conclusions so quickly about a person based on one unfortunate encounter..."

"I know," Claire interrupted. "It does not speak well of his character. It is very disappointing." She lifted her chin.

"I was going to say it sounds exactly like something your father would have done." She smiled at Claire in an infuriating way. "Or something which my daughter might have done. Driven by our passions, we sometimes strike out in unintentionally foolish ways. Even when love and loyalty may be at the heart of our deeds."

She touched Claire's cheek. "Did you not similarly misjudge Mr. Campbell the first time you met him? Perhaps also the second? Only to learn there was more to him than you had first thought?"

Claire looked away.

Her mother rose and brushed off her skirts.

"These things have a way of working themselves out, Claire. Miss Rutledge has the support of her father and true friends. Nothing will change that. If Thomas's brother does love Fanny... Well, then in the end, he will not be so easily dissuaded. Or else he is not the man for her after all."

"As for you, Claire, the same goes for you as well. Fanny is a sweet girl but of a timid nature, and now she has been badly shocked. But you are of an altogether different character. What will you do next?"

Claire stared at her mother's back as she walked away.

What did she mean? She wanted to ask but did not want to sound as if she were so empty-headed, she could not put two and two together.

Then it came to her.

Claire pulled herself to her feet. It was late afternoon. The call would have to wait until tomorrow.

She would ask Rosalind to accompany her. When a man prepared to duel, he would bring a second. When Claire met with the Mortons, she would bring a sister.

Heaven help Charles Morton if he tried to cross them both.

Thomas knocked firmly on the Mortons' front door. It was long past the usual time to call and he knew his arrival would be viewed as rudeness. He did not give a toss.

The Mortons' manor was of average size for a middling, gentry family. As minutes passed and Thomas stood waiting, he took in more of his surroundings and saw signs of decay. Nothing that would be obvious at a glance. But the windows were dirty, the paint of the door badly peeling and chipped, and the grounds looked rough and untended compared with Northwood's well-pruned greenery.

A poorly run estate, Thomas noted with displeasure. Much like the Mortons' poorly-run family.

The door opened. An unimpressed-looking, elderly butler stared down his nose at Thomas.

"Is Charles Morton in?"

No introductions. This was not a courtesy call.

The butler's face became pinched. "He is not."

Thomas glared.

"Do you know where he is?"

The sour face became positively tart.

"I do not." He shut the door firmly.

Thomas was irked.

Where would Morton go? If there was to be any large social gathering in Beauford, Thomas would already know about it. It was too late in the day to ride, too late to hunt.

He remembered Morton heading straight to the pub after leaving Miss Rutledge. He turned heel and strode back to the carriage.

The more he thought about it, the more questions Thomas had for Charles Morton. He recalled the Mortons' grotesque insults towards Miss Rutledge at the Northwood dance. Charles had claimed to be repulsed by Miss Rutledge.

So how on earth had he wound up in the throes of passion with her? If, indeed, that was what had happened.

Thomas was beginning to have his doubts.

He pushed open the door of the Bull and Bear. As it was early evening, the place was not yet crowded. A few men sat at tables, drinking. A low hum of talk and laughter filled the air.

Thomas scanned the room impatiently.

There. Charles Morton sat at a table in the back, surrounded by three other young men. Red-faced and gregarious, Morton was gesticulating wildly as his trio of friends laughed uproariously at whatever he was saying.

Thomas walked over and waited.

One by one, the young men fell silent, looking up at him. Charles was the last to notice.

Thomas saw shock on his face, then a shadow passed over it and shock was replaced momentarily by anger, then irritation.

What a callow young dandy. Had Thomas ever been this bad?

"Leave us," Thomas commanded, without sparing a glance at the other men.

"Now see here a minute..." Charles began. But his comrades were already pushing back their chairs.

Thomas sat across the table and eyed his catch. Long scratch marks, now scabbed over, ran up one side of Morton's face. As he noted them, Thomas knew every word Miss Gardner had told him was true.

"How did you get those scratches?"

Morton instinctively touched his face. He glared at Thomas.

"My valet. Cut me while shaving. Man's incompetent."

Thomas folded his arms and looked at Morton in silence. Well-dressed, plain features, tawny hair. He supposed some women might find him attractive. If they could see past his smarmy expression, his weaselly eyes. Thomas was ready to bet only a dull wit lurked behind those eyes. That was something he could make the most of.

"Tell me what occurred with Miss Rutledge," he said bluntly.

Morton set his mouth in a stubborn line.

"No idea what you're talking about. Even if I did, not your concern, is't?"

He folded his arms behind his head and slouched back in his seat with a slight smile.

Thomas leaned forward, his palms flat on the table.

"It is my concern, because my brother has been courting her."

Thomas had the satisfaction of seeing Morton blanch slightly.

"Thus, her virtue is very much my concern. I do not wish for my brother to marry a doxy."

He looked across the table and smiled pleasantly.

"I should think it would also be of concern to you, Morton. For if you do not tell me what occurred, I will pull you across this table and throw you onto the street by your collar."

He leaned back in his chair, steepling his fingers. "Speak up."

Morton was giving him a look of the utmost suspicion.

"Didn't do nothin' to her," Morton said sulkily. "You saw 'er at the dance. All over me. Follows me like a stray dog."

Thomas certainly did not see.

Charles Morton leaned back and put his arms behind his head, gaining steam as he spun his tale.

"Saw me in town, asked for a ride home. Threw herself on my lap when she got in. Tried to stop her—gentleman's honor and all that—but when the little minx wouldn't give up, saw no harm in a bit of sport."

"It was bad luck that you were spotted together." Thomas tried to conjure a look of masculine sympathy.

"T'was, wasn't it?" Morton was eager to accept commiseration.

"'S'pose your brother won't be courting her now?" Morton's eyes lit up mischievously.

Thomas chuckled. "I should think not." He shrugged. "I thought it was an inadvisable match anyhow."

Morton nodded sagely.

Thomas leaned back. "Well, Miss Rutledge has been thoroughly compromised. What do you plan to do next? Will you marry the girl?" He kept his tone neutral.

Morton sat a little straighter.

"Would be the decent thing to do, I s'pose," he said solemnly. "Poor girl. No one else'll want her now. Spoiled goods and so on. Thousand pardons to your brother and all that. If I'd known, never'd allowed Miss Rutledge to—" He coughed delicately. "—have her way with me."

Thomas barely managed to maintain his poker face.

"And what's in it for you, Mr. Morton? Having to marry Miss Rutledge when you could have your pick of any number of prime articles..." Thomas shook his head.

"Could, couldn't I? Can't be a bachelor forever though. Must settle down sometime. Bit under the hatches, you see. May's well a chit with blunt than a pretty one with nothing in her pockets. Practical, see?" He tapped his head. "Practical sorts, we Mortons."

Thomas recalled the poor condition of the Morton estate.

"How much is she worth?" He asked casually.

"Not so much as some, more than others." Morton grinned, glanced around, then leaned towards Thomas conspiratorially.

"Ten thousand pounds up front, old chap. Three thousand a year after." He smirked. "Father isn't in best of health. Might get more when he kicks the bucket."

Thomas felt close to kicking a bucket himself, right out from under Charles Morton.

He tried to grin back. A serving woman was passing by. He flagged her down and asked for ale.

When Morton had downed most of his mug, Thomas decided to push his luck all the way.

"Tell me, Morton—man to man—" He tried to manage what he hoped was a lecherous leer. "—was she a wild one?" He gestured again to the scratches.

Morton eyed Thomas speculatively a moment before breaking into a wide grin.

"You seem a bang-up cove, so why not. Could hardly hold her down, to tell the truth. Scratching and screeching till I thought I'd go deaf. Didn't get far. Not even up the skirt. For such a plain chit, thought she'd be dying to take what she could get."

"No offense to your brother," he added hastily, putting his hands up. "Each their own and all that. Man like him, probably wasn't dangling after her anyways. Not too moon-eyed, eh? All about the blunt for him, too, I s'pose."

"Indeed." Thomas took a swig.

Well, there it was.

He pushed back his chair and stood.

"Get up," he ordered.

Morton's face was a study in confusion.

"What the devil for?"

Thomas smiled sincerely for the first time since he arrived.

"Because I like to look a man in the eye before I plant him a facer," he said, adopting Morton's silly jargon.

Morton looked around the room. People were starting to stare as Thomas stood waiting. He gave a strained smile.

"Must be jesting. Ha ha. Very funny, Campbell. Got me good, I'll say that."

His eyes flitted around as if hoping for rescue.

"I assure you—I am utterly serious. You assaulted the woman my brother loves, and as he is not here now, I shall act in his stead."

Moreover, he mentally added, as soon as this was over, he would return and apologize to William. Then to Miss Rutledge. He would beg her forgiveness. He would get down on his hands and knees and apologize for not doing what he should have done in the first place—going to her immediately.

"Pardon me, let me rephrase—" Thomas had remembered the distinction Miss Gardner rightly pointed out. "—You did not *compromise* Miss Rutledge. You attempted to rape her in the middle of a public street in the refuge of your family's carriage."

He had raised his voice as he spoke and could feel the eyes of others in the pub upon them.

"And you did so in the hopes of compromising her so thoroughly she would be forced into marrying you. So that you could collect her ample dowry. Am I close enough to the mark now?"

Morton looked as if he were about to slither under the table.

"Now—get—up." He drew the words out very slowly, then glanced behind him to see how much space he had for his task. "Unless pistols at dawn are more to your liking?"

Morton paled.

A few burly men who looked like they could be tenant farmers had risen from their seats and now stood a little way off, arms folded over their chests, not interfering but observing with interest.

For the first time, Thomas wondered what kind of reputation Charles Morton had cultivated with women about town who were not of the gentry.

"Will you rise, sir? Or must I drag you up by the collar?"

"Drag him up!" A man's voice called from behind. There was a chorus of male laughter.

Morton's face was swiftly becoming shiny with sweat.

Thomas felt a twinge of something like pity. But he had been more than patient. It was not his fault if Morton were so craven that he could not face the consequences of his choice to prey on a defenseless woman.

He reached down and grabbed the young man by the scruff.

For a moment, he held him up in the air, dangling a few inches off the ground. Letting the room get a good look.

Ruefully he knew it was going to be too easy.

He propped Morton up, giving him ample opportunity to strike the first blow.

When it did not come, Thomas struck.

When his fist returned to its place blood was trickling from Morton's nose.

"That was for Miss Rutledge." Thomas said quietly.

He hit him again.

"That was for my brother."

A few of the men whooped behind him.

"Good one, sir!" Someone called.

He heard a woman's voice shout, "Hit him again! Hit him for Mary Parker!"

"Hit him for my friend, too, sir," another female server called, "Wouldn't even provide for his own babe, the cowardly arse! And him a proper swell!"

Thomas eyed Morton with greater displeasure.

"I was going to say this one was for myself." He eyed him coldly. "But it seems this one should be for them."

The last blow laid Morton out on the well-worn hardwood floor.

As the young man lay there groaning faintly, Thomas brushed himself off and turned to go.

The two serving women standing at the bar were beaming approval. A few of the men grabbed his shoulder or patted him on the back as he passed.

The Mortons were not popular in Beauford.

But it seemed like the Campbells were going to fit right in.

William was in the study when Thomas arrived home. His head was bent low over his desk, looking at an estate account book. Northwood had a competent steward, but the Campbells nevertheless preferred to be more involved in the day-to-day running of their estate.

Thomas stood in the doorway, looking at his brother, and wondering if it was now his turn to be the one receiving a blow rather than dealing it. If so, he was more than ready. He and William had not struck one another since they were boys. But this had been a monumental error and Thomas was ready to accept whatever punishment William thought fit.

More important was the question of whether what Thomas had done could be undone. Did William still care for Miss Rutledge? His brother had so far excelled at hiding his pain and disappointment. Thomas had underestimated how naturally reserved William was in temperament, how much he preferred to keep his own counsel in most matters of the heart.

How firm was the belief Thomas had planted regarding her dishonesty? For Miss Rutledge's sake, he hoped William's heart was as constant as he had taken for granted it would be.

Thomas swallowed hard. He had to try. Or else never be able to look Miss Gardner in the face again, let alone Miss Rutledge.

"William," he said quietly, waiting for his brother to look up.

"What is it, Thomas?" William replied distractedly. "Some of these rents are exorbitant and must really be lowered. A widow like Mrs. Taylor has no way of paying such an amount with five children to care for. I truly wonder at some of the arrangements Darby had in place. But no mind. Not all men look over their books more than once a year, I suppose." He sighed and rubbed his eyes.

Thomas had avoided his brother for days. Now he saw the signs of weariness on his person. William's clothes were wrinkled. His face was stubbled. There were dark shadows under his eyes.

"Yes, do what you think is best." He hesitated.

"I must ask something unrelated to the estate, however. Do you... still think of Miss Rutledge, William?"

William was silent a moment. Then he brushed a hand over his hair and nodded.

"I do," he said simply. He put a hand over his mouth and stared past Thomas. "She was... very dear to me. The feelings have not simply vanished, though part of me wishes they would—for clearly, she never felt the same way."

He sighed and shook his head. "Well. It is of no consequence. Though I do wonder what shall become of her. I cannot imagine a man like Morton being able to make Fanny happy. But there it is..." A forlorn look came over his face. He took a seat near the window and leaned his head on one hand.

"It is of consequence," Thomas said quietly. "I am certain Miss Rutledge returns your feelings most sincerely and always has. She is innocent of all that I claimed, William."

"What are you saying?" William's hands gripped the arms of his chair, his knuckles whitening.

"I am saying that Miss Rutledge was lured into the Mortons' carriage. Once she was inside—" He paused, feeling cowardly about delivering the truth, knowing the pain it was sure to cause, knowing he could not prevent it. He drew a breath. "Once she was inside, she was accosted. By Charles Morton."

William rose from his seat. Thomas stole a glance. His brother was tight-lipped, his jaw clenched, his fists curled.

It was as he expected. He would not fault him for his rage. Not when he was just beginning to absorb how badly Thomas had failed him.

"When I saw her on the street..." Thomas hesitated.

"Go on," William said harshly.

"She had escaped from nearly being raped, William."

William let out an angry hiss. He looked as if he were about to head for the stables, so Thomas quickly went on.

"I spoke with Charles Morton, William. Less than an hour ago. I found him in town. I confronted him, had the story from his own lips. At first, he denied it, but then the truth came out. It was part of a disgusting ploy to compromise Fanny, force her into marriage. A greedy and despicable scheme. Although I do not believe this would have been the first time Morton stooped to something so low."

He met his brother's gaze.

"I am terribly sorry, William," he said softly. "Sorrier than I will ever be able to say. When I saw Miss Rutledge, I should have gone to her without hesitation. I should never have returned home until I had spoken to her myself. When I think of what she must have gone through..."

William looked back at him coldly.

"Where is Morton now?"

Thomas took a deep breath. "I do not know where he is at this moment, but when I last saw him, he was lying on the floor of the Bear and Bull."

"You knocked him out?"

"I did. And took my time about it. Oddly, there were no objections from our onlookers. Quite the contrary. They seemed delighted by the spectacle. Not a popular fellow. Based on the comments some of the women made... well, I doubt Fanny would have been his first victim."

William sank back down in the chair and passed a hand over his face.

"Laying him out was too good for him," he said, almost absently. He looked Thomas in the eye. "Why the devil did she tell me she had done such a thing?"

Thomas sighed. "What did she say, exactly? What were her words?"

"She acknowledged she had been in the carriage with Morton, alone. She did not argue that you had seen her emerge in a dishevelled state. Nor that she had run off rather than face you. And then... I stopped questioning her. The idea of pressing for the details of such a matter seemed utterly vulgar. I could not look at her. I left her there in tears, Thomas. When I think of it, I feel sickened with shame. All she had said was the truth. She had merely not tried to excuse herself, or to explain the circumstances. Perhaps she thought it would be of no use."

William seemed bewildered. "Did she think I would not believe her?" He stared at Thomas. "But then...I had been only too willing to believe you. Perhaps she thought it would be no use."

"To feel as if she would be contradicting my word. That must have been part of it. To feel as if I had already condemned her, and turned you against her." Thomas swallowed. "I behaved like an utter rogue and will tell her so when I beg her forgiveness."

"She must have still been in shock," William continued, as if to himself. "Experiencing something like that... I cannot imagine how frightening it must have been. And then, to see you there..."

"She must have believed she would lose you because of what had transpired, although she was blameless. Regardless of the truth, she knew that was how it would be viewed by others." Had not Thomas said the same to Miss Gardner? How he wished he could undo those harsh words.

"She appraised me too accurately. She knew I would be faithless..." William said slowly.

"The blame is not yours. It rests on my head. You would never have believed such a thing if I had not put the idea there first and stubbornly insisted my version was the truth."

"And yet I was all too ready to believe it. I am disgusted with myself."

"Only because it came from my mouth. If anyone else had said such things, would you ever have listened?" Thomas sighed and leaned against a wall. "We have all acted despicably, when it comes down to it. Perhaps against the whole of the female sex if we are going to be completely honest. Miss Rutledge is a lovely girl, but it is not in her nature to advocate for herself. Indeed, she was likely brought up to believe she would never need to—for what else are a husband and father for?"

"There is truth in what you say." William met his eye levelly. "This is not the first time I have considered how shockingly different the standards of conduct are for women as opposed to men."

"If you are not-so-very-subtly suggesting that I have gotten away with things which would have resulted in any woman being quickly shunned from polite society you will face no opposition here. I fully agree with you. When I think of how Elizabeth will soon enter a society in which a man may maul a woman and yet only the woman pays the price and might even be forced into marriage with such a man—well, it turns my stomach. And Elizabeth will have every advantage of birth on her side. Whereas Isabel..."

Thomas's heart pounded as he thought of a man trying to take advantage of his daughter as Morton had done.

"We are preoccupied by the notion of the innocence of women. As a result, they are kept in ignorance of much of the world's evils, but that can also be their undoing." William's rubbed a hand over his face.

Thomas made a mental note to discuss with Elizabeth how one might disable a man with a few well-placed kicks, should it be required. He would teach Isabel the same some day. Heaven forbid they ever need the information. Heaven help them if they did not have it.

"Will she forgive me?"

William seemed to be talking to himself, but Thomas answered regardless.

"If she is anything like you, she will."

"She is a thousand times better."

Thomas nearly smiled. "There is your answer." He cleared his throat. "I will ride out for Hillcrest now. After I have prostrated myself, rent my clothing, and put ashes on my head, you may follow and hopefully she will be even more inclined to show mercy."

William narrowed his eyes.

"Not a joking matter, no. Too soon. I suppose I am simply nervous," Thomas said with a repentant look.

"Yes, how rarely is the infallible Thomas Campbell ever asked to apologize." William still looked grim. "How many times did you punch him?"

"Morton? Three times. Very hard. Knocked him down, as I said. No one appeared eager to pick him up again either, I must say. He might still be lying on the floor if you'd like to go and see. We can drag him to Fanny and let her have a turn?"

William snorted. "You are incorrigible, Thomas. No. I will go first. I wish to speak with Miss Rutledge alone. But do not think your debt is paid. Not yours or Morton's. We all have much to make up for."

Chapter 18

Gracie had insisted on coming along to the Mortons.

Claire had protested. Rosalind had pointed out that taking her might not be such a bad idea. Perhaps the presence of a child would keep things more civil, or even spur Charles Morton's conscience. One could hope.

Now Gracie's feet dangled from a sofa, her legs kicking back and forth restlessly. She wore her Sunday best, a periwinkle muslin dress that brought out the blue of her eyes. She looked as if she were already regretting her decision to come.

To be fair, even Claire was beginning to find the waiting tedious.

The Mortons' butler, a man Rosalind would later describe as "lemon-faced," had shown them into a gloomy morning room. The furniture was shabby, the surfaces dusty, and with the heavy curtains partially drawn it felt dark and confining. It had been a long time since Claire had last seen the room. Her mother visited the Mortons' from time to time, but Rosalind and Claire usually managed to come up with convenient excuses for not accompanying her.

"What can be taking so long?" Rosalind whispered. "Are they at home or not?"

Claire shrugged. They had mentioned they wished to speak with Mr. Charles Morton when they were escorted in. The butler had merely shown them to the room in silence.

Now that they were there, Claire wondered how easy it would be to wrestle a confession from Charles Morton. What would they do with it when they had one? If she were to approach William on Fanny's behalf, would he listen? Would he ask forgiveness? Or was his heart so changeable that he had already moved on.

She stubbornly refused to think about her own position or anything that had passed with a different Campbell brother the day before. It was Fanny's reputation that was in jeopardy. It was Fanny she was concerned with.

After twenty monotonous minutes, the door creaked open. Harriet Morton walked in, alone, clad in a bright violet silk gown and a white turban decorated with a peacock feather. Rosalind and Claire exchanged glances. Miss Morton was fond of ostentation. They were decidedly underdressed in comparison.

Harriet had a smile plastered on her face, which looked as if it might crack under the strain of maintaining it.

Once greetings and niceties about the weather and one another's attire had been duly exchanged, Rosalind spoke up.

"We were hoping to speak with your brother, Harriet. Is he at home?"

Harriet's smile thinned slightly.

"He is at home. But he is indisposed."

The two sisters glanced at one another. A wasted visit.

"I assume you are here because you have heard of the events last night in the village," Harriet continued, her smile growing even tighter. "I should have known you would come to gloat."

Rosalind frowned. "I assure you, that is not why we are here. We do not even know what you are referring to, Harriet."

Harriet sneered. "Of course, you do not. You have no idea. Even though it was her paramour who beat my brother senseless in front of half the town." She pointed at Claire.

"My paramour?" Claire choked out. "I have no paramour, Miss Morton."

Harriet's irritation changed to smugness.

"That is not what I hear, Miss Gardner."

She leaned forward.

"In fact," she said slyly, reminding Claire of nothing so much as a serpent. "I am surprised to see you are still calling on your neighbours at all. If it were not for the presence of your sisters, I am not sure we would have opened the door."

Claire clasped her hands tightly in her lap.

"And why is that?" Rosalind asked.

Harriet's eyes darted to Rosalind.

"Why Miss Gardner—" Her tone was as sweet as sugar yet dripping with poison. "—surely you must know of your sister's shocking behaviour." She turned back to Claire. "So very shocking that I am surprised you have the nerve to show your face in public after what I have heard about you."

Claire began to feel ill.

"Heard from whom, Miss Morton?" Rosalind said crisply. "Kindly provide the source of your slander before spreading your noxious gossip."

The gleam in Harriet's eye did not bode well. She was convinced she had the upper hand. Claire was terribly afraid she did.

"I suppose you are right, Miss Gardner. It was not very charitable of me to mention it, perhaps. But when it is all anyone in Beauford can talk about..." She gave a dainty shrug.

Claire looked at Rosalind helplessly.

"Stop beating around the bush, Harriet. Either tell us or don't, but make up your mind." Rosalind was losing patience. She adopted the school mistress tone she used when Gracie was not paying attention to her lessons.

Harriet narrowed her eyes.

"I do not appreciate your tone, Miss Gardner," Harriet said slowly. "However, as I know you speak merely out of concern for your sister and seem to be utterly in the dark about all of this, I will overlook your rudeness."

"Now let me see. I believe it was a Mr. Ned Evans—" Claire's heart sank as she heard the name. "—who has been telling anyone who will listen at the Bear and Bull about a strange scene he walked in upon a few weeks ago. A most improper scene. In which your sister was found being fondled and embraced by Mr. Thomas Campbell."

Harriet's eyes were lit with excitement. Much as they had when she had falsely informed Claire of Thomas's two mistresses.

Rosalind took a breath.

"In fact, Miss Morton, I was present at the scene you refer to. I assure you there was nothing—" she paused just for a second. Claire closed her eyes. She did not wish for her sister to lie on her behalf. Besides, it was clearly much too late. "—improper about it."

She glanced at Claire, who kept her eyes lowered, looking at the worn rug beneath her feet, the scratch on the mahogany legs of the sofa, anywhere but at Harriet herself.

Harriet looked surprised a moment. Then a look of understanding passed and her pious smile returned. "Of course, Miss Gardner."

She leaned forward to pat Rosalind's knee condescendingly. "Of course, you wish to do anything you can to protect your sister. Most noble of you."

"Yes, sibling loyalty is such a virtue," Rosalind ground out. "And now perhaps you might enlighten us regarding your own sibling's behaviour. Specifically as to why Mr. Campbell thrashed your brother, Miss Morton. I do not suppose it could have had anything at all to do with his outrageous conduct towards Miss Rutledge in your family's carriage the other day."

"Are you suggesting my brother deserved to be beaten, Miss Gardner?" Harriet exclaimed, outraged.

"That depends—" Rosalind smiled sweetly. "—on whether or not your brother is a would-be rapist, Miss Morton. Since to us, and I daresay most of the village, Miss Rutledge's word is irrefutable compared to that of your weasel of a brother's, I would say the answer to that question is a resounding yes. I hope Thomas Campbell trounced him thoroughly. Are you sure we may not have a peek?"

She rose from her seat and peered around with interest as if she might find the door to Charles' sickroom nearby.

Claire looked at the ceiling. So much for maintaining a veneer of civility.

If Harriet could have felled Rosalind with a single look she would have.

"Miss Rutledge," she hissed, "would be lucky to land my brother. No one else is going to want that pathetic girl. Now take your slattern of a sister and get out of our house."

Rosalind had already turned to go so the full effect of these words were lost, but nevertheless it was a cruel term.

Claire could not even meet Harriet's eye. She would not refute the accusation. If, in the eyes of all of Beauford, she was a fallen woman then it was hardly slander for Miss Morton to say so.

Moreover, considering the events of yesterday, she was doubly guilty of this crime of conduct; though Harriet had no way of knowing that.

Gracie's eyes flashed and she darted across the room before Claire could stop her.

She had been so quiet up until now Claire had forgotten she was there.

"You are a horrid woman, Miss Morton! Were you raised by wolves?"

Rosalind put a hand over her mouth, while Claire stifled an urgent cough. It was something Mrs. Gardner would say playfully to Gracie when she returned home too late in the evening or too covered with grime from playing outside. Apparently, it had stuck in her mind.

Harriet appraised Gracie coolly, clearly not put off. "I am so sorry, my dear, that your sister has ruined her prospects in life. But perhaps becoming Thomas Campbell's courtesan will at least put bread on your table. Heaven knows you and your sister will not be able to find any other men to do it now."

"That's quite enough, Miss Morton," Rosalind cast a look of the utmost loathing. "As the daughter of a wastrel, a gambler, and, from what half the village says, a cheat and a debtor, you do not exactly have much moral high ground on which to stand."

Rosalind tilted her head. "But out-and-out criminality? Ravaging women? That seems low, even for a Morton. I suppose your brother was so desperate for a well-dowered wife that he believed he could get away with such revolting conduct. Do you really think anyone will ever accept him into good company once word gets out of what he has done? No one will want him within an inch of their daughters.

He'd best consider a life on the Continent. Somewhere no one will recognize his worthless name."

Harriet flushed with anger and opened her mouth, but Rosalind pressed on.

"And while your miscreant brother will be lucky if he is not brought up before a magistrate and hung from a gibbet, my sister is engaged to Mr. Thomas Campbell and will soon be a married woman. Do you really suppose anyone will hold it against Thomas Campbell for wishing to steal a kiss or two from his future bride?"

Harriet's curled her lip in rage and disbelief, but Rosalind had turned her back.

"Come girls, let us leave this den of vipers." She swept from the room with a flick of her skirts.

"Den of wolves, Rosalind, not serpents," Gracie chirped as she ran after her.

Claire had accidentally lingered. Now she rose, trying to avoid Harriet's eye.

"Your sister is a bold-faced liar, Claire," Harriet said softly. "Your silence tells me everything I need to know."

Claire did not turn back.

"You must think me a fool if you think I'd believe for a moment that a man like Thomas Campbell would ever marry you when by all accounts he has already had you for free. You have stained yourself beyond reproach, Claire, and I am sorry to say anyone could have seen this coming a long, long time before this."

Claire thought that highly unlikely. If Harriet Morton possessed foresight to have anticipated any of Claire's actions over the past few months, she was a much wiser woman than any of the Gardners had ever given her credit for.

But what more was there to say, really? Claire would not stoop to cowardly excuses or further lies.

She swallowed her pride and left the room.

Rosalind stood outside with Gracie by the carriage. Her arms were wrapped around herself and she was trembling.

"I'm sorry, Claire," she burst out, looking near tears. "I knew it was pointless. But I could not sit there another second and listen to that dreadful woman! Besides—" Rosalind looked her sister in the eye. "— He has offered to marry you, Claire. Now you must accept. Surely, you must see that."

"He has." Claire swallowed hard.

She did not wish to show weakness outside the Mortons' manor. Knowing Harriet, she was peering out a window right now with Charles right beside her.

"Let's go home," she said quietly, and stepped past her sisters into the sanctuary of the carriage.

Chapter 19

A s they drove into the yard of Orchard Hill, Mrs. Gardner was standing waiting for them, hands clasped in front of her.

As they emerged from the carriage, she came over quickly.

"Did you see him?"

"Who?" Rosalind asked, somewhat crossly. The mood in the carriage had not been an uplifting one. Claire had been silent most of the way, while Gracie had fallen asleep on Rosalind, leaving a damp spot on her shoulder.

"Why, Mr. Morton, of course!" Her mother said in surprise. "Was that not your reason for going out in the first place?" She waved a hand and smiled broadly. "But never mind, it is of no consequence. Come inside, come inside."

A true mother hen, she shooed the girls into the house. Gracie trailed behind still yawning.

Claire could not find it in herself to muster enthusiasm for whatever had excited her mother.

Or so she thought, until she entered the house and Fanny Rutledge stood before them, a joyous expression on her sweet face.

She held out her hand wordlessly, and after a moment Claire registered the ring on her finger. A gold band with an amethyst cross.

"Fanny!" Rosalind cried, her energy returning. "Do you mean to say you are betrothed?"

Fanny nodded, her eyes shining. She carefully pulled the ring off her finger and shyly held it out. Rosalind took it carefully, exclaiming over its beauty, as Mrs. Gardner stood near, oohing and awing her appreciation a second time around.

"To the faithful empress of my heart." Rosalind read slowly, turning the ring so as to see the inscription.

"How romantic!" Gracie contributed from the nearby sofa where she had put her head on a cushion.

"The amethyst is a lovely stone, Fanny. He must have known its symbolism when he chose it," Mrs. Gardner said quietly.

As Fanny put the ring back on, Claire's mother clapped her hands together.

"Oh, I am so glad this has all been sorted out. To think what might have been. I could just about strangle that Charles Morton," she declared fiercely. "The Mortons have always been a strange and unneighbourly lot, always believing too strongly in their own superiority. But they have lived in Beauford for generations. I truly wonder if they will remain after this if that scoundrel's actions become widely known. Although they likely cannot afford to go elsewhere. I have heard their father's gambling debts have absolutely ruined them."

Fanny paled slightly.

Noticing, Mrs. Gardner looked abashed and gently put a hand to the girl's cheek. "Pardon me, my dear. I will stop this chatter. I promise I will not speak his name again this evening. We will speak only of your happiness. Now tell us, when is your wedding day?"

Claire still stood in the doorway, observing but outside of the happy circle.

"How did this happen?" She blurted out.

Her mother had just promised not to mention the Mortons again, and yet Claire did not see how she could go another minute without some explanation.

Fanny looked a little surprised. "Oh! Of course, you were not here when I told your mother the story."

She smiled at Claire and began her retelling.

"Mr. Campbell... William... He came to Hillcrest last night."

Last night.

Their disastrous visit to the Mortons had been completely unnecessary.

"My father was at home. It was all very proper," Fanny added, in case they should misunderstand.

Rosalind laughed aloud. "Of course, it was. None of us can imagine the *elder* Mr. Campbell doing anything improper, can we?" She shot a grin at her elder sister.

Claire did not return the look. She was not yet prepared to jest about anything to do with the Campbell brothers.

Although she was beginning to grasp that Thomas had done something she would have considered unthinkable—he had believed her.

More than that, it seemed he had done all that he could to extricate Fanny from the mess he had created with his rash words.

Fanny looked a little perplexed. "Yes, well... Where was I... It was rather late in the evening, but William—" She blushed each time she used his Christian name. "—insisted on being shown in. Papa later said he had debated not telling me, but in the end he did, thankfully. When I went into the room, William was on his knees."

She paused.

"He begged my forgiveness." Her voice was a trifle more than a whisper. "He said he should never have believed I was capable of... what he had implied. He said he would understand if I could never forgive him. But... I could. Perhaps I should have been angry, but I was not. When I saw his face, I simply had to." She looked beseechingly at her audience of women for understanding.

"Of course, you had to, Fanny." Mrs. Gardner said tenderly. "That kind of forgiveness is called love."

A shiver ran through Claire. All at once she was lightheaded. She leaned against the door frame.

Love? Was that what it was? Willingly forgiving another? Accepting them as they were?

While also wanting to kiss them until you were both breathless? Yet still wanting more, always more?

She closed her eyes, as if to shut the door of her mind to such thoughts. But they persisted.

"Did he tell you he loves you?" Rosalind asked eagerly, her face lit with curiosity. That was Rosalind—never afraid to ask a question.

Fanny colored. "He did."

There were stars in her eyes. "He gave me the ring, and said he had been planning on asking me in a completely different way, of course, but if I was sure I could really, truly forgive him, then would I be his wife."

She put a hand to her mouth and giggled. "Papa was standing just across the room watching us. Yet somehow it was the most romantic moment of my life."

"Oh, Fanny." Mrs. Gardner had a hand to her heart.

"When I said yes, he said I was making him the happiest man..."
She choked. "But it is him who is making me the happiest of all. To
think that less than a day ago I had no hope of ever seeing him or
regaining his regard." Her eyes glistened.

Mrs. Gardner drew Fanny into a motherly embrace.

"You have come through the crucible and your love will be forged
the stronger for it," she said softly.

"We are so happy for you, Fanny," Rosalind said with feeling.
"Aren't we, Claire?" She shot a prompting looking at her.

"Oh, yes, Fanny. It is wonderful. I can hardly believe your good
news." Claire gulped.

She could hardly meet Fanny's eye. She felt ashamed, an utter
hypocrite. Fanny was fortunate. Her love was a pure bright light, not
a cheap and tawdry thing to be hidden beneath a basket.

Claire bit her lip. She looked at Rosalind, suddenly worried about
her sister's tendency towards forthrightness, but she had already
turned back to the bride-to-be.

"And what of Mr. Campbell's younger brother?" Rosalind was
saying. "Did he admit the part he played in all of this? It seems to me
that it is he who—second only to he-who-Mother-said-shall-not-be-
named—was at the vanguard of this debacle in the first place."

"Oh, yes, Rosalind, Thomas is very sorry," Fanny assured her.
"William told me that he wished to come that very night, but he had
dissuaded him. And it was Thomas who found...Charles... at the
tavern in town and got the truth from him."

"And knocked him flat in the process," Mrs. Gardner announced.
"Don't leave out the best part, Fanny."

Claire's eyes widened.

"Not that I would have required any such thing," Fanny said swiftly, before allowing a small smile. "But yes, it is rather thrilling. To have someone do what I would wish to do, if I were a man." She thrust her chin out rather ferociously.

"Why, Fanny, I never took you for the bloodthirsty sort," Rosalind teased.

"I hope he blackened both his eyes," Mrs. Gardner said firmly. She glanced over at Gracie who had fallen back to sleep on the couch and was snoring softly. "He deserves far more than that. Should Mr. Rutledge and Fanny have decided to take the matter further—though I know to do so would have been most distressing for you, Fanny—he would be in far worse trouble than he found at Mr. Campbell's hands. He has gotten off lightly as far as I am concerned."

When Harriet had complained about Thomas's vengeance, Claire had not had a real chance to take it in.

Now she imagined Thomas, his fists clenched in righteous indignation, his fine lips curled into a threatening scowl, as he loomed over a cowering Charles Morton... and she felt a surge of pride.

Before she could help it, she touched her fingers to her lips, a warmth running through her as she recalled that handsome face tilted down towards her own, and those strong hands wrapped around her.

Thomas had done the right thing. He had secured her friend's happiness.

Perhaps another man would have been more prideful and would have refused to accept the possibility of being wrong. In which case, they would be gathered here now discussing a tragedy rather than a romance.

And had Thomas not shown her time and again that he was willing to do the right thing, even when difficult?

But instead of offering encouragement or acknowledgement, she had scoffed at him, scorned him. Even laughed in his face.

If her mother were to be believed, she had not even given him a second chance to propose.

She had not allowed herself to dwell on it, but could it be true?

Fanny's situation must have made him think of Claire's own. He must have not only thought of her but worried about her. And then swallowing any pride, he had made himself come to her again.

Only to have her run off like a silly child.

His strength could have been hers for the taking.

His arms, around her forever.

How could she ever expect him to make another offer now?

"What an impressive and redemptive display!" Rosalind was declaring, once again grinning significantly in Claire's direction.

Claire ignored the look. She felt sick with a feeling she feared was regret. Excusing herself to Fanny, and hoping her friend would not interpret her demeanor as envy, she ran up the stairs to her room.

William had been exuding an aura of happiness since announcing his engagement to Miss Rutledge.

And so, when just a few days thereafter he appeared on the terrace where Thomas was sitting smoking and reading and enjoying the fine weather, wearing an expression of frank displeasure it was startling.

Thomas put down his book. "Is everything all right with Miss Rutledge?"

"Fanny is fine," William said shortly. "She is not the one I am concerned for." He remained standing, hovering in a way Thomas did not appreciate.

"Do you have something you wish to tell me, Thomas?"

"Not that I can think of." Thomas kept his eyes downwards, smoking steadily. He had a sinking feeling he knew what was coming.

"Excellent. Then you will have no trouble reassuring me that your conduct with Miss Clare Gardner has, in every way and on all occasions, been absolutely beyond reproach."

Thomas sighed.

"What have you heard?"

William gritted his teeth. "I have heard that one of our tenants has been telling most of the men of Beauford, whilst he is in his cups, that you have seduced one of the daughters of one of the most respected families in this neighbourhood. The neighbourhood into which we moved your daughter in the hopes of providing her with a sense of stability, of community, and most importantly an opportunity to establish her name as she grows—a name which, for obvious reasons, needs to remain as unblemished as possible if she is to have any chance of one day making a match of any respectability whatsoever."

He paused to catch his breath.

"Now," he continued. "I will not dishonor Miss Gardner by repeating the details of the story I heard, but suffice it to say that the tale appears to be growing with every retelling and involves the use of Mr. Evan's bed for something other than rest."

Thomas choked on his cheroot.

"A bed!"

"Indeed. A bed. How could you do such a thing, Thomas? The way Evans tells it, one might think you were both stark naked when he walked in," William exploded. His face was flushed with anger, an emotion normally foreign to him.

"Have you learned nothing? Are you really so reluctant to take on your responsibilities that you return to such rakish habits?"

"While I may have been a moderately proficient seducer of women, in my defense, I was never prone to pursuing innocents. Even when I was what one might call a rake," Thomas said lightly.

William glared.

"But yes, I see your point." Thomas cleared his throat.

"Tell me that Ned Evans is a liar, Thomas, and we will go to him now."

Thomas did not meet his eye.

"In that case, why the devil haven't you done the right thing by Miss Gardner? Does the girl's virtue mean so little to you? Is this how you would wish a man to treat our sister? Or Isabel? Have you learned nothing from our recent experience with Fanny?"

Thomas reddened. "Miss Gardner has not lost her virtue, and I would thank you to stop making mention of any such thing. It was a few foolish kisses. Nothing more. There was certainly no bed involved. Nor, to my great regret, was anyone naked."

He should not have said that. William was not in the mood to appreciate flippancy.

"No one was naked. I did have my shirt off, however," Thomas amended. "We had both been out in the rain for hours. I was soaked to the bone and hung it to dry. Perhaps it was foolish of me, yes."

"Furthermore," he added quickly, seeing William's face. "I will have you know that, unbelievable though it apparently will seem to you— thank you for that vote of confidence in my honor, by the way—I have tried to do the right thing."

William narrowed his eyes suspiciously.

"On more than one occasion, in fact." Well, he would have if he had had the chance. That should count for something.

William continued to look skeptical.

"I have! It is not my fault that Miss Gardner is so... so...pigheaded!"

"It does not seem in your best interests to refer to your future spouse in that manner. But truly? She refused you?" William sank into the iron-wrought chair across from Thomas and stole a puff of his cheroot. "Does she truly not understand the precariousness of her position?"

His eyes narrowed again. "Did you mistreat her?"

"Of course not!" Thomas hissed furiously. "What do you take me for, William? Really!"

"I do not know what to take you for, Thomas. Of late, you have been doing any number of things I would never have anticipated—from seducing one of our neighbours to accusing my fiancé of immorality to starting a public brawl."

Thomas sputtered furiously, but William was rolling on.

"It is impossible for me to believe you conveyed your proposal in such a way that Miss Gardner could accept."

"Yes, all of the fault lies with me and none with Miss Gardner, even though she is stubborn as an ox," Thomas grumbled.

"Regardless, she is to become your wife. You will need to learn to accept her nature or you will both face great unhappiness." William took another puff. "Of greater concern might be the fact that you are equally—what was the flattering word you used a moment ago? Pigheaded. Or are you the ox? A pig and an ox. A comical pairing, I must say."

William looked pleased with his own wit, but seeing his brother's expression swiftly moved on.

"Now, you must return to Orchard Hill. This very day. And this time, you might wish to try a different tactic. Perhaps begging would do the trick."

"I am not going to beg a woman to marry me!" Thomas replied hotly.

"You are and you can, for Isabel's sake and your own. You will swallow your pride, accept the blame for your mistake, and remedy it or so help me—"

"It is not as simple as that." Thomas interrupted. He raked his fingers through his hair. "I... do care for her. But she does not return the sentiment."

"And she has made that quite apparent," he added stiffly.

William did not look sympathetic in the slightest.

"The time is passed for sentiment, Thomas. Perhaps you and Miss Gardner believed that you could go on with your lives and pretend nothing had happened—"

"That was exactly what Miss Gardner had hoped. I spoke with Ned and she spoke to the others..."

"There were others?" William exclaimed. "Did a crowd gather to watch you both? Next you will tell me you sold tickets!"

Thomas rolled his eyes. "I cannot force the girl to marry me, William."

"No, but you can try. Try harder. Ask her again. Speak with her mother. Perhaps they do not understand how far this has spread. If you do not succeed, I will speak with them both."

"You will not! I have allowed you to play the parent with Isabel, to make decisions in that regard. God knows you are better at it than I am. But you are not *my* father and I would thank you to remember that. This is my life and it is my decision."

"You said you cared for her." William looked him in the eye.

"Did I?" Thomas said petulantly, looking away. "I believe the cheroot is affecting my faculties. Nasty habit, smoking." He stubbed it out.

When he lifted his head again, William was still staring.

"It's no use, Thomas." He smirked. "I know you too well."

Thomas looked away. "I will make yet another attempt. To smooth things over at least. But it will be by letter. Too much seems to go wrong when Miss Gardner and I meet." Though also very right, but he did not think William would agree were he to elaborate on how exactly.

William donned a serious expression. "Would you like me to bring you a book of verse?"

Thomas narrowed his eyes.

"Sonnets? Byron, perhaps? Shelley? Shakespeare? I can go on. Stop me when you hear one you like. Marlowe? Dear Miss Gardner, yours is the face that launched a thousand ships, or so I humbly..."

At this point Thomas stalked off the terrace and the rest of his brother's words, as well as his maddening laughter, faded away.

If he were to quote anyone, it would be John Donne.

If ever any beauty I did see,

Which I desired, and got, 'twas but a dream of thee.

But Thomas was not sure Miss Gardner—Claire—if he could not use her name inside his head, how on earth would he ever become accustomed to saying it to her face-to-face?

He was not sure Claire would appreciate verse.

Though there were some which could be considered apt.

Licence my roving hands, and let them go,

Before, behind, between, above, below.

Apt... but rather bawdy.

With all that had happened with Fanny, he wished to strike the right tone. And that would not be it.

He groaned and crumpled up another page, tossing it over his shoulder. The room was becoming littered with scraps.

He bit his quill and leaned forward in his chair.

Dear Miss Gardner,

Your first impulse upon seeing this missive may be to crumple it into a ball and throw it away. I understand, for I have already done so— several times. But, please, I beg you—stay your hand. I do not write to vex you, but in the hope of beseeching your forgiveness.

You were right. I was wrong.

He chewed his lip. That seemed short, not to mention insufficient.

I know that the way I treated your friend was unforgiveable and so this may be too much to hope for. I have thought, more than once since then, of how I would wish for someone to act were they to see my daughter in a similar situation. Truly, I cannot even imagine the sorrow and rage I would feel were a man to so hastily assume her disloyal and dishonorable as I did with Miss Rutledge. Let alone comprehend the sorrow and rage a woman might feel being so unjustly accused after narrowly escaping such horror.

I acted unpardonably. Without feeling, thought, or consideration for your friend.

I have said these same words to Miss Rutledge—I wish for you to know this. I have said them to William—though he and I do realize he was not the one most injured by my fault.

I have left you for the last.

I am sure you have by now been informed that my brother and Miss Rutledge are to be wed. I take no credit for this reconciliation—it is solely the work of Miss Rutledge's generous nature and the love she bears William. And he, for her.

Strange is it not, that love can overcome such great mistakes?

I am exceedingly grateful that it has worked such a miracle. Your friend's happiness means a great deal to you, I know. You care for those around you with a strength and a depth of feeling that is most admirable. I feel the same of William—I could not have lived with myself knowing I had destroyed his chance at happiness. I believe Miss Rutledge represents such happiness for him as he does for her.

Not only was he rambling now, but the mention of love made Thomas pale a little. He was drifting into uncharted waters. Territory into which Miss Gardner might not appreciate being tugged, were he to go further.

With a sigh, he rested the quill once more. Despite what William may have demanded, he found he could not ask her the question—

not in this way, not yet, perhaps not ever again. He shrank within himself a little at the memory of her previous rejections, the way she had taken flight as guilt overcame her. He already knew what answer she would make and so why put himself through that again? Why put her through it? There was simply too much to make up for to hope her answer might have changed.

I know I have not brought you similar happiness. You mentioned, if I might paraphrase, wishing you had never set eyes on me. I have thrown your life into upheaval, thrown the lives of some of those you hold most dear into chaos. In every case, I ask myself what lies at the foundation of these mistakes and the answer is my own foolish pride.

What else can I say but that I am truly sorry I have cost you so much and given you so little in return. It is clear to me now why you have been so hesitant to throw your lot in with such a rogue and I cannot fault you for your prudency.

I do ask, however, that if there is anything I may do, any way in which you might permit me to render assistance, then at any time please believe you may count upon me steadfastly.

I know I have no reason to inspire your trust or your confidence, but nevertheless, know I remain,

Your humble servant, in every way,

Faithfully,

Thomas Campbell

Claire had nearly burned Thomas's dispatch. But it was not for the reason he might have imagined.

She had been standing near the hearth with the fire lit on a cool September day. As she read, her hands began to tremble so intensely that the letter almost fell from them.

Never in a hundred years would she have expected to receive such a missive from Thomas Campbell. At least, not until very recently.

It was written modestly, respectfully, and most of all, unpretentiously. He made no boasts of having singlehandedly restored Fanny's honor with his feat of strength. He made no mention of his dealings with Charles Morton at all. One might think he had put forth little effort into righting his wrong, rather than a great deal.

At least, it meant a great deal to Fanny.

And to herself as well.

She bit her lip. How should she reply?

He had mentioned his foolish pride—but made no mention of her own. She was ready to admit she had been equally a fool.

And now?

Her heart beat faster at the thought of this man begging her forgiveness and offering himself as her humble servant.

Her heart beat faster at the thought of this man—full stop.

Be honest, Claire. At least with yourself.

She crossed the room to the writing desk that stood near a back window and opened the drawer. Taking out the required materials, still standing, she leaned over the desk and quickly began to write.

Chapter 20

Thomas put down the letter and looked out over the parklands. It was a fine autumn day. Yet he stared unseeing.

A face clouded his mind, and it blocked out all other images.

If ever any beauty I did see,

Which I desired, and got, 'twas but a dream of thee.

The sound of a human voice broke through his daydream.

"Excuse me, sir."

A footman stood a few feet away.

"There is a visitor to see you. She is waiting in the hall."

Claire's back was to him when he entered. She was gazing up at one of the large oil paintings in the foyer. She had turned her head slightly for a better view, allowing him a better glimpse of her face in profile.

Thomas could hardly remember what his opinion of her had been the first time they met.

All he knew was that now, to him, she was lovely.

She was wearing a deep green dress with short sleeves that showed the soft bare skin of her arms. Her long hair was loosely plaited into a chignon at the back of her neck. A few strands curled around her ears, lending simple yet beautiful adornment to her face. She was not the kind of woman to care overly for adornments or ostentation. He knew that about her intrinsically.

She cared for books. She loved her family dearly. Country walks. Her village. Her neighbours. A stirring debate. He knew these things unasked. He knew more about her than she probably realized.

She was fiercely loyal. Honest to a fault. Painfully so. She had courage—recklessly at times, but what else could you call it when a woman insisted on standing by her convictions rather than taking the easy way out?

Her lips were slightly parted, head tilted upwards as she tried to read the inscription on the frame.

Her hands were clasped behind her. She stood straight and tall.

Thomas remembered the feel of her willowy body in his arms. Slender yet supple.

He would not think about the noises she had made when his lips were on her...

A coughing sound startled him and he looked around to see a maid carrying linens mounting the stairs to the next floor, a hand to her mouth.

The silence of the hall had been broken. When he turned back, Miss Gardner was looking at him with wide eyes.

As he met her gaze, she quickly dropped her eyes to the floor.

Claire stared up at the painting of Juno discovering Jupiter with Io. Poor Io was about to be turned into a cow.

Cows did not have to worry about their reputations, and so Claire rather envied her at the moment.

Oh, why had she come. Was it too late to leave?

A noise caught her ear and she turned to see Thomas standing a few meters away.

How long had he been there? Was he watching her?

She looked at the floor. She had never noticed the exquisite marbling before. The swirls of grey and black were quite mesmerizing.

"Miss Gardner?" His voice was deeper than she had remembered.

Her head shot up. She forced a smile.

"Good day, Mr. Campbell..." she began. Thomas raised a hand.

"Please." He was staring at her in a way she found disconcerting.

He softened his tone. "I think we may dispense with the formalities. May we not?" When she did not reply, he went on.

"I am Thomas. You—" A pause. "—are Claire. Please, continue, Claire."

She stared.

She had kissed this man. More than once. His lips had been on her breasts.

And yet it was the first time she had ever heard him say her name.

She liked the way he said it.

"Claire," he said again. This time expectantly. He stepped closer towards her.

"Please..." She faltered. Breathed deep. "It is a lovely day outside. May we walk?" She gestured to the door.

Once outside, they strolled in silence for some time. The day was warm but not overpoweringly so. There was a cooling breeze rippling through the trees and over the little lake that lay just below the rolling hill on which Northwood stood. As they crossed over a footbridge leading over a stream which flowed into the lake, Claire wished she could tell what was passing through Thomas's mind. He had spoken to her gently. He had seemed, if not pleased, then certainly not unpleased to see her.

Thomas was by no means a dandy, but he cut a fine figure with his height and broad muscular shoulders, paired with well-tailored clothes. He wore a blue cotton tailcoat, a lighter material on the warm day. Silver buttons drew the eye to his chest. His white linen shirt was topped by a cravat, but he had tugged it loose a little, exposing a triangle of bare skin that Claire found captivating. It would be the work of a moment to reach out a finger and touch him there, run a finger down, beneath the cravat...

He was too composed for her to discern his true feelings. She remembered a time when she had disdained his confidence as arrogance. Now she was merely envious of his composure. Perhaps their situation no longer perturbed him.

But it was all she could think about. It was the reason she had come.

She put a hand on the rail of the bridge and paused to look out over the water. Thomas had walked a few steps ahead but now returned and rested his arm companionably alongside hers.

It was quiet and calm. There had not been much of that between them. It was rather pleasant.

Their arms were only an inch or more apart, and Claire's awareness of this made her realize he had not yet touched her. She almost wished he had. It might have made this easier.

She sighed and sensed him glance at her.

It was now or never.

"Mr. Campbell..."

"Miss Gardner..."

They both spoke at the same time.

"I thought you wished for us to use our Christian names," Claire said accusingly. But there was laughter in her voice.

Thomas's lips twitched. "I did, didn't I? My apologies...Claire."

She was not sure why, but she felt her face coloring, and kept her eyes on the shining surface of the water.

Thomas shifted his body to look at her.

"Shall we begin again?"

"Yes, please," she said quickly. "Thomas, I..." But at the same time, he spoke again.

"I would like to apologize for..."

They stopped.

"What do you wish to apologize for? Have you not already done that quite adequately?" She arched a brow, finally turning to face him.

He looked at her intently.

The gaze was so intense it was all she could do not to look away. It was also all she could do to keep herself from touching him, so she gripped the rail tightly.

"I mean, the letter," she said, lamely. "It was..."

"Acceptable? Tolerable? Not altogether displeasing?"

She quirked her mouth and he looked sheepish.

"I am glad it did not displease you. Nevertheless, I should like to apologize to you face to face. For disbelieving you. For being so quick to rush to judgement. For jeopardizing your friend's happiness. For being all of the things you so aptly accused me of the last time we spoke." He smiled a little.

"And also—" His voice turned serious. "—for the way I presumptuously..." Now it was his turn to stare at the water.

"Yes, well," she said softly. "I was not precisely an unwilling participant, was I? Nor am I entirely blameless. I have not been as fair to you as I should have. And while you were very wrong about Fanny —" She looked at him, standing there, waiting for her approval and forgiveness. It was rather empowering. "—All is well that ends well, I suppose. I do understand, too, that you were motivated by loyalty to William and not any vindictiveness."

She glanced away. "I hope you are not too sorry. For... the kiss." And the other things.

She cleared her throat, let go of the rail, and stood up straighter.

"Because I have come here today to ask you to marry me."

His lips twitched.

"It is not funny," she cried. It was, of course, but she did not wish to be laughed at. Particularly when he had not answered.

"You must admit, it is a little funny. To an outside party, we must be exceedingly comical."

"Yes, well, it is the worry of an outside party that is the reason we are here in the first place," she muttered, looking down at her feet.

A finger was placed gently under her chin, lifting her head up.

"Pray, continue." His dark eyes were serious, his lips playful. It was an irresistible combination. "It is the first time I have been proposed to and I must admit I find the experience intriguing."

Her eyes flashed. "I have already asked. It is now your turn to answer."

His amused expression deepened.

"Oh, no. You have not asked. You merely announced your intention to ask. There is a large difference between stating the purpose of your visit and posing the question. Wouldn't you say?"

"Perhaps you would also like me to provide you with a ring, like William gave Fanny?" She glared.

"It would be nice, but is not necessary." He pressed his lips together as if trying not to laugh.

She sighed. "Very well. I suppose I may at least try to do a better job of it than you did."

"I resent that," he protested. "But... touché. It was not the most eloquent of proposals, I suppose. I look forward to you improving upon my methods."

Claire gritted her teeth. This infernal man. Was she truly about to request that he join himself to her for all eternity?

She suddenly knew what to do next.

She looked up at him, raised her arms, and clasped her hands behind his neck, pulling him down towards her.

His lips parted instinctively and met her own, warm and sweet.

She put everything she had into the kiss. She had no ring, but she had this much. Her passion. Her warmth. Her eagerness to touch him, to be near him. That she could convey.

She hoped it would do, and perhaps render him speechless for once in his life.

Then her thoughts trailed off as she gave herself up to the sensation of simply being close to Thomas once again.

She gently nibbled his bottom lip, then brushed her lips against his. Stroking herself against him, ever so softly, then with a firmer pressure, parting his lips with her tongue, tasting and touching him. Intimate, and yet not enough. Still not enough.

She pressed her body up against his, as she had begun to do that fateful day in the cottage. Today there was no damp and musty cottage—only the fresh summer air, the sun on their skin, and the sound of the wind in the trees. The setting was made for this, lending nature's approval to what suddenly felt to her like a most natural act.

Her breasts pressed against his chest. The light muslin dress she wore felt like unwanted armor. She imagined what it might be like to shuck all such armor off, to lay in the grass beside him, her long-legged body stretched along his, skin against skin. She pressed closer, letting him feel her through her dress, through her thin chemise, pushing herself against his groin, barely resisting the urge to run her hands along him. She kept them firmly behind his neck, letting herself tug and toy with the hair on his nape, receiving satisfaction from his sounds of pleasure as she did so.

He smelled incredible. Of the outdoors, summer grass, smoky cheroot, and an underlying scent that was purely Thomas. Foreign but familiar. It was their third kiss after all. She rather liked that she could recognize his scent.

Thomas's hands were running eagerly over her. At first he had gently cupped her face, but quickly he shifted, sliding his hands down her shoulders, down to her hips, clutching her waist and pulling her even tighter towards him to the point where she was nearly breathless. Nearly but enjoyably. When his hands began to cup her lower, kneading and grasping in a startlingly pleasurable way, a small, more rational part of her brain said that perhaps it was time the proposal moved to the next stage.

When she managed to pull herself away from him, it was he who gave a deep groan of reluctance this time. But he released her, taking one step back.

She put a hand to her hair, patting it back in place. Thomas's fingers were on his lips, which looked flushed and full—much like her own must appear, she assumed.

"I have never been a mistress..." Where in God's name had that come from?

Thomas's eyebrows shot right up.

She ground her teeth. "But I believe, in time, I may be able to learn the..." She swished one hand in the air, frustratingly lost for words.

"Art of pleasing men?" He offered. "Yes, you seem an apt pupil."

"Thank you." She narrowed her eyes. How had he gained the upper hand again so quickly.

"Be that as it may..."

He interrupted.

"Not that..." He cleared his throat. "There is more to marriage than that, you know."

Her eyes widened. Was there? Had she missed something?

He looked amused at her expression.

"Perhaps we may even enjoy one another's company in time," he said gently. "This marriage may not be our first choice—" Claire felt oddly hurt as she heard the words, which was ridiculous. Of course he had not chosen her.

"—but we do not have to make one another miserable. This may be hard for you to believe but... I respect you, Claire. I enjoy our..."

"Witty repartee?" She supplied, sticking out her chin. "Yes, I suppose are adequate in that area as well."

"Indeed." He smiled.

She scrutinized him a moment, then lifted her chin.

"If you are quite finished?"

He nodded slowly.

"Will you marry me?"

He looked at her with an odd mixture of amusement, fascination, and something else she could not put her finger on. Perhaps he was merely impressed. She was certainly doing a better job of this than he had.

He inclined his head. "I would be honored."

He stepped towards her and automatically she stepped back. Her body hit the rail.

He looked down. Then gently rested his forehead upon her own.

"And may I suggest, Claire—"

His breath was warm on her face. She closed her eyes. She never expected to be thinking this, but it was rather a romantic moment. Almost worthy of Mrs. Radcliffe. She would have to get Thomas to read her someday. Perhaps he would pick up some pointers.

He was saying something.

"—that the bans be read with all haste and a license be acquired as quickly as humanly possible." He lowered his mouth to her ear. "For I am not sure how much longer I can wait to have my wife in my bed."

And then his lips met hers again and all doubts were thrust aside, and she was melting.

Chapter 21

"How did it go?" Rosalind eyed her curiously. Claire touched her lips. They felt a little chapped, fuller than usual, even warmer perhaps. Could Rosalind tell from looking at her?

No, her sister was brash and bold, but as lacking in romantic experience as Claire had been up until a few short months ago.

"It went very well," she said, a little too prissily apparently, for Rosalind raised her eyebrows and gave her a sly smile.

"How well?"

"He has accepted my proposal."

"Oh ho!" Rosalind crowed. "Did you ever think a day would come when you would be proposing to a man? Never mind a man by the name of Thomas Campbell?"

"He was not the rake I thought he was," Claire reflected.

"Nor that I was led to believe he was," she added, thinking of Harriet and Charles and her foolishness in ever believing anything that came from their mouths. She would never stop feeling ashamed of that gross error in judgement.

"He is very handsome." Rosalind sighed and flung herself back on Claire's bed, her arms outstretched. "I would like one somewhat similar. Perhaps fair rather than dark." She patted her own honey-colored head.

"Then we would make a fine pair of couples." She smiled sweetly at Claire.

"Yes, well, I hope you go about finding yours differently than I did mine," Claire grumbled.

"I am not ready to find him yet. There must be adventures first. Travel. Expansion of the mind." Rosalind looked dreamy.

"I am not sure just how much money you think Mother will be saving by not giving me a season after all, but I am not sure it will be quite enough to carry you around the globe."

"Well, I will start in London then, and go from there. London must have more opportunity for adventure than sleepy little Beauford, you must grant me that."

"You have just returned for London. And did Gwendolen's experiences teach you nothing concerning the very fickle nature of adventure?"

"Yes, but that was a very brief trip, merely to encourage her through her confinement. There was no opportunity for true adventure. But point taken. I shall strive to avoid that kind. Although if Gwendolen had been able to avoid that kind, then I am sure she would have. It is not that simple, is it?" Rosalind looked thoughtful.

She sat up. "The wedding is only next week. What will you wear?"

Claire looked towards her wardrobe. She fingered a sunshine-yellow dress she had only worn a handful of times.

"Thomas could surely buy you a new one. If Harriet lied about his mistresses, then she is sure to have lied about everything else. He cannot be as penniless as she claimed."

"He is not. He lives with his brother by choice not necessity, and has not squandered a fortune away as Harriet claimed. But I do not wish him to purchase one for me. I want to come wearing something that is already mine."

Rosalind looked as if she understood.

"In that case, the buttercup is an excellent choice. You look beautiful in that shade and it is light and fresh-looking."

Claire smiled and smoothed out the skirt of the dress, checking that no mending would be needed ahead of time.

"The scalloping along the neckline and back are also pretty. Particularly in the front, where they draw the eye downwards." Rosalind coughed significantly, a glint in her eye.

Claire grabbed a pillow to hit her with.

"I would thank you not to think of or mention my bosom or my wedding night if you please."

Rosalind sobered. "What about his daughter?"

"Isabel? We discussed her as well."

"And?"

"They care for her very much. His sister has only met her a few times, but Thomas says Elizabeth is very sweet and accepting of Isabel in their lives. Perhaps it is unconventional but..." She glanced at Rosalind. "I wish for her to live with us. Northwood is large enough for us all to start. Or perhaps Thomas and I shall move into Stoneybrook."

"At least, until you have ten children and need a larger residence. Maybe the Mortons will move out." Rosalind cackled.

Claire shuddered. "No, thank you. I would not wish to live in the Mortons' manor. Or even to step foot in it again, preferably."

Rosalind flipped onto her stomach, her chin resting in her hands.

"What is it like to be in love?"

Claire gaped. "I am not in love!"

"Whatever is the matter? Are you embarrassed?" Rosalind looked surprised.

"No... It is just that..." Claire thought a moment, before raising her eyes almost shyly. "I am not sure what this is. We have not really exchanged many words on the matter."

"Because you were too busy embracing one another passionately? I shall pen a note to Harriet immediately informing her of how correct she was after all, shall I?" Rosalind chortled wickedly and this time, Claire did not hold back as she jumped onto the bed to pummel her with the pillow.

Later, alone in her room, she blushed a deeper shade of red as she turned the word over in her mind.

Love.

Did she love him? Was the roiling of her stomach and the quickening of her heart simply nervousness over the imminent loss of her freedom, her singlehood, herself?

Or were they the symptoms of a much different condition?

One in which she was certain to lose not only herself but her heart, perhaps most painfully.

William and Fanny wandered slowly out of the dining room, hand in hand, looking fondly at one another.

Thomas lingered a few steps behind, not wishing to intrude on a newlywed moment.

It had been an excellent dinner. Miss Rutledge was a comfortable addition, fitting in quickly. She added rather than detracted from their interactions. Although mild-mannered and timid at first, she was wittier than Thomas had realized, and quite well-read. Like Miss Gardner, she liked novels, but was also fond of European history. They had enjoyed a lively debate over Elizabeth I and whether or not she had been the most successful English monarch.

William preferred Henry V, while Thomas had taken Fanny's side. After all, Elizabeth had cultivated a court in which Shakespeare and Marlowe thrived, the British Empire expanded, and incredible exploratory voyages were made. Fanny pointed out that Elizabeth had claimed to have the "heart and stomach of a man," but not a man's brains. And thus, clearly women's minds were more than adequate, perhaps more so, and they were more than intelligent enough to be excellent rulers.

If Thomas could get used to calling Fanny by her Christian name, he supposed he would soon grow comfortable doing the same with Miss Gardner.

Claire.

The word rolled off his tongue in a pleasing way.

He still could hardly grasp that tomorrow was his wedding day.

Nor could he reconcile himself to being so reconciled to it.

Nay, to looking forward to it even. Though some aspects more than others.

Strange that he would never have predicted this path for himself, but now that he was on it, he was peculiarly content.

After Serafina's machinations and cruelty, he had thought himself incapable—no, not incapable, *unwilling*, to care for another woman.

But he did care for Miss Gardner. More than care.

The trio came into the drawing room and made themselves comfortable. The last of the evening light was streaming through the open windows. A lovely summer night in every way.

Fanny had already adopted a favorite spot in a winged-back chair near the fire, where a small dark oak table was conveniently placed, lending itself well to an ever-growing stack of books. She had one in her hand already, while William stood, one hand affectionately on his wife's shoulder.

William stifled a yawn and looked at his brother.

"I believe I shall retire soon. I do not wish to be yawning through your nuptials tomorrow morning."

He grinned at Thomas. "I would much rather memorize the occasion as it is one I certainly never expected to see."

"Will Isabel be there?" Fanny asked, a little absently, as she turned a page.

"Yes, Miss Gardner insisted upon it."

Fanny looked up at Thomas with a smile. "That is very like her. I think she and Isabel will go on very well together."

Thomas was inclined to agree. His daughter would have, if not a true mother, then certainly a woman to teach her and care for her as she grew. To offer what he and William could not, as men. As Mrs. Gardner had said, a girl needs a mother. And Isabel had been so sorely lacking.

The thought of her father marrying the sister of her new and closest friend had brought an exuberant reaction. As had the news Claire had gently conveyed regarding their sharing of a residence soon.

Mrs. Mowbray would remain in their employ, of course. Isabel was fond of her and the governess was a kind, steady soul who was genuinely attached to her charge. She may not have been a fine lady, but what she lacked in teaching the arts of feminine refinement, she more than made up for in affection.

Tomorrow, they would converge on the church at the early hour of nine. After the ceremony, attended only by family, he and Claire planned to spend their afternoon with Isabel, picnicking and exploring the grounds at Northwood. They would spend their first few nights there, with Isabel returning to Stoneybrook, before he and his new bride would journey to London. Thomas would meet Claire's elder sister; Claire would meet Elizabeth. A true blending of families.

His bride. She was his, or almost his, wasn't she? To care for in sickness and health—obligations which he planned to take as seriously as William did his to Fanny.

But also, to hold and to treasure. To possess.

A little shiver escaped him. He decided William was correct. Well-rested was the way to be.

"I think you have the right of it, William. Good night to you both."

Adieus being said, he started upstairs, thinking about the last night he would be truly alone.

Chapter 22

*J*ealousy is most inexcusable in a woman.

 There is nothing which more exposes her to ridicule. It is the fatal source of innumerable indiscretions, an inlet to every possible evil, and the sure destruction of the peace of families. Recall, Dear Reader, that the libertine is given up to unalterable evil and guard your heart against their wiles.

The Beauford Chronicle, September 1818

It was done. Claire was a married woman.

The wedding had been surprisingly pleasant.

She was not sure what she had been expecting—Harriet Morton to pop up from a pew screeching reasons why they should not be wed, perhaps. Or Charles Morton with a pistol seeking his revenge.

But the Mortons must be getting on with their own lives, as she and Fanny were with theirs.

Once news of the engagements began to circulate, quickly followed by Fanny and William's marriage, the Mortons must have cut their losses and moved on.

She had not seen them around the village since that last unpleasant visit.

And so, the wedding morning had not been marred in the slightest by the bride and groom's hasty joining nor the events which led to it, as a small part of Claire had been concerned it might.

All in attendance seemed convinced of the suitability of the couple for one another. Their enthusiasm was a kind of bulwark for Claire.

Now it was over.

She looked ahead to where her husband and step-daughter walked hand-in-hand across the rolling green lawn.

It had been a charmed afternoon. The sun smiled as they ate chicken salad and jam puffs on blankets spread on the grass, then followed Isabel all over the grounds.

She led them about to show off her favorite spots. A place below the footbridge with rocks the perfect size for a girl to balance on. The hollow of an oak tree so large Isabel could curl up inside. A little patch of honeysuckle to nibble when one wished for a small, sweet snack. A grove of willow trees with a fairy circle in the center.

Isabel was more at home at Northwood than Claire had expected. She visited so frequently the grounds were familiar and dear to her (although she had very seriously explained to Claire that Stoneybrook would always be her first love).

Now as they strolled leisurely back towards the house, the sun had passed behind a cloud and dark spots further off suggested rain would soon arrive.

But Claire's mind was not on the weather. Nor on the morning, nor the afternoon, nor even on the supper they would share as a newly enlarged family. No, her attention was almost fully consumed by the night that was to come.

When she had stood with Thomas on the bridge, the prospect of their marriage and wedding night had felt like the natural next steps. They had been close then, comfortable.

But now... Although the day had been enjoyable and Isabel's presence lent greater ease to their interactions, Claire felt much more uncertain. They had hardly touched. A hand to lift her into a carriage, a brush of fingers when opening the picnic basket. Nothing which might be called intimate.

Even their glances had been short. Sometimes Claire wondered if she was the only one stealing looks at all, so infrequently did she seem to catch Thomas's eye.

But his daughter was there—it was not the proper time; so she had told herself all afternoon.

Yet now that they walked towards the house, the small cloud of doubt continued to threaten. And a voice whispered she was as green as grass and knew nothing of what to expect or what to do and this had all been a mistake, a horrible mistake, and what were they really, but strangers to one another, knowing little about each other at all, and certainly not enough to be comfortable sharing a bed.

Let alone a lifetime.

But with determination she pushed those thoughts away, and lifting up her trailing yellow skirt with one hand—the same light dress she had worn that morning; sentimental, but she had not wished to change it though she would do so now before dinner—picked up her step to catch up with the man and the girl who walked a few paces ahead and who were now her family.

This man was hers. To hold and to keep. And he was certainly a fine specimen of manhood, she thought, as she once more appreciated his strong and sturdy body, his long legs, his dark tumbling hair. He was handsome. Intimidatingly so at times.

Thomas was lifting Isabel up with his hands and spinning her in a circle, not too quickly, but fast enough that she was shrieking with glee. As he saw Claire approaching their eyes met and he smiled—a wide, reassuring smile that said all was well and he was glad she was there. A smile so splendid that her breath caught in her throat, and she had the sudden feeling that a fire had been kindled somewhere deep inside.

Warmed through and through by his expression, she smiled back and walking past the pair, looked ahead to the house.

That was when she glimpsed the fine carriage that stood in front.

It was not one of the Campbells. The horses were not theirs, for one. And for another, it was a daintier vehicle than any of theirs. It spoke of elegance and taste. It spoke of London.

Claire wondered who it could be, and turned back to see if Thomas was expecting anyone—his sister perhaps? Although they had planned to go to her.

But as she saw his face, there was no need to pose the question.

His smile was gone and it had been replaced by something entirely different. She still did not know him well enough to pinpoint it. But it was a strong emotion, that much was clear, and she felt an unreasonable prick of fear.

Setting Isabel down abruptly, her husband strode past them both without a word, leaving her to take the girl's hand and follow a little way behind.

He had outpaced them so quickly that by the time they entered the foyer, shadowy and dim compared to the bright outside, he was gone.

Claire stood there with Isabel uncertainly for a moment. They had both been abandoned. Should she suggest they go up and dress? Isabel was looking at her expectantly.

But then the choice was taken from her.

Voices carried into the hall from behind a closed door off to one side—a small sitting room she had only been in once or twice.

And hearing the voices, Isabel's eyes widened and with a cry of "Mama!" she sprinted towards the room.

Claire stood, shaken to the core, her hands clenched by her sides. She was not sure why but based on all that Mrs. Mowbray had said, she had assumed Isabel's mother no longer played a part in their lives.

But that was idiotic, she now realized—the woman was Isabel's mother. Of course, she would wish to see her child. Even a child she had neglected.

Perhaps she even visited regularly. How was Claire to know? She had not even thought to ask.

How did one pose such a question to the man one was about to marry?

Do you see your mistress often? Pardon me, your former mistress. Do you see Isabel's mother from time to time? Will she be at family Christmas gatherings?

She was so stupid and so naïve that she had simply believed him when he had told her in the cottage that day that he no longer had a mistress. And besides worrying about how she might measure up that evening, she had not given the matter a great deal of thought. Certainly, she had not expected to meet his former lover in the flesh on their wedding day.

Claire felt numb and cold. Her nails were cutting into the palms of her hand.

Slowly, her feet were carrying her towards the room. As she approached, she saw Isabel remained in the entryway, peeking around the door. When she noticed Claire she cast a troubled look and stepped back a little.

Claire knew what she was about to see even before she saw it.

The loveliest woman she had ever set eyes on in her life stood inside, and her long slender arms were around Claire's husband's neck, drawing him down towards her for a sensuous kiss.

Thomas's mistress was a petite woman—she had to stand on tiptoe to even reach his mouth. Yet somehow this added to the charming picture she made, reaching up to him. Silver slippers peeked out from under her beautifully tailored midnight-blue skirts. They were small and dainty. Everything about her was. Claire knew she would feel like a giant beside this woman. Oversized and clumsy. She must be used to having that effect.

Her figure was womanly, rounded yet delicate, with a waist so small a man's hands could easily meet around it. Her hair was a shining jet black, pinned in loose curls that hung around her face and neck. There were jewels in the combs which fastened her hair, in her ears, and on the lovely fingers cast around Thomas's neck—dark red stones, rubies perhaps.

Had Thomas given them to her? He had not even thought to give Claire a ring as William had Fanny. That had not troubled her in the slightest before, but now she remembered and felt it like a cut to the heart.

Perhaps the kiss had just begun, or perhaps it had been going on since Thomas had entered. Had he swept her into his arms immediately? With no disregard for his daughter...or his bride?

Claire took a step, meaning to back out of the room quietly without them ever knowing she had been there. But she had forgotten Isabel and, in her hurry, nudged the girl who leaned harder on the door, sweeping it fully open with a creak.

It happened so fast. Thomas pushed the woman away from him, saw Claire and Isabel there, and took a step towards them.

But Claire darted out, brushing past Isabel, leaving her with her parents. She ran towards the staircase without a backwards glance. Only when she had reached her room did she slam the door and stop to catch her breath.

Her marriage was over before it began.

Thomas was furious.

"What have you done?" he snarled, turning back to Serafina. She stood there calmly, a picture of innocence and fragile femininity, her hands clasped gently in front her.

Ignoring his anger, she stepped past him.

"My sweet darling!" she cried, spreading her arms wide. Thomas was reminded of all the nights he had spent waiting to hear that voice speak out from the darkness of a full theater. That ringing, lilting beautiful voice which carried effortlessly from years of practice and which could convey most any tone in the repertoire of humanity.

Right now, it was conveying adoring motherliness. A mother separated from her daughter for far too long, reunited at long last.

Serafina played the part well. It made his heart ache for Isabel. He turned to see how the girl would react. Would she fall for Serafina's old tricks or see through her insincerity now that she was a little older?

Isabel expression was inscrutable.

"Have... have you come back?" Her high, sweet voice was halting and hesitant.

Thomas's heart wrung hearing the faint suggestion of hope it held. The child longed for her mother still.

"Come back, my love?" Serafina smiled kindly, her arms still open, waiting for the girl to run into them.

Isabel stayed where she was.

"Have you come back for good? You missed the wedding..." Isabel looked at her father, then back. "Did you come to take me back with you? Or to stay with us? With Mrs. Mowbray and I, at Stoneybrook?"

"Stoneybrook?" Serafina looked at her daughter with amusement.

"It is the house in which she lives," Thomas said quietly.

"Oh, my darling." Her tinkling laugh filled the room like silver chiming bells. "Of course not. How silly. I must return to London. I have a performance tomorrow evening. You would not wish to come back there with me anyhow—the smoke, the crowds. Your health is much improved here. Oh! Look at the roses in her cheeks, Thomas." She clapped her hands delightedly.

Thomas gritted his teeth, stifling the urge to say she had not cared enough for her daughter's health to write to her even once all these months. Oh, he had opened the letters she had sent to him eventually, glanced them over quickly before tossing them into the fire. None concerned Isabel. If a single one had, he would have kept it to show the girl her mother had asked after her.

But she had not. Not once.

"Then... why are you here?" Isabel asked slowly. "Papa was married this morning. To Claire. Why have you come? You have not come for me?"

To Thomas's horror he saw Isabel close her eyes. Then shake her head.

"Of course, you have not come for me." She sounded weary.

She opened her eyes again and looked directly at her mother. "You would never come for me. You came to take him again."

She shook her head again and this time he saw the tears fall, splattering to the carpet below. Serafina was negligent, but still the only mother Isabel had. How many times had she cried for her mother since he and William removed her from London? Never once had Thomas thought to ask Mrs. Mowbray if his daughter cried herself to sleep at night. His fists curled tighter still.

"You will take him. And you will leave us both alone, Claire and I. Just as you did before. And I will never see him. I will have no mother, and I will have no father." She choked.

"Oh, my dear one..." Serafina began in her softest voice.

But Isabel had already turned and run from the room.

"The poor child," Serafina said tenderly, looking after her with concern.

"She is your poor child, Serafina. And if you were truly concerned about her you could have done any number of things about it at any time since her birth."

She looked up at him from under long dark lashes. Her eyes were a speckled golden amber. He remembered how moved he used to be when she would look at him with that intense, beautiful gaze in the past. Now he felt nothing.

Except perhaps hate.

Yes, he was fairly sure he hated her now. Hated what she had done to him, to Isabel. And now, what she was trying to do to Claire.

"Do not shout at me, Thomas," she said softly. "You know I cannot bear it." She lifted a hand as if to touch his cheek, but he pushed it away.

"You will come with me. Now. Upstairs. You will tell my *wife*—" He emphasized the word. "—how you embraced me without provocation, without encouragement, and how I rebuffed you as soon as you did."

She tilted her head to one side.

"But you did not do so, Thomas."

"Did not do what?"

He felt feral and reckless, and disgusted by his feelings. Almost, not quite, but almost he wished she were a man so he might strike her. He had never touched a woman in anger before and he never would, but in this moment, the urge to hit another human being was strong.

"You did not rebuff me." She put a finger to full pouting lips.

"What is this rubbish?"

"I am saying, Thomas," she purred slowly, "that if your...wife...had not entered, I do not think you would have stopped me at all. At this moment, we would still be..." She parted her lips slightly and touched the bottom one with the tip of her tongue.

She had incredibly full, sensual lips. And her latest paramour could enjoy them well for all he cared.

"You are sorrily mistaken if that is what you think happened or would have happened." He looked down at her coldly.

His indifference might have more effect than his rage. She liked him hot-tempered. In the past, each time he had discovered another one of her indiscretions their verbal altercations had peaked and culminated in pleasurable reunions. Until he could forgive and forget no longer, and she grew bored with trying to persuade him to stay.

"You have run out of funds? Is that it? Your newest toy has not provided for you as well as you had hoped? Are you perhaps expecting a greater ransom than we paid you for Isabel? Annual tribute? A chest of treasure to take with you?"

"Do not be ridiculous, Thomas." She held out her hands imploringly. "I care nothing for gold or riches. As you well know, my love. My art is my passion. A life of truth. Freedom. Beauty. That is all I desire. And once all you desired, too."

"A life devoid of responsibility, of honor, of any inkling of care for another's welfare. There is no beauty in that, Serafina. For a while you had me convinced that there could be. But it was an utterly empty existence."

Her expression hardened slightly. "You spent many years in my bed enjoying your 'meaningless existence,' Thomas. You were more than content there as I recall. Shall I share some of those memories with your wife?" She picked up her skirts delicately, and turned towards the door.

"You wished me to speak with her, yes? Shall I tell her about you? About us? How devoted you were? The promises you made me?" She looked out from under her eyelashes again.

He struggled to hold back angry words.

"Shall I tell her how to please you best, my love? For surely you would wish your new bride to know what you like." Her voice was low and husky now, almost a purr.

He stared down into the lovely face of this enchanting actress. The mother of his child.

It was impossible not to remember why he had fallen in love with her. No, why he had been completely and utterly obsessed with her.

Serafina was enthralling. She always would be. She had a power that drew people to her. It was why she was such a magnificent performer. In every way.

But he was no longer capable of being enthralled.

He wanted to tell her held no power over him any longer, that her lips had been as bitter as wormwood when they touched his.

But there was no point. He did not wish to fight. She would be only too glad to draw this out.

He wished her gone.

He wanted to go to his wife. To his daughter.

"Are you quite finished?" He assumed a look of boredom.

Serafina's eyes narrowed. "Finished?"

"This conversation grows tedious. Our business is concluded, Serafina. If you are not here to see our daughter, you will leave this house. If you are in need of lodging overnight, there is an excellent inn in town." She need not know it was a tavern without a single room to let.

He began to walk towards the door.

"Don't you dare turn your back on me, Thomas!" Her voice was pleading. The broken-hearted, spurned woman, betrayed by her love.

The hypocrisy was nearly comical. But this was farce, not comedy.

He kept walking and only when he reached the door, did he turn back, a hand on the frame.

"If you require rest before you go, you may sit here a spell. If you change your mind about Isabel, ring the bell and a servant will endeavour to locate her for you. Though if she does not wish to see you..." He shrugged eloquently.

Then he closed the door as she raised her voice. The heavy oak drowned out whatever she was saying.

He turned towards the stairs.

There must be some way to fix this.

If he must spend his wedding night alone, so be it. Claire could have as much time as she needed.

But she had to know that he had not planned this, had not wanted this, had never meant to hurt her.

Claire sank back against the door, her mind in turmoil. Should she pack her things? Call for a carriage and return to Orchard Hill?

It would be humiliating to return, but not more humiliating than staying in a house with her husband's mistress.

Why had he done this to her? Could he not have left her alone from the start? Certainly, she had given him no indication she wished to be pursued. He had enticed her, stolen her freedom in exchange for what? A few guilty kisses?

He had almost convinced her he was an honorable man, trying to do the right thing, that he was concerned for her reputation and her future.

What did he mean to do with her? Why did he need her at all?

A horrible thought struck her. Was she simply to be a kind of Mrs. Mowbray? To serve as Isabel's caregiver while her true parents returned to London to lead their lives?

She covered her face with her hands. Poor Isabel. She wondered if the girl was still downstairs.

Or perhaps she had it all wrong and they were a trio, embracing together and reconciling as a family. While she was left outside in the cold.

She felt a spark of hope. It was not too late. There had been no wedding night. Could there be an annulment?

Her heart sank just as quickly, remembering nonconsummation was not sufficient. Thomas was unlikely to go along with a claim of impotence. Alienation of affections then? Rarely did that go in a wife's favor.

Not to mention the fact that any dissolution of marriage would be social suicide.

But better than remaining captive to a man so cruel and so deceptive.

A sob escaped her lips.

Ridiculous, foolish passion had gotten her into this situation. She had sworn to learn her lesson from her older sister's troubles, but evidently, she had not learned it as well as she should. Men were not worth trusting. Not worth marrying. She should have remained a spinster and lived with her mother the rest of her days.

There was a light knock on the door. She sat up, trying to remember if she had locked it. Surely no one would enter without her permission either way.

Oh God. Was it Fanny? She and William shared the wing across the house, but perhaps she had gotten wind of Thomas's visitor.

She could not face her friend right now. The contrast between her happiness and Claire's misery would be unbearable.

"Claire?"

Thomas.

She wiped her face quickly. Why had she wiped it? She would not open the door.

Yet she found herself rising to her feet.

He knocked again.

"Claire?" His voice was soft and low. She heard him sigh after a moment of her silence.

Was he alone out there? Or was that woman with him? Had they come to mock her?

"Claire... It is not what you think. Won't you please allow me to explain? Please. Allow me to speak with you."

It was more tempting than she liked.

"There is nothing to say. We both know what I saw."

She paused.

"Now go away." Her tone was as aloof as she could manage between tears that would not stop.

She saw the handle turn.

"Don't you dare!" She took a pre-emptive step back.

But he did dare. The door opened slowly.

"Are you...dressed?"

"Of course, I am dressed!" she said furiously. "I am packing. Kindly have a carriage ordered." It was a lie but he would not know that. Her case was still open on the window seat.

He pushed the door open wider.

He did not look like a man who had come from the arms of another woman. His face was not flushed with desire. It looked rather drawn in fact.

But what did she know of such things? Perhaps that woman had merely exhausted him.

"I did not invite her here, Claire. I did not even know she was coming."

He pushed locks of dark hair from his eyes. Claire bit her lip, thinking of how she had looked forward to touching those waves, brushing it possessively off his face herself.

"Serafina does what she pleases. As you can see, she has no sense of propriety or discretion. She believes she owns Isabel and I even still. Even though, after her unforgiveable actions, she quite thoroughly relinquished rights to us both some time ago. I do not believe Isabel has pardoned her yet. I certainly will not."

He looked at her, eyes wide and beseeching. Not a hint of pride or arrogance.

"She does not want me to be happy without her, Claire," he said softly. "She must have found out I was to be married and she came with all haste. This is exactly what she was hoping for—or nearly so. When you walked in..."

"Oh? Nearly so?" Fury twisted inside her. "I apologize for intruding so unexpectedly, for interrupting your passionate liaison. I suppose if Isabel and I had not walked in, you would still be there even now. On the floor together perhaps."

Thomas looked taken aback, then angry. "Of course not! Do you really think me so...? Is that what you believe, Claire? You did exactly what Serafina hoped you would do. Reacted with anger and jealousy, blamed me, and stormed out."

"Jealousy!" Claire exclaimed, drawing herself up. "I assure you—I am not jealous in the least. If she wants you, she is welcome to have you. I did not want you in the first place, as you will recall."

He flinched. If she did not know better, she might almost have believed him to be hurt.

She swallowed hard.

"What have I to be jealous of? The fact that you prefer your mistress to..." Oh, no. Her voice was catching in her throat. "...to... me..." She hiccupped embarrassingly, tears flowing over.

All of a sudden Thomas's arms were around her, holding her firmly to his chest. "Claire... No, no..." he whispered.

Her cheek was pressed up rather roughly against his tailcoat. He smelled so good. She closed her eyes, her body relaxing against him.

There was another smell there. An overpoweringly sweet scent of lilacs. She pushed herself away, hands against his chest.

"You smell of her."

He looked horrified.

Horrified that he did? Or horrified that she had noticed? Did he smell of her from head to toe?

Claire felt nauseous.

A loud tap on the half-open door surprised them both.

"Mr. Campbell?" A strident female voice. "Mr. Campbell, are you there, sir?"

Thomas frowned and pulled open the door.

"Mr. Campbell—" Mrs. Mowbray nodded to Claire as she saw her, before looking up at him. "Isabel is gone."

"Gone? What do you mean?"

"I was told she had come back with you, but I have yet to see hide nor hair. I have had the footmen searching but no one has found her. And now with the weather turned so savage..." She gestured to the window.

Claire looked out properly for the first time since entering the room. A hard rain was pounding against the pane, fogging the glass and making it nearly impossible to see beyond. A crack of thunder made her jump. She looked back to see Mrs. Mowbray's worried expression.

"I believe we must begin to search the grounds, sir," the woman said, looking expectantly at Thomas.

"Yes." Claire watched him run a hand over his face. More and more haggard. She wondered if Serafina was still in the house.

"Yes," he said again. He looked at Mrs. Mowbray more closely. "Gather the servants in the main hall if you will, Mrs. Mowbray. If you see my brother, let him know of your concern. I will be there in a moment." He glanced at Claire.

Mrs. Mowbray nodded and left the room.

Claire stared at her husband. Everything was worse than before. Her stepdaughter was lost on the very day she had gained her.

"This is all your fault," she said slowly, knowing the words were unfair, not to mention possibly untrue, as she said them but not caring, simply wanting to hurt him as much as he had hurt her. "When may your child stop paying for your selfishness?"

And it worked. His eyes widened.

Suddenly she could not bear to have him look at her another instant. She flew from the room, down the hall, her hand sliding along the bannister as she ran down the stairs. The servants were milling about below, pulling on coats, and gathering umbrellas. Mrs. Mowbray was overseeing their organization, wringing her hands with impatience. She looked up anxiously as Claire came down.

"Oh, Mrs. Campbell..." She began, starting towards Claire. But at the sound of that title, Claire walked even faster towards the front door, ignoring everything and everyone until she was past them and outside.

She stood beneath the overhang a moment. The beautiful weather was gone. As was Serafina's fine carriage.

It had become a day similar to the one in the ravine, though not as windy. Not quite as cold. She would be soaked in no time though, she knew, looking out through the curtain of streaming rain.

Somewhere on these grounds was a delicate girl still recovering her strength. A girl who, Claire now realized, must have fled not long after she had.

If Serafina was anywhere near as self-centered as Mrs. Mowbray and Thomas had described her to be, then she had not come there for her daughter. Merely to wreak havoc. And to intimidate Claire. Who had fallen into her trap perfectly.

Claire did not care anymore. Whatever was to happen between Thomas and herself, she had made vows that morning—and to her those vows had been made as much to Isabel as to Isabel's father.

What must Isabel be feeling? To be so casually abandoned once more by a mother more concerned with wooing her father away than in showing her child affection.

She tossed her useless silk slippers beside a potted fern and set off across the wet grass barefoot in search of her daughter.

Chapter 23

Thomas had failed a husband and as a father.

So easy was it to believe her new husband was already unfaithful, that his wife had already begun packing her bags.

So easy was it to believe that her father would again abandon her, that his daughter had fled into the wild and the wet rather than trust him to do right by her.

And the worst thing of all was there was no one to blame but himself.

Serafina may have lit the match, but the flames were all his own making.

He was more than willing to pay for his past transgressions—but to have the ones he held most dear do so was intolerable.

He treaded the stairs in silence. As he entered the hall, the chatter ceased abruptly.

He could easily imagine what they must have been saying.

How could this man be called one of their betters? A man whose child had fled from him. A man who could not manage to keep his fornication a secret for a single day but instead flaunted his courtesan before his poor young bride.

How grateful they must be that William was the true master of Northwood, and Thomas merely the prodigal brother, forgiven but forever a wastrel.

Only Mrs. Mowbray was brave enough to approach him. She came over with a folded cloak in her hands.

"I have brought this for Isabel." As he took it, she looked at his attire. "But perhaps you wish to bring one for Mrs. Campbell as well?"

He stared uncomprehending. He had expected Claire to flee somewhere. To go and find Fanny perhaps.

"Mrs. Campbell walked out only a moment ago. But she was not dressed for the weather." Mrs. Mowbray hesitated. "Shall I have a maid bring something warm? In case you find them both together?"

Find them. At her words, Thomas was suddenly swept back to the day he found Miss Gardner—Mrs. Claire Campbell now, though it was currently impossible to believe she would ever wish to answer to that title—in the ravine with Fanny. His heart clenched. If Isabel managed to get that far...

It was exceedingly unlikely. She was a small girl, unaccustomed to walking such long distances.

But he could easily imagine other perils.

The lake—a single slip and a soundless fall. No one to hear her cries over the sound of the rain. Or a crack of lightning hitting a tree she sheltered beneath.

He looked wildly about the room for William, hoping he was at home, hoping he had been summoned.

His brother had just entered from the opposite hallway. He was striding towards Thomas with Fanny close behind. Both were dressed in warm, practical clothing.

William's face was stern, but it softened as he saw Thomas's.

"Yes, well." He clasped his brother's shoulder firmly. "Shall we begin?"

Thomas was about to nod, then he looked back at Mrs. Mowbray. "Will you please have warm clothing ready for my wife?"

Seeing William and Fanny's startlement, he elaborated. "She has gone after Isabel already. Alone." He looked at William, who seemed to understand.

"We have heard that Serafina was here this afternoon," his brother said awkwardly.

"She was." Thomas spoke shortly. "She came and she has gone. Her visit was unexpected." He looked at his sister-in-law. "And unwanted."

William nodded. Fanny looked relieved.

"I am not the rake you fear I am," he wanted to cry, but he stayed silent.

Within minutes, they had divided into pairs and singles to cover the grounds. A few of the grooms were to go out on horseback to check the trails and main road.

Fanny and William walked with Thomas at first, but he quickly outpaced them.

William would understand. And so, he walked on alone, trying to recollect every place Isabel had ever mentioned, and thinking how best to reach each one in the quickest amount of time, in the most expedient order.

He would not think of where Claire had gone or where she might look first for Isabel.

He would find his daughter first, and then his wife.

Or God willing, they would be found together.

Claire held a small tired body in the shelter of her arms. Isabel's head rested on her chest, her wet dark hair hanging around her shoulders. Claire reached a hand down gently to brush it off the girl's face and doing so was reminded of Thomas's. The same shade, the same tumbling waves.

She had been shivering when Claire had found her in the hollow of the oak tree. The perfect place for a small girl to crawl in and hide.

Her already sore heart had nearly broken when Isabel looked up at her from red-rimmed eyes.

"Is he gone?" she had asked brokenly.

Claire had knelt beside her, disregarding the soggy leaves, the muddy ground. Her wedding dress would never be the same, but what did it matter when there was a little broken-hearted child so certain her father and mother would readily forsake her.

So certain her father had left Claire, too, but she would not dwell on that.

"Your father is not gone, Isabel," she said softly, touching her cheek. "He would never leave you. He is very worried about you. I am sure he is outside looking for you at this very moment. And he is not alone. There are many people who love you."

Isabel did not seem persuaded.

"She came for him. I knew she would. She has never wanted me. Never, never, ever. Only him." Her face was tragic.

It was no childish exaggeration on her part. Claire had no idea what it must feel like to know that your mother preferred your father, that she did not wish to see you, to visit you, to live with you.

"Oh, Isabel." She sighed, brushing hair off the girl's face gently.

"I do not know your mother. But I know this much—your father has not left you. I promise you he has not."

She hesitated a moment. "Your mother's carriage is gone," she said quietly. Isabel looked up. "But she left alone. Your father is still here."

Claire did not know much, but she was suddenly certain that all she was telling Isabel was indeed the truth. Thomas loved his daughter. He was committed to her beyond a doubt.

As for his new wife...Claire was not as sure.

"Now," she said, peering into the snug hollow where Isabel sat shivering. "Am I to take it you wish this small cave to be our new home? Or will you accompany me back to the house?" She smiled encouragingly and held out her arms, relieved as Isabel scooted towards her.

Thomas had checked the lake. He had looked beneath the bridge. He had searched the grove with the circle of mushrooms. He was wet and exhausted and most of all he was afraid.

He was walking through a part of the woods he felt sure they had passed with Isabel earlier that afternoon. He was repressing the urge to turn back to the lake once more. What if Isabel had fallen in and Claire had come across her and gone in after? He imagined their bodies floating on the surface of the water face down and felt bile rising in his throat.

He put out a hand to steady himself on a tree. The bark was slippery but reassuring under his skin. Tall ancient oak and elms surrounded him, their canopy shutting out some of the rain but also much of the light. Soon it would be night.

They could come back with lanterns, of course, but...

Touching the tree reminded him of the hollow oak that Isabel had excitedly shown to him and Claire a few hours before. Big enough for a small girl to sit in. He had imagined Isabel bringing a stash of books, her Matilda, a blanket perhaps, and enjoying her secret hideaway. Now his heart leapt as he realized he was not far off.

He crashed through the bramble as clumsily as a bear, impatiently shoved aside branches until he reached the small clearing he remembered and saw the enormous oak.

But the little hollow at the base of its trunk was empty.

The leaves inside were crumpled as if someone had sat on them recently. He tried to remember if Isabel had actually gone into the hollow when she showed it to them that afternoon. He could not remember.

He ran his hands over his face.

The thought of the lake was still on his mind. He would go back to it, look more carefully. At least his mind would be more at rest if he found nothing.

And in the meantime, perhaps William would have come across Isabel. Or Claire.

He walked back through the trees, feeling tired but maintaining a brisk pace. He would cut through the woods, then across the main road that wound through the estate, leading to the house and over the open fields that lay before the lake.

As he emerged through the trees into the clearing and spotted the muddy road, he heard his child scream. The sound came the right.

He looked, as if through a fog, and instantly felt the dread of knowing he would be unable to move quickly enough to prevent what was unfolding.

In a matter of seconds, a curricle had come barrelling around a bend in the road at an incredible speed. The black stallion pulling it was foaming at the mouth and covered with sweat.

At the same time, Isabel and Claire had exited the woods a little further along. They had come from the same direction as Thomas but must have gotten off course.

As the woman and girl had begun to cross the road, the curricle appeared from around the curve. At first, with the sound of the rain they must not have noticed it, but as it sped towards them Isabel looked up and screamed.

The driver made no attempt to slow down. Thomas could only watch in horror as the vehicle converged upon the two figures.

He saw Claire take in in the speeding horse. Then she turned to Isabel and gave a great push.

Isabel fell onto the lawn a few steps away.

At the very last possible moment, the curricle driver noticed the obstruction before him and whipped the horse fiercely. The crack of the whip cut through the air. The poor beast tried to swerve. The whip cracked again as it passed by Claire, the carriage coming within inches of her body. Thomas saw the tip of the whip fly down and catch his wife on the arm. The curricle wheel brushed against her and she fell.

And then the vehicle was past, and coming towards him, its pace slowing.

Shaking with fury, he stepped onto road, shouting "Halt!"

The stallion reared a little. Thomas grabbed the bridle as the conveyance rolled slowly to a stop.

"You will remain here," he snarled, not sparing a glance at the driver. "Do not leave this spot. I will deal with you in a moment."

He ran towards his wife.

Claire was already on her feet. The fabric of her dress was ripped along the sleeve and he saw a trickle of blood. But instead of minding the wound, her arms were already outstretched as Isabel ran into them with a cry.

Claire's hand was on the girl's head. She was murmuring soothing words as she looked up and saw Thomas.

She may have been angry with him still. As for himself, he had nearly forgotten what had passed between them only a little while ago.

The feeling of relief was so strong, he could do nothing but join them where they stood, wrapping his arms around them both.

His eyes closed with exhaustion. They were unharmed and whole.

Mostly whole. He opened his eyes and stepped back.

"Your arm..."

Claire was shaking her head.

"A scratch. It's nothing."

It was more of a gash, but the bleeding was not heavy. He pulled off his cravat and ignoring her protests, tied it firmly around the cut.

He remembered the driver and looked behind him to make sure they had not disappeared.

To the contrary, not only were they still in place but William and Fanny had arrived and from the look of it, angry words were being exchanged.

The look on William's face alerted Thomas to what he should have already guessed.

The driver was Charles Morton.

He looked not the least bit apologetic, but stood with the whip still in his hand, shoulders back, and his head jutting forward in what was uncomfortably close proximity to William's.

What was more, he reeked of spirits. Which explained his belated braking.

Thomas was not interested in whatever was being discussed.

He yanked the whip from Morton's hand, getting his attention quickly. It was all he could do to not use it on the young man himself.

"You could have killed my wife and child," Thomas said in quiet rage.

Morton's face was puckered unpleasantly, red with drink and anger. His lips were already curling back in disregard.

"But I didn't, did I? Now get out of my face. Trying to discuss important matters here, can't you see."

Given this second opportunity, Thomas's fists were itching to collide with Charles' face. He caught William's eye first.

"Morton," William said coldly. "I presume there is a good reason for your appearance at Northwood or you would not have been stupid enough to come. Perhaps the village is on fire? An outbreak of plague?"

Charles gaped, too intoxicated to comprehend. He shook his head as if trying to clear it, like a dog trying to shake off fleas.

"You know 'xactly why I'm here..." he began, taking a step towards William and Fanny. Thomas saw William gently push Fanny behind him.

"Indeed, I do not. In fact, I am surprised to see you in the vicinity of Beauford at all," William said icily.

Charles sneered. "Thought you'd drive us out, did you? Been here five generations and thought you'd drive us out like dumb cattle."

"Yes," William said quietly, not breaking his gaze. "That is exactly what I thought."

William looked towards Thomas and Claire.

"Apparently Mr. Morton has just come into the knowledge that his family shall be removing themselves from Beauford forthwith. In a fortuitous turn of events, some kind benefactor has paid off his father's debts." William looked on Charles with distaste. "It would seem fools run in the family for not only has Morton's father squandered his family's income, but he also went so far as to use his own estate as collateral in a gambling den."

Charles looked like a balloon about to burst. "You took advantage. Cheated him, my father, he..."

William cut him off. "Took advantage? I merely acquired what he had already bartered away. What kind of a man wagers his own home, the residence of his wife and children, in a game of cards?"

"He planned to pay it," Charles burst out. He was shaking—whether from rage or spirits, who could say. "We had things well in hand..."

"Yes," William interrupted again coldly. "Attempting to rape a woman so that she would be forced into marriage with you, so that you could redeem your estate. Was that the plan you had in mind? How incredibly noble."

Charles seethed silently.

"What did you come here for today, Morton?" William asked quietly. "On the day of my brother's wedding, you come to our home. You must have known we would not be the least bit sympathetic to your case. Why are you here?"

Charles's hands were curled by his side. He sputtered. "I came to say that you, sir, can go straight to hell. We will not be leaving Beauford."

He looked at Fanny who stood behind her husband, her face a mask of calm composure.

Charles pointed at her. "And I came to say I hope you enjoy that pathetic bitch—" He turned to generously include Claire in his gesture. "—and your precious doxy. You both can..."

But that was as far as he got. William grabbed him by his cravat and yanked him forwards.

William exercised far more restraint than Thomas would have.

He gripped him firmly by the throat until Morton's face had turned a dark mottled shade. Then he thrust him to the muddy ground and stood over.

"I do not believe you are well-informed as to your situation, Morton, so allow me to make it painfully clear. Your family *will* be leaving Beauford. I have not paid off all of your father's creditors and I shall not do so until every last pustule you call a relative has departed never to return. You may bless some other town or another country for all I care, but you will not come back here again."

He took a breath. "If you do not depart, due to idiocy or thick-headedness, there are two things which shall happen next. First, your mother and sister will be visiting your father in debtor's prison—for that is where most of the merchants in this region believe he belongs and they have been far more than patient. You shall not attend him there, however, for you will be in a far less hospitable place where my brother and I shall visit you—in Newgate, where you will await trial for the rape of several young women, as well as the attempted murder of my brother's wife and daughter."

Charles stared. "You're bluffing. There are none who..." He trailed off.

"None who would testify?" William looked sick at the sight of him. "You would be surprised. There are at least three who I assure you would. I have taken the trouble of reassuring them they would have the Campbells' full support. Before you ask, my wife is not one of them. There is no need of her testimony when you have already left such an adequate trail of heartache and pain in your wake. Many of your young victims have fathers and brothers who have assured me they would like nothing better than to see your neck in a noose."

Charles took a step back. He eyed his horse and curricle.

"Yes, what an excellent idea." William spoke almost pleasantly. "Get in and set yourself back on the road. Unless there is anything you wish to add, Fanny? Thomas?"

He looked at Claire and her arm. "Or perhaps you, sister?"

Thomas raised the whip as if to strike and seeing it Charles leapt almost comically into his seat and drove off.

Only a few minutes had passed, but it felt like much longer.

Isabel was leaning heavily on Claire, her eyelids heavy.

"Let me take her," William said softly, seeing Thomas's gaze. "Fanny and Mrs. Mowbray will put her for a hot bath and then to bed. We will treat her with the greatest care."

Thomas had no doubt of it, and he appreciated that William was trying to give him the opportunity of a moment alone with his wife.

"Call for Doctor Greyson," he requested. He looked at Claire who shook her head. "For Isabel then. Please."

William nodded and lifted Isabel up into his arms.

Thomas turned back to his wife.

She would not meet his eye.

He looked at the white linen cravat which covered her injury. No redness showed through the fabric which was a good sign.

"It has been a long day," he said quietly. "May I give you my arm?"

She shook her head mutely and began to walk ahead of him, her pace slower than usual.

She must have been more fatigued than she realized for only a moment later her foot slipped on the wet grass, and letting out a gasp, she extended her arms to steady herself.

Thomas caught one arm gently. But having steadied her he stepped closer and swiftly catching her by the waist, lifted her up before she could object.

"I am too heavy," she protested, squirming a little. It was untrue. She was taller than Serafina, but lithe and only slightly more substantial.

"You are not at all." And lifting one of her arms he placed it firmly around his neck. In a moment she had settled against him, her head on his shoulder.

His exhaustion abruptly evaporated.

It was his wedding day. And finally, his bride was in his arms.

Isabel was safe in William and Fanny's care.

Now as he walked, he could dwell on Claire. So much had occurred since morning. He had nearly forgotten about Serafina. Nearly. He was sure Claire had not.

Claire had been so quick to assume he would prefer his former mistress to her. Why? Did she still truly have no idea of the effect she had upon him? Of how lovely she was in his eyes?

True, she was no sophisticate like Serafina. He could not imagine Claire as comfortable in a similar milieu, basking in the adoration of rich Londoners or lounging amongst bohemian artists.

Physically speaking, they were a contrast as well.

A contrast he adored. He loved Claire's height, her slimness. She was not voluptuous like Serafina, but perfectly rounded in all of the right places. He loved her long-legged stride, the easy and confident way she carried herself. Her dark autumnal hair—which right now was filling his nostrils with its scent, a mix of her own smell, the soap she had used that morning, and the fresh rain.

He recalled their first meeting. He had thought her obstinate and outspoken. He could easily admit now that he had been the same. And while in him it was a failing, he now loved Claire's outspokenness. She was blunt and sincere and above all, refreshingly honest— whereas Serafina was all contrivance and manipulation.

His wife had already displayed more care for Isabel's well-being than her own mother ever had. Had Serafina given a single thought to the wreckage she was leaving in her wake before she departed in her fine carriage? If she had, Thomas felt certain it would only have brought her pleasure to know she was leaving him to clean it up, to take the blame.

She would have scoffed at the idea that she had anything to do with Isabel's reaction or her running away.

As they drew near the house, Claire wriggled in his grasp and he let her slide down to walk beside him. Though he would have preferred to carry her over the threshold.

"I am coming upstairs with you," he said softly, as they entered, and when she said nothing, he followed her up.

When she entered her suite of rooms, she turned as if considering whether to shut the door on him. He stood there for a moment until she turned away, walking over to the mirror on the wall and touching a hand to her face.

"You look lovely," he said softly.

She looked shocked to hear the words and he cursed himself for not having had the consideration to ever say them before.

"Shall I call a maid to dress your arm?" She shook her head—a gesture he was growing used to.

Would she ever speak? She untied the cravat and inspected the cut, then moistened a cloth in the basin on the dressing table and patted it clean.

Thomas watched in silence. It was no longer bleeding and she did not appear to be in a great deal of pain, but the thought of how close the whip had come to doing real damage to her made his blood boil. If it had struck her face, or an eye...

William had dealt with the situation well. Thomas had no complaint. But if he saw Morton again after today, he would not exercise the same restraint.

He fumbled in the pocket of his coat a moment, patting himself to locate the small packet he had placed there before leaving the house that morning.

"I do not know if you will want this..." he said slowly, unfolding a cloth wrapping and holding a small object out to her. "But I meant to give it to you this evening."

He glanced at the window. It was essentially night now. The windows still let in a little light, but a maid had already lit the candles that were held in sconces along the walls beside the bed.

She glanced at it but did not take it.

"What is it?" she asked shortly.

He picked up the object from the cloth. A ring. A single circular emerald was set in the center of a gold band, surrounded by two smaller ones on either side. The band was engraved with intricate swirls of leaves and flowers.

He had ordered it from London. The design was his. A ring that alluded to natural beauty, made for his country bride.

Claire was staring at the ring.

"It...is lovely." She reached out a hand hesitantly, picking it up and turning it.

She looked at him and held it out to him again.

"But perhaps we should admit this has been a terrible mistake now, Thomas."

She looked down and away. "Though I fear it is too late."

"It is too late, though that does not give me any reason for fear. Quite the opposite. You are stuck with me. While you may wish to bar the door to me tonight, or for however many nights you must take —" He took a breath. "—someday I hope you will forgive me. I will be patient until then."

He looked into her eyes. "You have forgiven worse of me before this."

She looked back, her lips trembling.

"Oh, Claire," he said quietly. "Do you wish me to leave? I promise, if you say the word, I will do so. You may lock the door behind."

A moment of silence. He stayed quite still.

She shook her head.

Should he push his luck?

He reached out a hand to stroke her cheek.

"Will you believe me when I say again that I had no knowledge of Serafina's visit? That I did not encourage her attentions?"

He swallowed, looking at her stern face. "While you may be unhappy to be here, please know that I would never wish to mar our wedding day in such a way."

She was silent.

Then she nodded.

He let out a breath he had not known he was holding.

"I am not..." She stopped. "Altogether unhappy. To be here."

She looked up at him, the hint of a smile on her lips. His heart leapt.

"Will you..." He hesitated. "Will you allow me?" He held out the ring again, then took her hand, cool in his own warm and larger one, and slid the ring carefully onto her finger, before turning her hand over and planting a kiss on her palm.

She sighed and pulled her hand away. She turned back to the dresser, fumbling to pick up a brush, a comb. Something to distract herself.

He would have to try harder to distract her in a different way.

He stepped up behind her, seeing her reflection in the large oval mirror and himself reflected behind her. They made a handsome pair, both tall and dark.

He put his hands gently on her shoulders.

"Your dress is soaked, Claire," he said. "You must be freezing. Shall I summon a maid?"

She shook her head slowly, meeting his gaze in the reflection.

"Do you remember that day in the rain?" he said softly, moving his hands carefully down to her waist.

She shivered a little.

Somehow, he suddenly knew, every moment had been leading to this one. So many meetings in the rain and the wet and the muck. Yes, it was England, but nevertheless, this had been truly excessive. All culminating in this—her standing before him, her dress soaked to her skin, with him behind her, hands poised to finally do what they had been longing to do from that first day when he offered her a ride and she so rudely refused him.

"I was loathe to go anywhere with the disreputable Thomas Campbell," she replied, looking at him steadily in the reflection.

"Not so disreputable anymore, I'm afraid. I renounce and retire from all my rakish ways." He put his lips to her neck and kissed the soft skin. "Indeed, I fear you will have made a true gentleman of me before you are through."

It was a start.

But there was so much more.

Neither of them had eaten since the picnic, but he felt he could go days without sustenance, staying right here in this room for however long she would permit him.

"Do you know how much I want you, Claire? For how long I have wanted you?" He whispered.

His hands moved up to the front of her wet dress, cupping her breasts. He breathed down into her ear softly. "Only you."

He moved his lips down and over her neck, kissing her shoulder.

"From that first day we met. You were...infuriating...but intoxicating. Each time I saw you, I found myself wanting more."

She gave a shaky laugh. "You called me mulish, I believe."

"You heard that? You little eavesdropper!" He nibbled her neck.

"To be fair, you were not exactly trying to be subtle." She raised her eyebrows.

"I don't suppose I was." He grinned boyishly. "Will you ever forgive me?"

She swirled around suddenly and reached her hands up to grasp the back of his neck—in the way she had done before, in the way he was becoming incredibly partial to—and pulled his lips down to meet her own.

She was trembling. He could not tell if it was with cold or fear or longing, perhaps all three. He wrapped his arms around her, running his hands over her body. To warm her, he told himself. Also, because he could not do otherwise.

Her lips quivered beneath his own, soft and full. They parted eagerly for him, a foreshadow of things to come, and he groaned at the thought. She opened to him with an ardency and freedom all her own, and he teased her with his tongue, tasting her sweetness, feeling her heat, the heady promise of her kiss.

"Am I to take this as forgiveness?" He leaned away from her.

She bit him then. First gently on the lip, then moving to his neck she licked and bit again, gently at first, then harder, until Thomas closed his eyes and held onto her waist, losing himself in the feeling. Her hands were running over the back of his neck, through his hair. He loved the touch of her hands.

"Harder," he whispered, and she complied, just for a moment before coming back to his lips and kissing him again with even more intensity than before. Her breasts were crushed against him, her body flush against his own.

So many places still to be kissed.

"Oh, Claire. What are you doing to me?" he whispered, moving his mouth away from hers slightly as he spoke.

He looked down at her flushed face, her red lips, her wide eyes. She was beautiful, fragile. His.

"This is no mistake. I think you know that. Perhaps we knew it that very first day." She closed her eyes as if overwhelmed by his words. Or as if she still did not fully trust them.

He pushed the thought aside, and kissed her forehead lightly. Gently he ran his hands over her hair, tugging out pins and letting it tumble down around her shoulders.

The fabric of her dress barred his way. He wanted it gone. He wanted her bare under his hands.

"Thomas," she whispered, leaning forwards and raising her lips to be kissed again.

"My beauty," he whispered in reply, giving her the kiss she required as his hands moved to the fastenings at the back of her dress.

His fingers were deft and practiced as he undid her dress, pushed aside her shift, and loosened her stays. He hoped she was not thinking about where he had learned to remove a woman's garments. He wanted her thinking only of this moment, only of him.

"Wait," she said, turning around and clutching her clothing to her chest before he could push it away. "You as well."

She arched a brow.

"'Tis only fair."

"Very well, my lady." He grinned. Should he make a show of it, or simply strip as quickly as humanly possible?

He settled for a compromise, removing his coat, then tugging his shirttails out and pulling the linen up and over his head.

When he stood bare-chested, her eyes were wide. She had seen him this way once before, but now she did not bother to hide her pleasure in his body.

He wondered what she was thinking. He had been told he was pleasing. Serafina had preferred her men attractive, so he knew he had been in good company. A stallion among the many in her stable, he reflected wryly before refocusing on the lady in front of him. The only one he cared about.

"You... are very beautiful," she said haltingly, then blushed.

"Thank you," he said solemnly, refusing to allow his mouth to turn up. "And now it is your turn, I think."

She let go of the fabric she held and let it slide to the floor.

Thomas drew in his breath.

She was not wearing stockings or slippers, and so she stood there utterly bare in the candlelight.

Her breasts were even more shapely and lovely than he had imagined. And he had imagined quite frequently.

He lifted a finger and lazily traced a nipple until it was hard and pert.

"Do you have any idea how incredibly, unimaginably desirable you are, Mrs. Campbell?" he asked her quietly. She quivered under his hand but met his gaze, lips slightly parted.

He smiled mischievously. "I do not believe a man would ever be in need of a mistress again, with you as his wife."

It was a misstep. He saw her eyes widen and her face fall. She took a step back, crossing her arms over her chest.

He cursed himself silently.

"Claire," he said hoarsely, stepping closer. "Forgive me. Forgive my foolish words. There will never be another woman. I swear to you."

He put his hands on her naked waist, ever so gently, and tugged her towards him. She allowed it. Her hands rose to rest on his shoulders, fingers running lightly over his skin.

And then he drew her to him fiercely, tightly, taking her mouth in a smoldering kiss, and running his hands over her body as if he were drinking her in with his touch.

Their mouths were hot and greedy, the kiss continuing to rise in intensity and heat, as Thomas's hands moved with a mind of their own over his bride's bare skin. Her hips, her waist, her back, the soft swells of her buttocks.

He groaned as he touched her, desperate for more, not wanting to rush her, desperate to rush.

Before he could hesitate, he leaned away slightly and dipped a hand between her legs. She gasped against his mouth as she felt his touch. His fingers came away wet and he plunged them back, stroking and caressing her.

"Thomas," she hissed.

A younger and more selfish Thomas might well have laid her on the bed then, entered her in a single stroke, assuming only his own pleasure mattered.

But this was different. A new start. He cared for her, passionately— yes, but also tenderly. So much more tenderly than he had ever known he could feel about a woman.

He wanted her to enjoy this. He wanted to leave her begging for more.

He was not solely without experience in pleasuring women, after all.

He lifted her into his arms, feeling her breasts against his chest, and carried her the few short steps to the bed.

Laying her gently on top of the coverlet, he stretched out over her for a moment, kissing her mouth, allowing himself the pleasure of feeling her nipples hard against his skin.

There would be ample time to pay devotion to her breasts. And he planned to be very devoted.

When he moved himself down the bed, she raised herself a little, looking curious, then saw him hovering.

He parted her legs gently, tracing his fingers up the insides of her thighs. Such soft skin.

"You look very wicked right now, Thomas," she said, a little nervously.

He gave a devilish grin and without warning lowered his mouth between her legs, ignoring her exclamation of shock and the hands that stretched out instinctively to claw weakly in protest before withdrawing to grip the coverlet instead.

As she felt his lips, her protests stopped as quickly as they had begun. He stroked her wetness with his tongue, tasting her sweetness, and she let out a cry half pain half pleasure.

"Too much," she whispered. "Thomas..."

But as he continued, her back began to arch and her fingers twisted in the fabric in frustration. From her responses, he suspected it would not take long to bring her to pleasure—not this first time.

He began to suck and lick and flick her bud, then, carefully, he slid a finger inside her. She clenched herself around it, then moaned and relaxed. He added another. Gently sliding in and out as he continued the ministrations of his mouth.

"What are you doing, Thomas... What are you doing to me..." Perhaps she meant to sound commanding, but her voice was as weak as a kitten's. Moans escaped between each word.

And then she was shuddering against his mouth, her body arching, as she cried his name and clutched her fingers in his hair.

When she was done, he moved up beside her and drew her into his arms.

"My love," he whispered, kissing her mouth, while delicately running his fingers over one beautiful breast, then the other.

"Am I?" She pulled back a little.

"What?" He raised his brows.

"Your..." She bit her lip and looked away.

He realized what he had said.

He looked down at Claire, his wife, her auburn hair streamed out around her face, her eyes looking at him for reassurance, not quite daring to hope, to trust him fully.

He thought of the day—their vows, her jealousy and pain, her care for Isabel, her forgiveness.

Most of all he thought of what had happened on the road. Of the curricle swerving at the last instant. Of how different things might have been.

"You are," he said huskily, lowering his lips to hers. "You are my love, Claire. I was blind not to see it from the start."

She pressed her lips together and closed her eyes. Was she displeased?

He saw a trickle of moisture roll down one cheek.

"Claire?" The word was an expression of confusion. He touched a finger to the tear. "What have I done, Claire? Should I go?"

She bit her lip and shook her head. Her eyes stayed closed.

He kissed her cheek. Then just below her eyes where the tears strayed. Then her lips, softly, gently. A kiss of comfort, of care.

She did not respond at first, and his heart sank.

Then she wrapped slender arms around him and pulled him to her chest.

"Oh, Claire. My love. Don't cry," he whispered. "Please, don't cry. Not over me. I am utterly unworthy of it."

She looked up at him, stroking his face.

"Thomas." The look she gave him was almost aching. Her smile was sad. "I tried to protect myself from you."

"You were right to," he said seriously, kissing the tips of her fingers.

"No." She shook her head. "I was not. You were not what I thought." She gave a little laugh. "Do you have any idea how stupid a girl I am, Thomas? Perhaps you will hate me."

She met his eye. "I trusted the Mortons over you. The Mortons! It sounds so ridiculous now. Every evil thing I could make myself believe about you, I readily embraced. I did not wish to believe you could be anything but..."

He grinned. "A wicked rake?" His fingers danced over her breasts, sliding over her firm stomach, then weaving between her legs a moment until she gasped.

"You are very wicked, indeed," she said, narrowing her eyes. "But you are my wicked Thomas now."

She pulled him against her, then slid her fingers down to his trousers and began to tug.

"I wish to see you in all your wickedness, if you please," she ordered, an impish look in her eyes.

Now it was his turn to be oddly shy. He stood up, hands to buttons.

She raised herself up to watch, hair loose around her face and shoulders, breasts flushed with desire.

It was all the motivation he required. He shucked off the trousers and jumped back onto the bed, lowering his mouth to her nipples while tickling her stomach until she was alternately moaning and giggling under him.

"So, this is what I now possess?" she finally managed to choke out between gasps.

"Possess?" He paused, taken aback a little. "Am I your property, my lady?"

"It seems only fair, if I am yours..." She reached out a finger and trailed it lightly along his hardened ridge, then wrapped her hand around him gently.

He let out a moan, pushed her back down on the bed, and put his body over hers.

Their lips met. The time for talking had ceased.

Sliding a hand between her legs, she parted them eagerly, already excited for his touch. She was more than ready. He let out a groan, and let himself push up against her opening a little. Meeting no resistance, he pushed further, praying he would not cause her too much pain. Not all women were the same and he knew, from talking to other men, that not all women experienced the same pain, nor did they all bleed in contrary to popular belief. But still, he held himself back.

It took all his willpower.

"That feels..." Claire gasped. He paused above her immediately. She bit her lip and he did not think it was due to pain. "Please... Thomas... More."

He thrust again, slowly, then again. She gasped. His hands covered her breasts, rubbing her nipples to hard peaks, drawing her moans and her sighs.

"Thomas," she bit her lip, and he knew she was wanting something she could not express in words.

He stopped holding back, letting himself take her entirely. And then he was lost in her depths, as lost as she was in his.

When they were through, she wrapped herself around him, legs around his waist, and pulled him tight.

"Thomas, my Thomas."

He closed his eyes. This was bliss. More than he deserved. He would strive to earn it, in every way he could.

They slept in each other's arms for an hour, maybe more. Then woke and repeated it all again. When they lost count of how many times they had paired, he finally ignored her protests, and ringing the bell, wrapped a sheet around his waist and summoned a servant to bring them food and wine while Claire hid with her head beneath the covers, stifling giggles.

Near dawn they fell into a true sleep, limbs tangled together still and hands clasped tight, as the rain pitter-pattered softly on the windows.

Chapter 24

When Thomas awoke, Claire was gone.

A note rested on her pillow, beside a few strands of long auburn hair. Beneath it was a small stack of newspaper clippings, carefully folded and tied with a ribbon.

Resisting the urge to put his nose to the pillow and breathe deep, he opened the note and read:

"My Dearest, Darkest Husband,

It would seem that Fanny and Rosalind are devoted readers of the Beauford Chronicle—*our local newspaper (I mention this since you are so new to the neighbourhood you may not yet be familiar with this illustrious publication). I had no idea just how devoted until yesterday when they presented me with this parcel as a wedding present. The enclosed clippings were originally printed in a series of conduct articles concerning the safeguarding of local youths, particularly young women (of course), from the vices and wiles of libertines and scoundrels. Oddly enough, the series seems to have begun shortly before Your Rakeliness entered our neighbourhood. Nevertheless, Fanny and Rosalind are convinced it is you whom the editors must have had in mind from the start, and I must say, after perusing the contents of these clippings I am of a mind to agree.*

As the articles are written in an overpoweringly didactic prose and can be rather tedious, I have thoughtfully provided you with a brief summary of their contents. Roughly, they may be broken down into the following recommendations:

Avoid the reading of novels.

Trust not those with depraved reputations.

Avoid immodest dress.

Avoid improper diversions.

Seek a husband, not a rake. Good sense and good-nature are requisite.

Avoid foolish adventures.

Modesty and silence are a woman's best weapons against the rakes and libertines who hide among us.

Avoid the fantasies of a weak mind.

Discern between the rake and the common man.

Waste not your passions on a rake.

As I am certain you have already discerned, there are uncanny similarities between this wise list of adages and the, shall we say, unconventional manner of courtship (is this too strong a word?) conducted between ourselves these past few months.

In fact, one might almost believe we had broken each and every one of the rules on this list on purpose—when you and I both know that is the furthest thing from the truth. Certainly, I did not wet my dress intentionally that day in the rain when you picked me up. Nevertheless, I assume that the alluring figure I presented kindled your rakish passions uncontrollably and eventually led to the sequence of events I have been privately referring to as The Seduction in the Cottage. I know, it is not at all a romantic enough name for a novel. I feel certain Mrs. Radcliffe would disdain to use it. Be that as it may, perhaps I shall now admit there was indeed something romantic about that day—and so I find I cannot regret that foolish adventure. (Despite the pain it caused her, I am certain Fanny does not either.)

Now, as for the requirements of "good sense and good-nature," perhaps we must simply admit that these are areas we both must work on developing more carefully. While up until meeting you, I had every confidence in my good sense, you put that to the test in unanticipated ways—as I am sure I did with you. So, let us have no recriminations. That said, I cannot help but wonder about the advice of "modesty and silence." If I had turned such weapons upon you would a world of trouble have been saved? Surely a meek and modest miss would not have drawn your ire—nor your desire. If I had been more silent, more modest, why, perhaps I would never have found out about your harem of lovers from Miss Morton in the first place and thus not had my appetite whet for those terrible temptations of the flesh into which you so generously initiated me last night.

I shall not go through the list item by item. Number eight, for instance, is one I am certain does not apply. Surely neither of us shall ever admit to anything so mortifying as lying in our lonely beds in the dark of night and conjuring up a familiar face before lifting the hem of our night rail and darting a finger or two down into the fathoms below, while imagining the touch is that of a tall and handsome (or lovely) near-stranger. I for one would not, though if you have need of confession, I am all ears.

The last on the list cannot be ignored, however.

If it could have then I would have and we should not be here.

It is sensible advice, of course, and if I were as avid a reader of the Chronicle *as my dear sister perhaps I would not have been caught so unaware by said passions.*

But there it is—from the moment you walked into Orchard Hill, Thomas Campbell, you inflamed my passions and while your doing so has brought with it some not inconsequential measure of frustration and pain, I find I cannot regret it. Can you?

I must trust that you are shaking your head right now and answering in the negative, that you are thanking the heavens above that of all the little run-down houses in all of the small sleepy towns in all the world you walked into mine.

And so, I fear not for the destruction of the peace of our family, to loosely quote item ten. I believe the peace of our family—yours, mine, Isabel's—is just beginning, and I cannot wait to share it with you both.

Lovingly yours,

Claire

P.S. I did not say the words last night and wondered if you had noticed, but I shall write them now, happily, eagerly, and whisper the in your ear when next we meet.

I love you, Thomas.

Thomas had never dressed more quickly in his life. Sparing no thought for his valet, he was still hastily doing up the buttons of his tailcoat as he strode down the hall in search of his bride.

Chapter 25

I sabel was fascinated by Claire's ring. She asked to see it again and again, as they spent a quiet morning together in a pretty little sitting room attached to the bedroom Thomas's daughter used when she visited.

Claire did not mind. She was enjoying looking at the gleaming band too much herself. The next morning they would leave for London, and it had been decided Isabel would come to. Upon their return, they would reside at Stoneybrook. Perhaps a larger residence would be needed in the future, but for now Claire quite liked the idea of being close to her mother and sisters at the beginning of her marriage.

Mrs. Mowbray sat humming in a rocking chair, her knitting needles weaving furiously. She was making some baby clothes to give to a young family who lived in the village. By the look of it their first child would have a very full wardrobe.

In the afternoon, a carriage pulled up outside and Mrs. Gardner, Rosalind, and Gracie swept in like a small tempest, chattering incessantly and covered with smiles.

Gracie and Isabel immediately ran off hand-in-hand to play.

Rosalind drew Claire up to her, a feisty grin already on her face. Claire groaned silently. She could only imagine the interrogation her sister would try to give.

"Do not even think of asking whatever naughty thing is on the tip of your tongue, Rosalind," she warned in a low voice. "You have had ample opportunity to educate yourself on marital matters from Gwendolen. I will not be your second schoolmistress."

Then she blushed despite willing herself not to.

Her mother caught her eye from where she stood talking to Thomas, and smiling warmly, gave her daughter a bold wink.

Rosalind snickered. "Perhaps it is not me you must worry about. Who knows what Mama is asking your husband at this very moment?"

Claire's mouth widened in horror. "You truly think... That she would ask Thomas? She would never! Rosalind!" She punched her sister lightly on the arm.

But she was not at ease until Thomas returned to her side. He kissed her lightly on the cheek and wrapped an arm around her waist.

This time she ignored Rosalind's looks. Let her look her fill. Claire could become quite used to these little shows of affection as far as she was concerned. She squeezed her husband's arm, enjoying the feel of the solid muscle that lay beneath the grey wool of his coat, and smiling up at him.

Truly, her face was beginning to feel stretched from smiling so much.

She felt radiantly happy. She felt...rather beautiful, in fact.

Before she could help herself, she recalled the beautiful woman she had encountered the day before. But surprisingly, she did not recall her with pain or envy.

She looked around the foyer. Her mother and Rosalind were engrossed in a lively conversation with Thomas. Gracie and Isabel had just run across the hall shrieking as they chased each other. She spotted William and Fanny coming down the stairs from the other wing, hand in hand, their eyes lit up with shared happiness.

Taking in these surroundings, she felt nothing but pity for the woman who had rejected her own family and betrayed the man who had given her his tender young heart.

She would not make the same mistake.

She would treasure her former rake.

And interrupting his conversation, she pulled Thomas towards her, took both of his hands in her own and tilted her head upwards to be kissed.

Epilogue

I t was Christmas.

The bells had been rung. The eggnog had been drunk. The greenery was hung; holly and ivy and laurel and, of course, mistletoe.

And Rosalind Gardner was bored.

They were in Scotland. Aberdeenshire, to be more exact. Staying at a manor belonging to William Campbell's cousin. It was a house exchange—a fun idea in theory.

The cousins' were back in Beauford enjoying a rural English Christmas at Northwood, while the Campbells and Gardners had journeyed north to the highlands.

The highlands were beautiful, but, in Rosalind's opinion, they were also very dull. There were only so many walks in the cold and biting December wind one could take.

Rosalind threw herself back on the scarlet damask sofa, feet kicking up in the air to throw off her slippers. There was no one to see her, so who was to care if her skirts were around her ankles.

Besides, kicking made her feel slightly less crochety. As if she were running towards a faraway destination rather than stuck in one place.

A destination far from Scotland and, ideally, much warmer.

Peals of laughter were coming from across the hall. It was not a disagreeable sound, for it was the laughter of family and friends, but it did tend to remind her that everyone was having a lovely time except for her.

Of course, Claire and Thomas were. Perhaps it was vulgar of her to say it even in her head, but truly, they were incapable of keeping their hands off of one another—so which was the more vulgar, the thought or the actions which they were all forced to watch or tactfully avert their eyes from?

Not that Rosalind minded Claire's happiness. She was pleased that her straitlaced sister had let loose her passions somewhat since her marriage. And pleased that her marriage to a former rake was going so well. Though she would not mind less kissing in public if it came down to it.

Then there was Fanny and William, soon to be increased to a threesome. Their love was the quieter sort, but no less plain to see.

Mrs. Gardner and Mrs. Mowbray had taken to one another wholeheartedly. And of course, Isabel had Gracie and vice versa. Those girls were truly inseparable. They would have to find matching husbands someday. Brothers perhaps, like Claire and Fanny.

And then there was poor Rosalind.

She flung an arm over her golden-haired head melodramatically— but self-consciously melodramatic which was quite a different sort.

She might be thinking "woe is me," but she would never actually say it out loud.

No, she was not the kind to complain but rather to plot.

And right now she was plotting adventure.

Step one, return to London. It was the hub of the nation and thus the fount of adventure.

Step two, acquire a means of travel. Perhaps she could advertise herself as a lady's maid. Or a governess. Or a ship's cook. Anything!

Step three, leave from Dover on a ship travelling to... Well, anywhere really as long as it was not Scotland or England. She would even take Ireland if she had to, though Italy would be far better.

And after that? Enlightenment. Expansion of the mind. Her very own feminine Grand Tour. And above all, Romance—in the original sense of the word, not the kissing kind: "the story, whether written or recited, of the adventures of a knight or hero."

She would be the hero of her own true Romance.

Scratch that, the heroine.

And she was leaving as soon as Christmas was over.

Thank You

D ear Readers,

Thank you for joining me on this romantic voyage! I hope you have enjoyed meeting the Gardner family.

If you enjoy following author newsletters, you can sign-up for mine at www.fennaedgewood.com. You'll receive the latest book updates, opportunities for ARCs (advance reader copies), giveaways, special promotions, sneak peeks, and other bookish treats, including a FREE special extended epilogue for the Gardner Girls series coming in late 2021, exclusively for subscribers.

If your time spent in Beauford was pleasant, I hope you'll consider leaving a review—your feedback is important to me and will help other readers decide whether to read my books as well.

I wish you continued happy reading! May your TBR list be never ending!

A Sneak Peek at The Seafaring Lady's Guide to Love...

AVAILABLE ON AMAZON

PROLOGUE

The woman was dying.

It was clear to see.

From the pallor of her skin—a sickly bloodless grey—to the sheen of sweat coating her brow.

Her hair was damp and tangled from the exertion of trying to stay alive and failing; with the exertion of trying to give new life and also failing.

Now she was fading away to nothing, like a wilting flower.

She, who had been everything to him, would soon be nothing at all, to anyone, ever again.

Perhaps it would always have turned out this way.

But perhaps it might not.

He clenched the bedsheet in his right hand, as hard as he could. Consumed by futile grief and rage.

His left hand held hers. Limp and cool. She had not stirred in he knew not how long.

With that thought, he raised his head from where it hung over the bedside and gazed at the window. Along the edges of the curtains, he could see a faint gleam of light.

A glance about the room revealed the candles lighting it had burned down to stubs.

Morning then. A new dawn. For one of them.

"Philip..."

It was the faintest whisper. He squeezed her hand involuntarily before he could help himself and leaned closer.

"Sarah."

The word was a plea.

He could hear the fear—and worse, the tears—in his voice and he gritted his teeth. She should not have to hear the sounds of his pain. Not now.

The small limp hand gave the slightest squeeze back before relaxing into passiveness again.

He swallowed hard.

How could this be? How could the woman lying in the bed be the same one he had known? The woman he had laughed with, touched with tenderness, embraced with passion? Been embraced by in turn.

She was supposed to be full of life. She was supposed to be with him their whole lives. Wasn't that what they had promised?

As long as you both shall live.

Promises could be broken. And ever so cruelly, too.

He choked back a cry.

"I'm sorry..." The words were so faint. He closed his eyes. He could pretend he had not heard her. Would that be best?

"I'm sorry...Philip." Her voice was a little louder. He could hear the effort in her voice, and that more than anything else made him open his eyes and look at her.

She was looking back, from behind those beautiful iris-colored eyes, with an expression so sorrowful it wrenched his heart.

"Don't. Don't look at me like that, Sarah," he said hoarsely. "I beg of you. Don't."

She held his gaze a moment longer, then closed her eyes.

"I..." She drew a deep rattling breath.

Whatever she had been about to say, he would never know.

Her hand trembled in his and then went slack.

She was gone.

Now that he was alone, he let himself do what he had not before. Stretching out over the bed, he wept.

CHAPTER 1

London, 1822

Rosalind Gardner had been skulking around the London docks all morning in a state of nervous anticipation.

Around her, the hustle and bustle of those who made their livelihoods from the seafaring trades carried on, oblivious to her mental quandary. Men—young and old alike, along with some no more than boys—scurried about, unloading and hoisting and carrying their rich cargos. Barrels full of wool and tobacco, along with more exotic items—coconuts, olive oil, sugar, cocoa, brandy, and spices— were carted across the docks to warehouses and wagons.

The air was filled with the salty scent of the seawater along with other, less agreeable smells of hard-working male bodies and fish.

Fish oil, to be exact. A few hours before—yes, she had been standing in one place for that long—a young dock worker had slipped and dropped the barrel he was carrying. It had smashed to the ground, bursting open in a ripe piscine puddle. An older man had loudly berated the boy, who had flushed with shame and run off to load himself up with another barrel—this time walking much more carefully until he reached the warehouse which was his destination.

The docks were fascinating, surely. But it was not dock life which most interested Rosalind, but ship life.

From these docks, she could travel to almost anywhere in the world.

She had already chosen her ship and her destination: Tortola, in the West Indies, via the Witch of the Waves.

Not only was the Witch a large and lovely galleon, it also bore the most romantic name she had seen on a ship.

Most of the ships along the quays were named pedantically.

The Lion—completely unimaginative. Half the ships on the quay seemed to be named the Lion.

The Mary-Rose, the Rose, the Primrose, the Rosemary. She was sure if she stood on the docks long enough, she would soon see a ship called the Rosalind. The names were pretty enough, though dull. They conjured images of captain's wives and daughters—and with them dull, English life.

The Castle of Comfort—while a little bit better, the name was either overly optimistic (Rosalind knew enough not to expect a ship to offer the comforts of life on land) or pessimistically ironic.

But the Witch of the Waves—now that was a name that thrilled!

Not only was the sound of it wonderfully alliterative, but the carved creature who bore it was beauty and mystery personified: A bare-breasted mermaid with long streaming hair and a fierce expression on her lovely face. Her arms were folded just below her breasts, giving her an even more imposing appearance despite her lack of clothing.

Rosalind had shivered when she saw the wooden sea lady.

No one could feel unsafe aboard a ship led by such a fearsome female creature.

Now there was only the matter of purchasing passage.

The Witch of the Waves was not a passenger ship. Primarily, it transported cargo and sometimes was rented out as a packet ship for mail between England and the West Indies.

Rosalind knew this for she had not only been eavesdropping all morning, but she had also worked up the courage to ask a kindly-looking older sailor who she saw going back and forth between the Witch and the shore.

No, the Witch of the Waves was not a passenger ship, he had explained—and Rosalind had felt her heart sink—but seeing her expression, he had quickly added that there were a limited number of cabins, for both men and women, set aside for passengers. Although they were a pretty penny, he added, looking her up and down in a mildly appraising way.

Well, Rosalind had been saving her pennies. Pinned to various locations of her outfit were packets of pound notes sewn into watertight pockets. Although she truly hoped she never had the opportunity to learn just how watertight they were.

For three years, she had been saving. She would not say scrimping and saving, for she was really not badly off for a single young woman. Her eldest sister, Gwendolen, had married a duke, after all.

Her second eldest sister, Claire, had not done too poorly for herself either with her marriage to a country squire.

In the two years since Claire's marriage, Rosalind had made her way to London and taken up residence with Gwendolen's family. Never one to be idle, she had also worked as a governess—much to Gwendolen's husband Angel's amusement.

Oh, of course, she could have had a season—or more than one—if she had wished it. But Gwendolen's experiences had not left Rosalind with a positive inclination towards the ton's marriage market. Nor was she ready to begin the life of the settled, married lady.

To the rest of the world, Rosalind was practically on-the-shelf as she drew nearer and nearer to twenty-two years of age. But then, Rosalind had never cared all that much for the opinions of the rest of the world.

It was her life. Therefore, it was her opinions that counted. Although she was well aware that in spite of the relatively enlightened age in which they were living, many men would still find such a view shocking in a prospective wife.

So, it was fortunate she did not have to marry out of necessity.

She had the security of her family—the knowledge that she would always have a place with her mother and Gracie, or with one of her married sisters—and that was something many single young women either did not have or did not wish to have. They wished to have their own homes and their own families.

Rosalind was fairly certain she wanted those things as well some day...but not just yet.

If she did not leave England at least once before she settled down, she knew she would never be able to live with herself.

Besides being laden with pound notes, she also carried something even more precious—letters of reference from her brother-in-law, the Duke of Englefield, commending her to some of the finest families in the West Indies, and another recommending her as a governess to a family he was acquainted with on Tortola.

Until today she was fairly certain he had not believed she would actually go through with what he had called her mad scheme. Well, when he and her sister opened the letter she had left them, they would see that she had finally followed her heart's desire.

She looked down at the ground.

Her feet had been moving on their own, while her mind wandered.

She had reached the small wooden building which served as the ship's office.

She straightened her back, raised her chin, and prepared to launch forward.

But abruptly, someone launched into her instead.

The door opened with a bang and a frowning man hurtled forward, straight into her. The door slammed closed behind.

With a wild gasp, she dropped her valise and began to tilt backwards. Her arms flailed wildly as she sought a handhold of any kind.

Meeting only air, she clutched hold of the only solid thing she could find: the man in front of her.

She grasped his coat with both hands and pulling herself upright again, stood there gaping up.

He had not even budged.

Which was no wonder, for he was the burliest man she had ever seen. She might easily have mistaken him for a dockhand were it not for his clothes, which marked him as a gentleman.

The combination of hefty strength and barely contained muscle filling out the finely tailored coat and trousers of an obviously-wealthy gentleman disconcerted Rosalind. There was something incredibly masculine and appealing about this man's body, yet intimidating about his overall person.

She was momentarily thrown off course.

Apparently, the gentleman—if indeed he was—had been similarly struck for he had not even moved to help her.

Rather, she realized with a start, he was looking down at her from behind cold brown eyes almost as if she was something he had found on his shoe.

That in itself should have been off-putting.

Not to mention he had made no apology.

Yet in spite of his gross lack of manners and his imposing physique, there was something behind the surface of his expression that transcended her inclination towards dislike. Something surprisingly boyish and innocent and—just for the blink of an eye—even heartbreaking.

He had thick jet-black hair. She had always liked dark-haired men.

It was overly long and a lock of it had tumbled down and was blocking one eye, softening the hard, masculine planes of his face.

The glistening piece of hair beckoned to Rosalind like a moth to a flame. Before she could think twice, she found herself reaching a hand out and gently pushing the hair back into place.

The man's hand shot out and caught her arm, firmly but not altogether roughly. His skin was darker than most Englishmen's, she observed, almost olive in tone. Perhaps he was Italian.

"I beg your pardon," he said, his gruff tone clearly implying he was doing no such thing. His voice was so magnificently deep and mellow it sent a thrilling chill through her.

But unintentionally captivating or not, Rosalind was not about to let this ox of a man try to give her a lesson in courtesy.

"Pardon you indeed," she retorted tartly. "Do you always burst through doorways with the force of a tempest and without looking where you are going? You might have knocked me all the way into the sea!"

His eyes widened as she spoke, as if he were totally unaccustomed to being challenged.

"Of course, you need not ask," she continued, smiling calmly in a way she could see infuriated him. "I shall forgive your terrible lack of manners, sir, if you will kindly step aside." She crossed her arms under her breasts and pointedly donned an expression of aloof boredom as she waited for him to step past.

For a moment, her opponent stood as if frozen, uncertainty written over his face.

Then his jaw tightened. Without another word, he nodded and went by.

Giving herself a little shake, she opened the door to the office building. A clerk sat at a desk across the small room.

She went towards him swiftly, determined to brush the unsettling encounter from her mind.

"I would like to purchase passage on the Witch of the Waves," she said, brightly. "I understand you have a number of cabins available."

The man looked up at her, eyes bugging out in a rather fish-like fashion. Was her request really so strange?

"You do have cabins available," she emphasized, sweetening her tone. "I was told so just a few minutes ago by one of the crew."

"Well... y-y-yes," the clerk stuttered. "But..."

"Excellent. How much will the passage to Tortola be?" She began to pull open her reticule.

"B-b-but..."

"My good sir, are you quite well?" Rosalind eyed him curiously.

The man sat down and put a hand to his brow.

When he looked back up at her a moment later, a glimmer of intelligence was returning to his features.

"To tell the truth—" he confessed. "—The gentleman who just left was quite..."

"Rude? Caustic? Abrasive?" Rosalind guessed.

"Yes, indeed. All of the above." The clerk looked grateful. "You understand then."

"I do, indeed." Rosalind tugged at her gloves. Once she was aboard, she would stow the blasted things for the rest of the voyage.

The man's expression had changed. Now he was the one looking concerned. She did not think it had anything to do with the gloves.

The clerk cleared his throat. "He also reserved all of the remaining cabins."

Rosalind raised her eyebrows. "All of them?"

"Yes, all. There are eight in total, I believe. Although I believe he is traveling with just one other companion."

"All of the ladies' cabins? Not only the men's?" Rosalind said, trying to keep the panic from her voice.

She noticed the clerk continued to use the word "reserved" rather than "paid," but evidently, they were the same thing to him.

"Yes, all four of the ladies' cabins as well. Though I believe he said only one would be occupied." The clerk rifled through a stack of papers in front of him, as if searching for a list or set of instructions that would enable him to deal with the stubborn young woman before him.

Rosalind watched, her mind momentarily blank.

This would not do.

She had not stood for hours in the hot sun trying to come to a decision about her entire future, only to have her decision thwarted by a man too rude to apologize for his rudeness and so rich he could buy out an entire ship on a whim.

Well, it was not as if she was a pauper. She had the means to travel, did she not? Why should she not proceed as planned?

All that was required was a little gumption, a little creativity.

Suddenly, it all seemed perfectly clear. Her mouth was opening without hesitation and before her mind could fully catch up.

"Well, that is quite all right then," she said cheerfully.

"It is?" The clerk's head snapped back up. "Is it?" The dear man looked quite hopeful.

"Of course, of course." She waved a hand. "I merely came in to make sure he had remembered. To reserve all of the cabins, that is—not only the men's."

"Not only the men's..." The clerk spoke slowly as if trying to make out her words.

"Yes, my husband—" She emphasized the word. "—can tend to be a bit forgetful. I would not wish to bunk on the men's side, of course." She gave a cheeky smile.

Understanding was beginning to dawn on the clerk's face. "Your husband..." He cleared his throat. "Yes. I see..."

She did not wish for the poor man to have to regret his earlier words.

"Yes, you must have seen us speaking outside just now." She shook her head sadly. "He is abrasive, isn't he? And demanding. Very demanding. You have no idea. He can be very difficult at times. Very difficult indeed." She was sure that was no exaggeration.

"Yes, I can imagine," the clerk said, looking sympathetic.

"But in any case, there is no harm done." She tugged her gloves back on.

She would board the ship, track down the man, and pay him her passage.

There was no reason in the world why he would need four women's cabins. The clerk said he was traveling with only one other person. Well, even if that person was a woman—and Good Lord, she could only hope it was not his wife—there were still six cabins between the two of them.

It would all work itself out.

"There is a larger cabin," the clerk said, quickly, before she could go. "That you and your husband could share. I could consult with the captain and once he understands who it is for..."

"Oh, that won't be necessary," she said cheerily. "We prefer it this way, truly."

She winked.

The clerk's eyes widened. Then he slowly winked back. "Ah, of course. Well, safe voyage then, Madam..."

But she was already stepping out the door, and whatever appellation the clerk called her by was lost in noise of the docks.

Want to Keep Reading?

Other Books by Fenna Edgewood

Childhood sweethearts become forbidden lovers in this Shakespearean-esque second chance romance where secrets and lies throw two opposing families into turmoil.

Romeo and Juliet, meet Henry and Caroline...

Caroline Gardner has always had her very own white knight. Her childhood sweetheart, Henry Gardner, is handsome, kind, and passionately in love with her. Or so she believes, until one day she is told everything she knows about Henry is a lie. In an instant, their long-time engagement is broken and Caroline's world is shattered.

Henry Gardner has been told that the girl he's loved all his life has cruelly betrayed him. But no matter what she may have done, his love for her will not dim. The only problem? She's about to marry someone else.

Less than twenty-four hours until he'll lose her for good...

Stealing an earl's bride on the eve of her wedding might be an insurmountable challenge for some men, but Henry is determined to make sure Caroline knows that forever is a promise he means to keep. Even if doing so comes at a perilous price.

One boy. One girl. One future they must fight for together.

Her one true love may have returned, but after all he's put her through, Caroline has no intention of falling back into his arms. But when she stumbles onto a terrible family secret, Caroline must make a leap of faith and put her heart in the hands of the one man she swore she'd never trust again.

About Fenna

F enna is an award-winning retired academic who has studied English literature for most of her life. After a twenty-five-year hiatus from writing romance as a twelve-year-old, she has returned to the genre with a bang. Fenna has lived and traveled across North America, most notably above the Arctic Circle. She resides in Canada with her husband and two tiny tots (who are adorable but generally terrible research assistants).

Fenna loves to connect with other readers and writers. If you'd like to get in touch, receive the latest news on her releases, and get access to free bonus material, please sign up for her newsletter at www.fennaedgewood.com or simply shoot her an email at "info@fennaedgewood.com"

Website: www.fennaedgewood.com
Facebook: facebook.com/fennaedgewoodbooks
Instagram: instagram.com/fennaedgewood
Newsletter Sign-up: fennaedgewood.com/newsletter/